COME LANDFALL

COME LANDFALL

a novel

ROY HOFFMAN

The University of Alabama Press • Tuscaloosa

The University of Alabama Press
Tuscaloosa, Alabama 35487-0380
uapress.ua.edu

Hardcover edition published 2014.
Paperback edition published 2017.
eBook edition published 2014.

Typeface: Scala

Cover image: *Distant Rain*, Brad Robertson, acrylic on canvas,
48" x 48", 2012; courtesy of the artist
Cover design: Michele Myatt Quinn

Paperback ISBN: 978-0-8173-5871-6

A previous edition of this book has been catalogued by the Library of
Congress as follows:
Library of Congress Cataloging-in-Publication Data
Hoffman, Roy, 1953–
Come landfall : a novel / Roy Hoffman.
pages   cm
ISBN 978-0-8173-1830-7 (trade cloth: alk. paper)—ISBN 978-0-8173-
8753-2 (ebook) 1. Hurricanes—Fiction. 2. Gulf Coast (Miss.)—Fiction.
I. Title.
PS3558.O34634C66 2014
813'.54—dc23
                    2013035972

In memory of
My sister Sherrell
who understood everyone's story
&
My uncle, Major Roy Robinton, U.S. Marine Corps
lost as a POW in World War II
who never told his

Contents

COME LANDFALL

Prologue

In dress blues the Army Air Corpsmen face each other down the aisle of the Presbyterian church and when the command comes—"Arch swords!"— they lift their sabers, point to point.

Beneath this steel canopy the bride and groom walk, her shining officer at her side, her satin wedding dress flowing. "'Til death do us part," echo their vows.

At their wedding reception in a Richmond hotel, they slow fox-trot to "Stardust," his heat enveloping her, like the time they first embraced on New Year's Eve 1940 at a dance in Georgetown, or brushed skin early summer frolicking in the surf at Virginia Beach. But more ardent now.

"A toast to Rosey and Christiane!"

She can still taste the champagne on her tongue.

The bouquet tossed, the rice thrown, they make their way to their suite and change. He is in dark blue pajamas; she, a peach silk nightgown. "I so love to look into your exquisite blue eyes," he says, holding her. Her Jewish poet first enamored her with that word.

He plucks loose the top string like a harp. Her shoulders shake beneath his palms.

"Give yourself up to him," her mother had said.

In the sumptuous bed, shy beneath blankets, she feels his fingers open the silk far down. She is trembling.

"Are you chilly? Here, my beloved."

When she buries her face in his neck, she catches the scent of his after-shave—a hint of cinnamon—and relaxes.

Exquisite.

The darkness is calming.

His long fingers press against her hip, sliding.

Pajamas whisked off, he is on top of her, and his chest, with its curls of black hair, is crushing. She wants to say, "I can't breathe," but hears her mother: "Surrender." She takes a breath, smiles, moistens his full lips with a sweet kiss, then a lingering one, deeper.

His skin is smooth as a young boy's as she floats her hands down his back and grasps him hard.

All her twenty-one years she has waited for this.

She gives, and gives.

Oh, my warrior, my love, where have you gone?

PART I

Nana's Soldier

ONE

Stardust Melody

When rain whipped the harbor windows of the Cotton Gin Casino, Angela looked up from her serving tray, past the hectic slots and feverish dice tables, and pictured Nana in her room at Coastal Arms. A few miles from where she carted orders of bourbon and gin, her grandmother sat at the assisted living facility wringing her hands with every uptick of wind. Tropical Storm Isidore, strengthening into a hurricane, was the third monster that year to taunt the Mississippi coast. Sixty-five-mile-per-hour winds would hardly close the casino down—party mania took hold and slots pumped faster—but every blow threatened to become Noah's flood to Christiane and her neighbors.

Angela's phone buzzed in her pocket: Nana or Max, an anxious grandmother or a surly musician boyfriend, one of them bound to get her fired. Four o'clock: an hour left on her shift. She kept on toting drinks.

"Hey, Angela"—it was Chip, the blackjack dealer on a break, always nudging—"be at Rudy's Club tonight?"

"Stick with cards."

Last weekend at Rudy's he'd danced so close she'd recoiled from his breath.

"Could be your last chance," Chip said. "We might all be blown to hell this time tomorrow."

"Send me a postcard," she said.

She felt the wind in her bones, no matter that five feet of reinforced concrete stood between her and the elements. She'd been born in a storm, graduated Biloxi High under a tornado threat, and spent the worst six months of her life in the aftermath of Helene. She still could not drive that street by Back Bay paralleling the coastal road.

The all-night couple in Hawaiian shirts and sandals, the plastic model on the arm of a loud Texan, the lovebirds necking by deuces wild video poker—around her the casino-goers carried on with glee.

Out the window, heavy gusts churned the shrimp boats hurrying in to harbor.

She took a screwdriver order from the Hattiesburg sisters, regulars at the nickel slots, and headed back to the kitchen.

When her phone rang again, she fished it out.

"Where are you?" Nana said.

"Earning my keep. Be there soon."

"I've lost my pocketbook," Nana said.

"We'll find it, don't worry."

"The lady said this was my pocketbook, but I think she took it. This one isn't mine."

"Well, I'll talk to her when I get there!"

"You're not out driving in the storm, are you?"

"No, no, I'm safe and dry."

"Thank the Lord."

"And you are, too," Angela said.

"The girl's playing piano," Nana said.

"We'll get her to play your song. Gotta go. Love ya."

"I love you, my Angel."

The Coastal Arms folks were staying put through this one. Under threat of a Category 2 last summer, management had loaded up the residents to transport them to Meridian. Nana had sat by a window in the bus, waving Angela good-bye like she was a girl going off to camp. When they returned in two days, weather dissipated, Nana was as frazzled as if she'd been lashed to a mast.

Angela watched two young men in USAF sweatshirts—airmen from Keesler, no doubt—swagger by while girls she worked with spotted them like birds of prey. Brandy, a leggy Tennessean, took out after the taller one with her drink tray.

Musicians and artists, waiting tables or pumping gas at the docks, were more Angela's domain. Or at least the curly-headed boy in poli sci at Gulf Coast Community College who'd pronounced himself "a lefty," a term she hadn't heard since her dad's day.

She loaded up her tray, did the rounds, smiling appreciatively as customers stuck bills in her tip glass. She jotted down orders, trudged the last of what she figured was at least five miles. Free booze, loose wallets—that was the equation.

In her three months she had been amid constant motion. Only yesterday had been different.

There had been a moment of silence at 7:46 A.M., that moment—8:46 in New York—that the first plane had hit the Twin Towers a year before. Having just started her shift, Angela had seen all-night partyers, Yankees in muumuus, breakfast buffet regulars in flip-flops, all pause and bow their heads. The machinery of the casino had whirred on, the flashing lights and slot machine bells, but everyone was motionless at their places like a playland of mannequins. Then "America" sounded over the loudspeakers, followed by a Rebel yell and the vow, joined by raised fists, "They'll pay for this!"

Nana had called her twice during the flyover from Keesler, worried there were bombers overhead. "It's okay, Nana," she had reassured her. "It's remembrance and prayers."

Finishing up her rounds, she filled out her time card, tallied her tips—four times what she had made on the graveyard shift at Krispy Kreme—changed into her jeans and blouse, and started out the door. The fitful rain had eased a moment.

She dashed to her Corolla, entered the flow of traffic on Highway 90, and took off west.

The heavy oaks that usually leaned down like well-wishers at the end of her shift gyrated like souls possessed. The Biloxi Lighthouse was a ghost ship in the shrouded light. As she passed the fake galleon of Pirates Plunder, then the antebellum home of Father Ryan, poet-priest of the Confederacy, her phone flashed Max's name.

She flipped it open. "You know you're catching me on the highway this time of day."

"Isidore's already turning," he said.

"You'd love me to go off the road."

"You know I care for you."

"By how you treated me the other night at Rudy's? With that dumpy teen hanging all over you between sets?"

"I've got fans."

"I've got a life!"

"I'm in my garage," he said.

How many evenings she had perched on a stool in the corner of that garage while Max's band practiced, charmed by his stubby fingers walking the frets of his gleaming guitar. The weekend before, when he had touched them to her neck, she had drawn back, as if they were talons.

"I wrote you a song," he said through the howling.

"I'm headed to Nana's."

"I was going to ask you about her."

"Play it for your favorite asshole. You." She snapped the phone shut.

At moments like this, she felt she might fly, pressing the accelerator harder and lifting her car's nose into the sky. She thought of Dorothy, spun from Kansas in a stupendous tornado.

But then there was Nana.

Pulling into a service station to top off her tank, she got in line—part of the pre-storm excitement, like scouting for "D" batteries—and glanced at the picture of Nana and Lucky in her wallet: Miami Beach, the Fontainebleau Hotel, granddad in his powder blue jacket, Nana in her rose crepe dress, posing between fox-trots for a photographer's flash. How she missed Lucky. He'd be proud of her for filling the tank.

She came alongside Jefferson Davis's historic home with its civil war veterans cemetery somber beneath the dancing trees, then turned into Coastal Arms.

On the side patio, in ponchos together like castaways, cuddled General Sam Wheeler and Francie Holcombe, who'd "fallen in love," as Nana explained it, after meeting in the antiseptic hallways.

"Isidore's a pussycat!" roared Wheeler to Angela as he peered from beneath the bill of his cap. "Camille was a five, Frederic a four, now that's power. I've flown missions through ones bigger than this puff on the horizon."

"But we've got to be cautious, dear," said Francie, who patted his hand.

"I'm not camping out with a bunch of sissies in the TV room," he said.

"I'm a sissie," said Francie.

"You'll be fine, I'll make sure of that," said Wheeler, pulling her closer. Francie smiled and leaned into him.

"How's my Nana today?" Angela said as she headed to the entrance.

"Christiane loves it when those C-130s pass overhead," said Wheeler. "She's been going on about the war ever since."

Inside, attendants were putting masking tape on windows and a few residents were watching a Weather Channel announcer with gale force winds scrambling her hair. From the social hall came the booming sound of a piano, the entertainment of the afternoon still on schedule.

"Hello, Angela," said Maria Torres, a caretaker. "Your Nana will be happy to see you. This makes her *muy emocionada*, very, you say, excited."

"What's the latest?"

"No more moving to Meridian like last time. *Dios mío.*"

As Angela passed down the hallways, she saw a chronicle of Nana's year-long habitation—the peg board with photos of last spring's Mardi Gras parade for residents, the Fourth of July festivities a couple of months ago. One section said, "Birthdays!" with Christiane Fields listed at February 16. At last year's party, for Nana's eighty-third, they'd enjoyed caramel cake and lactose-free ice cream. Angela had joined them to sing "Happy Birthday," then Nana and Lucky's theme song, "Over the Rainbow," afterward holding her as she sobbed in her room.

"How beautiful to care for somebody like that," she had said as she stroked Nana's hair.

How easily she could imagine being back in her grandparents' antebellum house with its double porches looking out to the Mississippi Sound, going to the second floor with its family portraits, seeing Nana pop out of her bedroom to greet her—petite, beaming, drying her short silver hair with a towel while reporting how she'd just bested Lucky in tennis or gotten back from a frolic in the Sound. In her seventies then, she was still capable of a smooth fox-trot with Lucky at the Broadwater Hotel, even a sexy tango.

"Anybody home?" she called outside Nana's door. She peeked in at a slight, disheveled woman facing the window.

Without turning around, Nana waved her in. "Come here, quick."

Angela walked up beside her. Seagulls hurtled and leaves rained down on the Jefferson Davis property, the sign at its entrance, "Beauvoir," pelted by rain. The Mississippi Sound was a canvas of turbulent paint.

Angela bent down and kissed her cheek. "It's kind of pretty, don't you think?"

"Did you hear the airplanes?"

"They're those big ol' Hurricane Hunters," Angela said. "Just heading home to Keesler. General Wheeler told me so."

"Not dive-bombers?"

"Everything's okay!"

"Really?" She turned and looked at her granddaughter, a hopeful aspect in her faded blue eyes. How bright Nana's eyes had been gazing up at her during her ninth grade dance recital, or as she received her high school diploma.

"Yes."

"Oh, good," Nana said, standing up. Her bracelet, a gold loop she'd worn as long as Angela could remember, slid low on her wrist. "You've put me at ease."

"Max is out of my life," she said.

"Which boy was he?"

"We came to visit last week, remember? The guitar player?"

"Oh, that one!" She shook her head. "I saw the way he looked at you. He was after one thing."

"Oh, Nana, it's not like that anymore."

"Since when!"

Angela laughed.

"You're not working too hard, are you?"

"No, my job's cool."

"Just remember who we are and what we stand for." Nana made a circling motion with her hand. "Let me have a look-see."

Angela spun. "A beautiful young lady," Nana pronounced, holding out her arms.

Even though Angela towered over her, her grandmother's hug, tight around her waist, made her feel protected as a child again.

"Here," said Angela, angling Nana to the side of the bed and sitting her there. "Let's fix you up."

From the side table she picked up the silver brush engraved "CF" and began to draw it through the fine-spun silver hair. "I love the name 'Christiane,'" Angela said, brushing slowly. "If I have a little girl one day, that's what I'll name her. Promise."

"Listen!" Nana exclaimed.

Through the noise of the wind came the far-off piano music. The notes rose and drifted, lost in the storm's churning, then coming back again like the swooping gulls.

"That's our song!" said Nana.

"That's not 'Over the Rainbow.'"

"Where's my scarf?"

Angela took one of the scarves off the peg on the door. "Lemme," she said, putting it around her grandmother's neck. "The red gives you nice color."

"Who said anything about 'Over the Rainbow'?" Nana said.

"Nana, you know your song was 'Over the Rainbow.' We used to sing it with Lucky. They played it when you got married."

"And you know what I know?" Nana reached up and pushed Angela's hand away. "This hurricane," she said, her voice turned flinty, "can blow us all to hell as far as I'm concerned."

"What?"

"Give me my brush back." She stood and grabbed at the brush.

"Here, it's yours."

"I hear the planes, and I hear the song, and I'm not a liar. If that's what you think, then just leave me alone. Go on." She pointed to the door. "Good-bye."

"Nana," Angela pleaded, "don't be like that."

"Well, I need my pocketbook. Somebody took my pocketbook."

Angela found it on the doorknob inside the closet. She handed it to Nana, who peered inside, went to the bureau and put in her lipstick, and slung the bag over her shoulder.

"Come on," Angela said, slipping her arm through Nana's and leading her to where the music cascaded down the hall, "let's just be like we used to."

Cam Nguyen leaned into the tired piano at Coastal Arms, summoning what she could from its beat-up keys. So much for the Bach two-part inventions she loved to race her fingers through, or the Chopin waltzes she rode deliriously like the roller coaster at the fair. In the three weeks she'd been playing at Coastal Arms for tenth grade community service credit, she'd learned a host of antique songs at the behest of the social director, who'd handed her a music book with pretty titles such as "Misty," "Autumn Leaves," and "You're Nobody 'Til Somebody Loves You." Cam had gotten annoyed at first when the residents gathered around and drowned out her notes singing like gray-haired drunks. But Daddy had told her: "To put happiness in the heart of an old person is to honor the wise."

"Stardust" made her think of Daddy, out on the *Miss Mai* with no company but cousin Thanh, who preferred whistling over talk, and a ship-to-shore radio that crackled with tiresome noise. The song's images—purple dusk, climbing stars, lonely nights—could apply to a man on a shrimp boat, too. Hurting for his late wife; bone-tired from five days on the Gulf; hurrying for some far-off harbor to ride out another bothersome hurricane—she pictured Daddy far away. "Quan Am," Cam prayed silently to the Bodhisattva she loved, "keep Daddy safe from this storm."

She began another stanza of "Stardust." How her music brightened old Mr. Smith with his glass lenses as thick as paperweights, and the skinny woman with long white hair, as long as a college student's, falling snowily over her shoulders, and the "newlyweds," as she thought of them—General Wheeler and Mrs. Holcombe—who sometimes held each other and fox-trotted.

And here came Mrs. Fields, too, snapping her fingers as if she were a girl again. Escorting her, as usual, was her granddaughter. Angela had pretty hair—brown, curly—and the faintest freckles on her nose. Cam's Laotian friend, Khampou, twenty-one, had gone gambling at the Cotton Gin and seen Angela working there. "She's got nice, strong legs," he'd wolfishly said. Was Angela trashy? Cam wondered. Did she do things to men for money?

Cam finished "Stardust" and began her last song of the hour as the winds roared overhead. "Satin Doll," it was called, and it reminded her of a cute little doll that sat on the couch at her mother's manicure shop, put there for little girls to play with while their mothers got their nails done.

Knuckles rapped on the piano. She looked up. It was Mrs. Fields.

"Why did you stop?" the old woman asked.

"Ma'am?"

"Why did you stop playing?"

"Nana," said Angela, "let the girl finish the song."

"What's your name, child?"

"Cam Nguyen," she answered, her hands still moving over the keys.

"When what?"

"Nguyen," Cam said, spelling it out. "It sounds like 'When.'"

"Play the one you just did."

"The 'Stardust' song?"

"Yes, that one."

Francie Holcombe, leaning in at the door, protested: "Don't you be trying to tell us what music to hear."

Cam quickly wrapped up "Satin Doll" and moved back into "Stardust," and Mrs. Fields started swaying to the music. Cam thought of an old movie she had watched with her mother in the nail shop, reclining on the couch during her break with the smell of nail polish thick in the air. A couple in the movie had danced to music like this; she imagined Mrs. Fields as the woman.

Mrs. Fields halted, opened her eyes wide as though startled by a ghost. "Stop. Please."

Cam had only reached the first refrain.

"Stop, I ask you!"

The wind was bellowing. Cam's hands froze on the keys. Nana reached to her neck and undid the scarf, held it out, and let it drop over Cam's wrists.

"You dropped your scarf, ma'am."

"It's a gift."

"Nana," said Angela, "it's a Hermès."

"I've got too many of the damn things. Let the girl have it."

Cam's heart beat to the rising wind.

"I'll take it," Angela said.

"Put it on," Nana commanded.

A long silence was filled by rattling overhead.

"Fine, fine," Angela relented, nodding to Cam. "Whatever makes her happy."

Cam slipped it around her neck, feeling the silk slide against her throat.

"Oh," Nana said, "it suits you!"

Cam nodded, mumbled "Thank you," and gathered up her music. It was time to get home before she got caught here in the storm, stranded in this hotel of crazy ancients.

Alone in her room after dinner, Christiane looks out to see no airplanes in the agitated darkness, their lights blinkered out by the turbulent night. But far overhead, she knows, they churn above the clouds, the roar of their engines rising.

Why does the calendar on her wall read 2002 when it is 1941? She fishes a golf pencil out of a drawer, leafs to December, and circles the sixth. She x's out the days until December twenty-third and counts them aloud. Seventeen—that many days until Rosey will be stateside. It is such a long journey for her husband, air hops from Manila, to Guam, to Honolulu, to California. The least she can do is spend a few nights in a sleeper car of the Union Pacific. Even then he will be west for just two weeks, then flying back east, the very Far East, to Clark Air Base in the Philippines. Oh, what a reunion they will have in San Francisco.

She faces the mirror, brushes her hand through her hair. "You're a sight," she says to the woman in the glass. She has little more than two weeks to get ready.

She turns on the radio and gets into bed. She enjoys the public radio station's two hours of big band music, and CDs that Angela has brought her of Sinatra and the Andrews Sisters and Dinah Shore, and late at night when she lies awake anxious for sleep, the round-the-clock talk shows with their annoyed and insistent callers.

On WWL-AM in New Orleans, she hears talk about the tropical storm and callers asking about possible flooding and evacuation routes. People phone in with storm stories—she hears the names "Betsy," "Camille," "Frederic," "Georges"—commenting on paths the big blows have taken.

"Oh," she moans, "where's my music?"

She turns the dial to WMAH, Mississippi Public Radio, where a discussion is wearing on about parallels between 9/11 and Pearl Harbor.

Pearl—the words snag her attention—*Harbor.*

"Rosey," she utters.

But he's in the Philippines, where his trans-Pacific call—far-off, tinny—comes on December sixth.

"Oh, Christiane, my love, my exquisite beauty."

There is a faint tremolo in his voice.

"Rosey, my Rosey, are you well?"

"Yes, love."

"Safe, rested, well fed?"

His long peal of laughter cascades halfway across the planet. She feels him pressed against her now.

"Yes, and you? Tell me."

"I ache for you. I can hardly go through the days without you."

"Seventeen more days," he says.

Seventeen. Yes, she keeps her train ticket on the bedside table.

She envisions him on the Philippine island of Luzon, aviator's cap off, face turned full to the sun. The curve of his profile is vivid to her, his large, brown eyes, prominent nose, and full lips. Even now she can reach out and touch him. Just as he's told her in letters, exotic plants and brightly plumed birds and thatched huts surround him, and he gazes out on it all as he is lifted in his plane, banking over the volcanos and palm trees and cratered lakes, dreaming of his bride as she does of him. She envisions their meeting in California. It will be their second honeymoon bed.

"*We interrupt this program to bring you a special news bulletin.*"

She sits up straight. The swirling night outside the Mississippi window revolves away.

"*The Japanese have attacked Pearl Harbor, Hawaii, by air, President Roosevelt has just announced.*"

Thank God, Rosey is far from there. She sees the boys on the blasted battleships, the cries for help, the sinkings, the planes destroyed in their hangars. Rosey's face floats over it all like a scrim, hovering.

"*Hostilities seem to be opening actually over the entire South Pacific.*"

"Angela?" she says aloud. "Angela!"

"*A second air attack has been reported on Army and Navy bases in Manila.*"

How could she even have a granddaughter when she is worried about her beloved captain, her warrior and poet, still seventeen days away?

The lights flicker; the radio shuts off. "No!" she protests.

The power surges back on.

She does not recognize this place now with its flower print walls, its bright paintings of shrimp boats and lighthouses and camellias, its uniformed attendants speaking foreign languages and saying their sons and daughters are carrying the American flag into new wars.

"This concludes our look back at 'the day that will live in infamy.'"

The wind rises and moans.

"Now we take you to Artie Shaw and His Orchestra."

She hears the grinding of jet engines and the churning of winds and claps her hands over her ears and hums along to "Stardust" so loud it fills her head with a vibrato that beats back at the roaring.

TWO

Men in Uniform

At the Nguyens' house on Oak Street in the early morning, three blocks from casino row, sunlight washed through the den that held objects precious to Phi Nguyen, Cam's father. In frames on the wall were Cam's honor roll certificates, a color photo of Cam as a little girl with her mother, Kieu, in front of Fancy Nails in Biloxi, and a black-and-white snapshot of her sister, Mai, as a toddler in Saigon. On a table was Bodhisattva Quan Am, a two-foot-tall statue that Phi had stuck into his duffel when the family was fleeing Vietnam, long before Cam was born on Mississippi soil. That Isidore had turned west two days before, then bore out to sea, was the goddess's bidding.

Cam had heard the story countless times of the tumultuous voyage on the South China Sea. Despite the tragedies that befell them, Daddy believed that, thanks to the goddess of mercy, they had not all drowned. Quan Am's face was lovely, delicate, her eyes all-seeing. Unlike the Buddha, who had transcended this world, Quan Am had stayed behind to show the way to her and others. At St. Benedict's, her friends had Jesus, and Cam had Buddha, but who matched their Mary? "Quan Am is more powerful than Mary," she had told them the first week of school. "A man was about to get his head cut off with a sword and asked Quan Am for help and the sword broke apart. Could Mary do that?"

On his knees, bending low, Daddy thanked Quan Am for sending Isidore away, then asked her to guide the spirits of Mai and Kieu, to keep them from being troubled. They had died years apart but their souls were linked, daughter and mother.

Supplicant beside him, Cam caught the smell of the shrimp boat on his neck and shoulders, in his mashed-up shirt. She tried to breathe evenly and clear her mind of all earthly concerns, as she had been taught.

She became distracted by Quan Am's hair—plaits woven neatly. If she fixed her hair like that, might Daddy open his eyes to see her, his living daughter, rather than always paying homage to Mai? He pushed her to work harder, yes, make top grades, especially in math and science, and excel in music as her mother had. But it was she, after all, who could communicate with her sister's spirit. Still, he made his pleas to the Boddhisatva, much as the teachers in the Christian school made theirs to the crucifix in chapel.

Daddy said he sent her to St. Benedict's because Catholic Charities had enabled them to come in America and root into the Deep South through the refugee resettlement program, making no demands on their Buddhist faith. But Cam knew it was because he believed the public schools, with their swaggering boys in baggy pants and sneakers, their girls with short skirts and bare midriffs, were no place for a young lady. The parochial school, he believed, was her protection. The priest in charge assured Phi that Cam's own religion would be respected, and dutifully Daddy took a wad of cash four times a year to pay the tuition. She did not tell him that she was preached to often, and took turns reading aloud in chapel from the Gospels like the other girls. If anything, being of a different religion seemed to quicken their interest in her, like she was a project to undertake. Whatever it took, she prized their attention.

There were two other Vietnamese girls at her school, but one had parents who'd become Baptists in a Philippine refugee camp, and the other, the child of an unknown American soldier, was just, well, weird. A Chinese girl a grade below said that the Bodhisattva's name was Quanying, but Cam told her it was Quan Am. They'd gone on the Internet together and seen that the goddess had both names, depending on the culture. In China, she sat on the head of a dragon. In Vietnam, she rested on a lotus blossom. Quan Am would shield her whatever came.

Daddy finished his recitations and rose from the floor. She had enough time before school to fix him breakfast. While he told her about his week on the boat, about the decent haul of shrimp and the calm waters before the storm blew, she heated up rice and grilled the fish he had brought home hauled up with the shrimp. It was bony, oily, but tasty enough when splashed with soy. Daddy lived to catch shrimp, but they were taken, every last one, to market.

From the next room, where he was putting on a clean shirt while she cooked, he told her he had imagined seeing Mai in the waves, swimming. Cam said nothing in response. "Quan Am," she whispered over the skillet, "keep Daddy from drinking."

"Did you play the piano at the home for the old people?" he asked, coming back into the room. "They were frightened because of the storm, I am sure."

"Yes sir."

"It is so sad that these elders are put out like sheep to the pasture. They have no children to care for them."

"It is the way here."

"You will do that to me?"

She shook her head. "I'll cook for you every day."

"It is good that you go there to give them pleasure with your music."

"A lady danced all by herself when I played an old song."

"Such happiness for her. This pleases me." He came and stood by the stove. "Mai," he said, "would be proud."

Mai. Always Mai. She was with them more than if she had completed the voyage.

"Look," she said, knowing something Mai could not offer as her accomplishment: from her pocket she drew out the scarf.

"What is this?" he asked.

"A lady liked my music so much she gave me this gift."

"You must take it back."

"You told me red is happiness."

"You can wear your mother's clothes, there in the closet. Not a stranger's."

"It will insult her."

"Maybe she did not understand what she was giving you—the old, it happens."

"Her daughter said not to, but the old lady practically threw it at me."

"You will take it back to her," he said firmly.

"Daddy!"

He said nothing, but glowered.

"You want me to take it back now? I'll be late for school."

He was a stone.

"After my piano lesson this evening?" she said, her voice softening.

"After your piano lesson," he said.

"Yes sir."

"More fish," he said.

The Cotton Gin was a sleek white hotel and casino along the Highway 90 shoreline, its harbor windows looking out to the curve of Deer Island, and toward the channel, where shrimp boats, in smooth weather, eased home with nets spread like wings and cabin cruisers thrummed by with rock 'n' roll pumping from their decks. Its neon marquee out front of cotton plant, straw hat, and plantation house, invited hotel guests and casino-goers to step into a land of snazzy boutiques, abundant buffets, and jackpot dreams. Across the asphalt, pawn shops and church steeples promised restoration as needed.

Nana had first brought Angela to the Cotton Gin on her fourteenth birthday for a performance of the Cirque du Soleil—Had eight years really passed since then? she marveled—and she had rarely felt more grown up than on that day, arm in arm with Nana in her cream-colored suit. Children were allowed to pass *through* the casino on the way to the theater, Nana had explained, but not so much as pause in front of the games. No matter. She had glimpsed a magical realm.

The coast had been defined in Nana's heyday by antebellum homes and seafood shacks, resort hotels and juke joints, but the casinos had transformed it into a redneck Vegas. When the Mississippi legislature outlawed gambling on land but approved it "offshore," the tricked-up riverboats appeared, then gambling palaces like the Cotton Gin on gargantuan pontoons lashed to resort hotels. Locals who had once waited in line for jobs at Waffle House, or manned the desk at beach hotels with kidney-shaped pools with umbrella tables, now worked in hospitality services at resort kingdoms.

Eight hours hard on your feet and tough on your back was what Angela called it, but she smiled on through. Since her mother had died, then Lucky, it had been just Nana and her. What funds Lucky had left Nana kept them both in the house with the gallery porches until the family attorney, Mr. Flowers, a kindly ninety-year-old, had informed Nana that upkeep on the historic home would soon eat up Lucky's dwindling estate, and she should sell before the next hurricane beat the property down even worse. Use the funds, he told her, to secure a spot in a good residential facility. She tried to give some proceeds to her granddaughter, too, but Angela said her dad could help her if needed.

"You won't get a plug nickel out of that sonuvabitch," Nana had said.

She was right. Getting even a card from her father was like hearing from the man on the moon.

When she had the chance to work a double shift at the Cotton Gin, especially the coveted Friday or Saturday night hours, the tips were so good that money worries eased completely, though, at least for a few days.

Covering for Marilyn from Moss Point, she was at her station at 9 P.M. Friday, tray loaded with drinks, when she heard a ripple of applause. The clapping started near the entrance, and followed a cluster of young men in sky blue uniforms who were walking by the dice tables.

By the craps players and pai gow poker enthusiasts, nodding to the well-wishers, the Keesler boys headed with calm, correct bearing toward the casino's sports bar restaurant with its giant TV screens.

"Give 'em hell!" shouted the rotund man at the roulette wheel.

"Osama'll be a dead sonuvabitch," cried out an old-timer in a VFW hat. "We'll get him."

"Thank you, thank you," called out the two women from Hattiesburg, who demanded their screwdrivers.

There had been no clapping for her father when he returned from

Vietnam, she had learned as a child. In 1969, after his long stint in infantry, he had landed first in San Francisco and walked through Haight-Ashbury in his fatigues, cursed at, spat at by shaggy kids in tie-dye tees with Maharishi beards. He'd shouted back, "I'm one of you," answered by "Baby killer!"

She'd been in fifth grade when he told her that's why he played Country Joe and the Fish obsessively on the tape deck in his truck, more than twenty years after he'd first heard the anti-war ballad. Its question of what people were fighting for was answered with curse words that shocked her in a song: "I don't give a damn," rhyming with "next stop" being "Vietnam." He'd been dragged right off the campus of the University of Georgia to go there, he'd said. He'd spent most of it "high," though she didn't find out what that meant until she was in eighth grade. She heard the story, Mama's version, when he left them shortly after her twelfth birthday, never to return. "Daddy had to wrestle his demons," her mother told her as they lay in bed, the windows open, the breezes from the Mississippi Sound like a demon of her own devouring her heart.

She remembered Lucky and Daddy screaming at each when Daddy said a Fourth of July parade was nothing but "saber rattling," and Daddy sitting alone in his study one Veterans Day, head in hands, when uniformed men marched down the coast road being cheered. He'd refused therapy, she later learned from Mama, not believing in post-traumatic stress disorder (that PTSD was a sham was one thing he and Lucky agreed on). The only therapy he insisted he needed, she'd confided, was "a new life."

A new wife was more like it. He was the only sixty-year-old dad she knew still having babies.

Phone again. No supervisor was looking; she answered. "Nana, this isn't a good time. We'll have a picnic tomorrow, on the beach, okay? I'll come get you at lunch. Yes, yes, love ya, gotta go, bye."

"Co'cola?" asked a man's voice at her shoulder.

"What?"

She turned to find herself looking into the deep brown eyes of an airman.

He repeated the request, then grinned at her.

"Mixed with?" she asked, taking up a golf pencil to jot it down.

"Dinner with a pretty lady."

"I hope you find her."

"Just did."

She put the pencil back down.

"Well, you know, you're not wearing a ring," he said.

"Well, you know you're a walking cliché, don't you?"

Why had she let that slip from her mouth? Always respect the customers was the mantra. Ignore them if they harrass you, call security if they're mean, but hold that smile.

"I couldn't help myself," he said.

"Uniforms don't impress me." She nodded to Brandy. "Try over there."

"I'm ridiculous, I know."

He was, she figured, a half-inch shorter than her, built like a rock, sandy-haired, and with a smile that said expensive orthodontic work as a kid.

She bit her lip, hiding her crooked lower teeth. *Why do I care?*

"It's just I was trying to find my buddies when I saw you, and couldn't resist."

"The pilots are that way." She stuck her chin in the direction of Sports 'n' Ribs.

"Weather warriors," he said.

"Pardon?"

"It's what we do."

"You mean, like"—she laughed, another taboo, ridiculing a patron—"fight the clouds?"

"Ride the winds, too!" He beamed.

"So it was you who saddled up Isidore and took him out of here?"

She noticed a supervisor looking her way now. "I'll get you your drink, sir," she said, picking up the pencil again and writing down the order. She stepped away.

"Isidore wasn't thinking about Mississippi," he said, following her.

"Vectors, water currents, temperature—we could have told you that."

She paused before an ancient crone, took her order. The supervisor had turned away.

"I don't need experts," she said to him over her shoulder. "I can read these things in the sky."

"A gal who loves weather. Go out with me!"

"Sure bet, rain man." She made her way to other customers down the labyrinth of slots.

He cut her off at the pass, held out his hand. "Franklin Semmes, Senior Airman, Keesler Air Force Base."

"Angela Sparks," she said despite herself.

"Call me Frank."

She reached out and touched his fingers, the barest gesture she could afford.

"Maybe," he persisted, "we could have coffee sometimes?"

"I'm moving to Paris tomorrow."

"I'll be back," he said.

"Have a nice life, Frank."

Dusk settles along the coast, consuming the storied homes and pensive oaks in first darkness, and Nana, on the side porch of Coastal Arms, looks across the street to the side gate of Beauvoir. On days when the wind lies low, she can sometimes hear the tour guide leading visitors about the grounds of the Confederate president's home, telling how the weary Mississippian buried his sorrows there after defeat. As the day dwindles, the lights begin to rise on the casino fashioned from an old riverboat at the end of a dock opposite the grounds.

Through the side gate, which seems to be open, Nana sees another light rising, this one gentler: the white headstones of the Confederate veterans cemetery behind the presidential home.

"Christiane," she hears someone say, "aren't you coming in for dinner?"

"I'll be right there," she says.

It is autumn and the days are shorter. As voices hum and dinnerware clatters from an open window of the dining hall, the darkness is settling quickly, the dusk like a wind moving through more forcefully. The tops of the headstones still hold the light, and begin to look like the caps of soldiers in a fog.

She sees a movement along the rows.

Her grandmother used to think that spirits dwelled in the upper reaches of their ancestral home, and there are residents of Coastal Arms who worry that the Confederate dead, buried so close, will wail and moan.

But she does not cotton to the notion of ghosts.

The traffic between her and the side gate has fallen to a lull. She glances around. She is all alone.

She steps off the patio and onto the scrub grass, and then onto the road, and the only car that approaches slows to a halt and the driver waves her across.

Are the grounds closed for the evening? Is there not one light on in Jefferson Davis's house, which stands far off in the darkness, an antebelleum phantasm of columns and porches?

"Rosey?"

Someone is moving along the grounds, cap a pale beacon showing the way.

Arlington Cemetery in Washington, the rows of headstones, fresh and white and marching, forever it seems, from the Civil War to the present to wars not yet imagined, over the curve of the earth. She sees Rosey walking through them, toward her, to meet up on a bright spring day when cherry blossoms suffuse the city with a heady languor, a softness that almost mutes, but never quite can, the sorrow of so many lost. She has a great-uncle buried close by who fought in the Spanish-American War. Rosey's people, he tells her, lie in Eastern European graves.

It is their last day together before he flies out from Bolling Field— the president is building his defenses against Japanese expansion— and where he is going, he assures her, the Philippines, it is safe.

"The war is raging far away," he says. The Germans, the British and

French and Russians—it is their war.

They walk by the Tomb of the Unknown Soldier, where a fallen one of the Great War lies in honor, the changing of the guard a slow, dignified ceremony before the tomb inscribed, "Here rests in honored glory an American soldier known but to God."

They pause, silent, hold hands.

"I'll be back home before you know it," Rosey says.

He looks so young, his angular face, his olive complexion, his sensuous lips meeting hers as they sit on a bench at the edge of the park, then continue on to downtown D.C., where they find a restaurant near the mall and drink wine. Their remaining hours together rise like verdant hills to traverse. She can see them stretching before her. One. Two. Three.

"I want," she tells him, "to start a family."

"Yes, love."

"I think," she whispers, leaning close over the goblets filled with sadly festive Burgundy, "this is a good time."

Then, so softly that it sends tingles up her back, he leans over and brushes her lips with his. He leans back, orders two more glasses of wine. The taste of it is smooth and dark on her tongue, down her throat. They eat lightly, drink again.

Before long it will be their first wedding anniversary, and she already has her present for him, but knowing now he will be departing, she pulls it down from the closet when they arrive at their apartment. He unwraps it. The silver goblet shines. In its curve Christiane can see their own reflections, her soft, choir girl's face, fair complexion, and yellow hair, his swarthiness, his almond eyes, and short, wavy black hair. He lifts the cup to his lips and pretends to drink. "*L'chayim*," he says.

"To life," she proudly translates.

"That's right, my love."

"You can use it when we go to your brother's for Passover," she says. "I've been reading more about it. Some people even say it was Christ's Last Supper."

"They accept you," he says, "you know they do. They love you, too."

"But we don't have to save it," she says, taking the goblet from him, wiping it out with a napkin, and setting it on the table. She goes to the refrigerator and takes out a bottle wrapped in sparkly paper. "All we need is a band playing 'Stardust.'"

He takes off the champagne bottle wrapping and pops the cork and fills the goblet, and they take turns sipping from it, filling it again, yet again.

When they stumblingly strip off their clothes and fall into bed, she relishes the smooth length of his body against her, and she presses her lips into the place in the crook of his neck she calls her own.

"*This is the time,*" she knows and whispers, but only to herself.

She hears a buzzing at her ear.

"Rosey?"

Groggily he answers, "Yeah . . "

"I love you."

"I love . . ."

She feels his body sag against her, and the depth of his night breathing, and then the first morning light is striking through the window. "Hold me," she is saying, but he is up, hurriedly dressing, saying he will be late, that he has fifteen minutes to make it back to the base, "No, hold me now," she is saying, but even as he is leaning over to kiss her deeply, he is, at the same time, pulling away, saying, "I will write to you every day, I'll be home soon, my exquisite beauty, my love," as she is saying, "Hold me."

And she is saying it now, looking down at her lined hands, at the wrinkles on her fingers.

Voices are rising and lights dance closer.

"Mrs. Fields?" It is the voice of a young girl. "Mrs. Fields!" She is waving a red scarf, like a danger signal.

She turns and starts to run through the headstones but trips, a hot pain coursing up her leg as she falls against the spongy grass. The night earth spreads around her like the Mississippi Sound swallowing a drowning woman.

"Mrs. Fields, what happened?" says the girl, who is kneeling next. "I went looking for you at the home to give you this but saw you out here and now you fell. Oh, Mrs. Fields, you must be hurt . . ."

"Leave her alone!" shouts another voice, a man's, and that is followed by the dancing lights—flashlights, Christiane sees, wildly waving as the Coastal Arms staff come running across the grounds.

"Nana!" What is Angela doing here, too?

"Nana," Angela says, coming close, "they couldn't find you, you can't just walk away like that. They called me at work. Oh, dear Nana."

A Coastal Arms guard is taking Cam by the wrist, wresting away the silk scarf. "You'll never steal something from one of our residents again!"

"She didn't do anything!" Angela exclaims. "My grandmother gave her that."

The guard lets her go.

"Nana, oh Nana," Angela says, helping her up. "You can't just disappear like that."

"I'd like to disappear now," she says, brushing dirt off her dress and looking around at the cluster of people.

"Oh, Nana, look at all the ruckus you've raised."

"Angela, my Angel, I'm so . . ." She covers her face with her hands.

THREE

At First Sight

Seeing Max head toward her across the casino floor, Angela could hardly imagine curling up with him under a slow ceiling fan. Without his guitar to give him stature, his lank body, stubbled chin, and Frank Zappa T-shirt turned him into a scrawny hound.

After dating him for three months, her world record, she knew that wild-eyed look. How much pot had he smoked before spiraling into darkness?

There was nowhere to hide.

"You don't answer my calls," he said.

"I'm working."

"I was gonna turn my life inside out for you," he said.

"Oh, please."

"Music's my life, but I was going to get a job, talk about our future."

"Your future's weed," she said.

"You didn't complain last weekend, when we were"—his voice softened, a familiar strategy, slipping into a refrain—"*dreaming in the heat of you and me.*"

"That song sucks."

"You're a liar. You loved it."

"And you're a loser."

"We had a thing, a thing! Feel it!"

"Don't raise your voice in here."

"You don't tell me what not to do."

"Stop it," she whispered fiercely.

"It's you who's shaking your ass for tips. At least I'm doing something creative."

"Nana was right about you."

"What does that broken-down old bitch know?"

She watched her hand as if it were someone else's, fingers wrapping around a bourbon and water on her tray and flipping it at his snarling face.

She counted the moments until she would hear the words from the station boss, "You're fired!" but a loud, triumphant bell sounded over a slot machine where a man tethered to an oxygen tank had hit three lemons. Casino managers were already headed his way. What a win! A frail elder, no less! What could be better for business! She knew their thoughts. As they took his picture to go on the jackpot wall, gawkers pressed around.

"Co'cola, Angela?" It was the weather warrior.

"Who the hell are you?" asked Max, standing his ground.

"I think you're bothering this lady," Frank said.

"Whoa!" Max roared, wiping at his face. "Captain America!"

"Both of you, both of you," Angela said, "just get out of here."

"You know this guy?" Max said, poking a finger in Frank's chest.

"Why don't we take this outside," Frank said, moving to within an inch of Max.

Brandy was there now, too. "What you got driving these boys crazy?"

Angela saw an even darker streak in Max's eyes, like when he'd thrown a microphone across the stage at Rudy's.

"Yes, Frank's my friend," she said, grabbing the airman's arm. "Save your neck, Max, go home. Go home."

"Go home," Frank repeated.

Max puffed up, took a step toward Angela, held his pose, then crumpled like he'd had the wind knocked out of him and slunk away.

Frank patted her hand. "Hey, friend," he said.

"You again." She let go of his arm, turned, and started taking drink orders. The tray was shaking in her hands.

"Beautiful time of year to take the ferry to Ship Island," he said.

"Would you do me the honor someday?"

"What?"

"Ship Island, it's—"

"I know what Ship Island is."

"Honor of joining me on an excursion there? The boat seats two hundred. That enough chaperones?"

"I've got a weird schedule," she said.

"Which means yes?"

Brandy was looking on, raising her eyebrows at Angela, giving the slightest little nod of the head.

"Okay," Angela told him. "I guess you helped me out."

"It's what I do," he said.

"Don't get carried away," she said. "Okay, okay."

"After church on Sunday? Two o'clock?"

"After *church*? This isn't going to work," she said.

"What's wrong with two o'clock?"

"No, never mind." She shook her head. "Meet you there."

When she drove by Keesler after work, she looked in to see uniformed men in formation ready to protect Mississippi from terrorist incursions, better yet, she thought, from boisterous fans overrunning casinos after New Orleans Saints games. If she'd had Frank's phone number, she would have called to cancel the date. What else could she do, hand a folded note to the guard and ask him to pass it on? She could not even remember his last name.

What did she even have appropriate to wear? She stopped in at the Gulfport Mall, looked over the summer clearance. "At least Nana will be entertained," she thought, her grandmother feeling low since her fall, her leg bruised purple, wrist sore.

At Coastal Arms the next morning, as Nana sat in her chair, Angela modeled the two outfits. One was a sleeveless blue print sundress, the other a yellow silk blouse with her jeans.

"Which one do you like best?" Angela asked.

"What's his name?" Nana asked.

"What makes you think this has to do with a guy?"

Nana waited.

"Frank," she finally answered. "He's Air Force."

"Wear the dress."

On the dock, the Sunday afternoon breeze felt good against her legs, the Gulf Coast heat subsided, the love bugs gone until next September. Biloxi fall meant a deep azure sky and the Sound sparkling with sunlight.

"Makes you feel tangled up in blue," said Frank, looking overhead, as the ferry moved out through the harbor.

"That's not original, you know."

"Bob Dylan," he said.

"I didn't take you for a Dylanite," she said.

"Is that like a Canaanite?"

"I didn't learn all that much in Sunday school," she said.

"My roommate at Kentucky Faith was a Dylan freak," he said. "'Slow Train Coming' gives me the chills. Dylan's faith journey's been amazing."

"My dad used to listen to him."

"Cool dad."

"I think he was getting a different message. Y'all wouldn't agree on much."

"I can get along with anybody."

"It's been three years since I've even seen him."

"I'm so sorry. No wonder you're hurtin'."

"Did I say I was hurtin'?"

"We all are in some way."

"Hey, this isn't some sort of church thing, is it, you're doing with me?"

He laughed. "We're all in different places," he said.

Gulls came close to the ferry, laughing, too, or maybe crying, she could never tell quite which.

As Frank named far-off clouds—cumulonimbus to the south with cirrus sweeping the horizon—she could not help but look at his bright teeth, his clean jaw. Max had favored a perpetual dark stubble. Frank was scrubbed by the wind.

Had she ever gone out with Max during daylight hours? They had always met up in his garage, or late at night at a club when she'd scrunch into her tightest jeans and don a black tee. Her dress whipped around her now, a delicious feeling, like waiting to dive into a pool.

"It's beautiful out here," she said.

"Air pressure"—he closed his eyes a moment, turned his head upward, then looked back at her—"I'd put it at a thousand and fifteen millibars.."

"Be my guest," she said.

"A thousand and seven being average. High pressure"—he made a sweeping gesture with the back of his hand, presenting the world to her view—"great weather."

"I thought all you Air Force guys wanted to be *Top Gun*."

"I was raised in Marks," he said, "in the Delta. Cotton as far as you could see. Summers I'd come see Grandaddy here in Biloxi. Big Frank, we call him."

"So you're Little Frank?"

He shook his head. "That's my daddy. We're back to just plain Frank again with me. Big Frank was a walking history of hurricanes, or half walking—he lost his leg in the war."

He told how Big Frank would regale him with tales of yesteryear storms—1938, 1942, 1951, and on to the named ones.

"Alice was the first girl name for a hurricane," he said, "in 1953. Bob was the first boy's name, not until 1979, just in time to make way for Frederic. A year earlier Hurricane Frederic would have been Florence or Fay. 'Modern times,' Big Frank would say.

"He kept his old hurricane tracking charts in a kitchen drawer, the kind you get at the grocery store, and I used to take them out and look at the lines. One dead-ended at Biloxi—Camille. 'How come you didn't draw her line further, Granddaddy?' I asked him. ''Cause she had us runnin', is why.'

"He taught me to respect the elements, he did. I remember one July down here when I was a young teenager, we just stood out in the yard together while the rain was falling—he had me turn my face upwards to taste it—and he said, 'That's my church.'"

"He sounds like he was a good grandfather," she said.

"Was? He's sitting on his Back Bay dock right now nursing a high-ball and a peg leg."

"Oh, that's nice to hear!"

"A blessing," he said. "Though he can test your faith when he goes on a tear about this or that."

"I take care of my Nana," she said.

"I heard you on the phone that day with her when I met you. I thought right then and there you could be the girl for me."

She felt herself blush, turned to look out at the Sound. Even as he was oddly appealing, going on about Grandaddy, she knew she had to dash his hopes. Otherwise it would prove a long afternoon on Ship Island.

"I'm Big Frank's best friend," he said, and she felt her heart open like a paper white.

"I just don't go out with military guys," she said.

"We've served our country in five wars," he said, as though he hadn't heard her at all. "Civil War, Spanish American, World War I, World War II, Vietnam. Now the war on terror makes a sixth. Franklin, Frank, Frankie, Big Frank, Little Frank, Me."

"I hate war," she said.

"I hate it, too. That's why I'm willing to fight to keep there from being an even bigger one."

"How come you're not a Marine or something then?"

"I read this book when I was at Big Frank's that summer he made me taste the rain," he said, "Heroes of World War II, and there was one story about Army Staff Sergeant Robert A. Dodson. He'd trained as a weather observer in New Orleans and in 1944 was assigned to a weather squadron in England. He was about to learn how to para-chute when the jump school was closed down to get ready for D-Day. He learned to mock-jump, never left the ground, until he went up with the Eighty-second Airborne. Then he got to do a real jump, his first and only—0230, June sixth, D-Day—over Sainte-Mère-Église, a little village behind the beaches. Tied to another chute were his instruments—

psychrometer, psychrometric tables, primitive stuff in terms of weather.

"But he had these, too"—Frank made a "V" with the fingers of his right hand and aimed them at his eyes—"and these." He touched his ears. "All the equipment in the world can't beat looking and listening, and instinct. That's what I like to think I have, it's what I hope I have. Instinct.

"So there he is, coming down behind enemy lines and he even injures his knee, but he gets his instruments and camouflages them for later because right at first there's combat. Germans everywhere. Dodson and his group are Air Support, sure, but they're riflemen, too—that's what's so great about it—and they hold them off, and the beaches are hell, you know, Utah, Omaha, Gold, Juno, Sword, but we're breaking the German hold. You know what happens then?"

Behind Frank she saw dolphins beginning to arc out of the water, but just watched his lips and teeth, saying, "Tell me."

"He goes and gets his weather equipment from where he'd hid it, and with a VHF radio starts sending dispatches. Dodson's giving our guys exact, up-to-the-minute information about mist and fog and wind and visibility in France. He saved lives, Angela. And he did his part to help the Normandy Invasion be a success." He fell silent, then turned to look out over the blue-green calm. "I want to play a part, too."

"In what?" she said.

"In the conflict between us and them, light and dark, that's going on now." He turned back to her.

"You make it sound like the end of time."

"Armageddon's coming, I can tell you that. And when that happens, like Mr. Dylan says, you won't need a weatherman to know which way the wind blows.

"You have nice hair," he said suddenly, then reached out and pushed it away from where the wind swirled it across her face. He let his fingers linger against her temple, then brush her cheekbone. She reached up and moved his hand away.

"You don't know the first thing about me," she said.

"I can tell you this," he answered. "Storm ahead."

"*Where?*" she said with alarm.

He pointed at her. She shook her head and laughed.

As the ferry came to dock, they disembarked to explore the island. A boardwalk coursed through dune grass and sand, cleaving the island in two. As they ambled over it, she told Frank that she had lost her mom when she was thirteen, only offering, "She just died, it was a car accident," and that she had spent a while trying to live with her dad, an angry Vietnam vet, who'd already started another family in Rochester, where he was working for Kodak. His new wife—"he finally divorced her and married yet again, he's one of those types"—had it in for her. "I did a year of school up there before Nana rescued me."

"I guess that's where you got your Yankee sass," he said.

"Could be."

Frank told her that the island had been a staging area for the British assault on New Orleans to the west in 1814. They entered a brick rotund called Fort Twiggs used by the Confederates until the Union warships came into the deep water harbor blasting away. "When your Yanks won," he said, "it became Fort Massachussetts. We're getting you back, though, every time a damn snowbird loses his pension in a Biloxi casino."

"Getting *them* back," she corrected. "I could jump rope to 'M-i-double-s, i, double-s, i, double-p, i' before I could recite the whole alphabet."

In the fort, as they wandered beneath the curved ceilings, Frank showed her the cannon emplacements with their oblong windows opening out to the harbor, and the cannons themselves, like century-and-a-half-old creatures petrified to iron. They came to a crude, brick oven out in the open. Frank laid his hand on it. "A hot-shot furnace," he said. "They got the cannon balls hot as blazes before blasting them at the ships. Technology."

Near the exit Frank paused and showed her a plaque with hundreds of names etched there, and the words above them: "In Memory of the Confederates Interred on Ship Island."

"There's a graveyard here?" she said.

"Look." Frank touched a name on the plaque. "Franklin Semmes."

"The first Frank!" she exclaimed.

He kicked off his shoes and she did the same and they left the board-walk and padded through a dry marsh area, paralleling the beach. Beneath her bare feet the sand was faintly damp, cooler than the air. Animal tracks—paw prints, the curving lines of snakes—wove into the scrub.

"Somewhere around here," he said as they arrived at a sandy stretch giving way to the length of the island, "is where Franklin Semmes was buried."

Angela looked around, seeing only sea oats and dunes and, far off, a lighthouse.

"The Union had a stockade on the island," he said sorrowfully. "Oh, Lord, can you imagine what it was like in the summer? He died a prisoner. They didn't even bring his body home. I figure this is where the burial ground was. Washed away, every last one of them. Vanished. Just like those poor folks in the World Trade Towers. Not a trace." He shook his head. "That's not right, Angela, not right at all. Something must be done."

She stepped up to him, put her hands on the sides of his smooth face, and kissed him once, gently. "I'm sorry," she said, pulling away. "I don't know what came over me. You suddenly just seemed so sad."

He seized her by the shoulders and pulled her back, kissing her hard.

The ferry sounded its horn. They raced to the boardwalk, got their shoes, and made it aboard, sitting next to each other in the stern, watching Ship Island return to a mirage.

When Nana heard the piano music, she felt the notes move up through her feet. There were others who danced on their own—swaying, clapping along, even doing a little box step—as Cam played from the book *Shows of Rodgers and Hammerstein*.

"Music makes you young again, Nana," said Angela with her in the lounge again.

Her sweet Angel, always so attentive. How was it that Angela's father had turned out to be such a wretched son of a bitch? How pitifully Don had treated Dorothy. Nana remembered how, when he was first home from Vietnam, they had all gone dancing together at the club. Don had sat, unwilling even to tap his fingers to the beat. She knew right then and there that their marriage would be in shambles. But there was nothing she could tell her daughter. She would make it up with all she could teach her granddaughter.

"You can tell a lot about someone from watching them on the floor," she said to Angela.

Nana saw General Wheeler by the window. How sad he looked, all alone with his sporty little mustache and bushy Gregory Peck eyebrows. Rumor had it that Francie Holcombe had gone for the weekend to visit her son, who had refused to let her return to Coastal Arms, looking into a residence for her in Pass Christian. The old general caught her gaze and smiled. She turned away, as if she had not noticed.

"Are you okay?" Angela asked.

"Why do you ask?"

"You just got so red!"

"Maybe I'm going through the change of life," she said.

"At eighty-three!?"

"I think he wants to dance with me," Nana whispered, looking back at Wheeler, who was giving her the faintest, most heart-palpitating nod. She dipped her head in response, like a swan.

Wheeler stood slowly, creakily, and made his way onto the floor. Cam finished her song. He made a circling motion in the air to her, to start again. Cam opened into a waltz.

With another gesture, as if signaling to a longtime partner, he summoned Nana.

"*One two three, one two three,*" she said to herself, as though she needed to count out what was already deep in her central nervous system.

The residents of Coastal Arms all seemed to appear at once, coming from the playroom with its Ping-Pong table and game boards, from the occupational therapy room with its macramé table and painting easels, from the lounge where the Christmas TV advertisements were rolling despite the fact it was not yet Thanksgiving. From the corner they gathered to watch as Nana took the general's left hand while he placed the right one behind her back, and they stepped into the music.

But as they turned slowly—*one two three, one two three*—Nana noticed that the residents were not looking at them but at the door. When Wheeler revolved her that way, she saw what they were looking at— Francie Holcombe, her mouth open in silence, her cane lifted off the ground, pointing at them like a shotgun.

"I knew you were after him!" Francie shouted.

"I thought you'd left," said the general, still waltzing Nana, "and were never coming back."

"So she moved right in, did she!"

"There was no reason for me to sit in the corner all by myself," he said, speaking to her over Nana's shoulder as they slowly spun.

"Get your hands off him!" Francie cried and started to rush at Nana, but the general let go and turned to Francie, saying, "There, there, it was me who asked her to dance."

"She's had her eye on you!"

Nana was aware that the residents had encircled them, looking stupefied but eager, as if hoping for a brawl.

"Him?" said Nana, turning her shoulder to them both. "I could have my pick of any man I wanted. He's a nice guy, but after all . . ." She joined her granddaughter. "Come on, Angela. Let's blow this joint."

Arm in arm, like haughty schoolgirls, Nana and Angela pushed through the onlookers and out of the building, walking the block to the traffic light at Highway 90. "Could you believe her!" said Nana. "The nerve. In my day I could have turned the general's head, and he'd have never looked twice at that . . . that . . ."

"Say it, Nana. Come up with a good word for her."

"That ragamuffin!"

"Oh, Nana, I didn't know you had it in you!"

"Common tramp is what she is."

The light changed. They crossed to the median, then to the other side, descending three short concrete steps to the sand. The manmade beach unfurled flat as an ironing board broken by the tinselly dazzle of casinos and the shiny rectangles of seashell emporia. They strolled westward, where the sun became an orange ball sinking over far-off New Orleans.

"Do you believe in love at first sight?" Angela asked.

"Not if it's Sam Wheeler."

"So you do, more or less."

"Have you fallen in love with that pilot?"

"He's not a pilot. And I don't believe it can happen like that anyway."

"You poor girls today. Of course it can happen like that, it can happen any way at all. Not sex, mind you, love. It's about here"—she touched her head—"and here." She laid her hand on Angela's heart. "Not . . ." She waved her hand in the general direction below her hips.

They came to a lean-to tilted toward the Sound and detoured around the front of it, the gentle surf inching toward their feet. Nana glanced into the little shelter and glimpsed a couple wrapped up together. Butt naked, the man lay against the woman, who was on her back, her legs wrapped around her lover's hips, her red toenails waving in the breeze. "Oh, my God!" Nana exclaimed.

She grabbed Angela's hand and tugged her faster. "Get a hotel!" she shouted behind her, then began to giggle, and Angela joined in. They continued on, raucous teens on a sunset stroll.

"There was this one boy," Nana said suddenly. "Oh, never mind."

"There was this one boy," Angela repeated. "And . . ."

"And nothing."

"And . . ."

"He had the softest brown hair, like silk, short of course, West Point short, and eyes the color of Hershey's chocolates. I was spending the summer with my Nana, in Newport, and my girlfriends and I sometimes came into the City on a weekend. We met these guys, these West Point men, I should say. His name was Walter.

"He said, 'Do you want to go to Roseland? We can double date with one of my buddies and one of your girlfriends,' so I said okay. It used to be near Times Square, maybe it still is, and the fox-trot was popular, so we did that, but the lindy hop was, too, they named it after Lucky Lindy, who flew over the ocean. It was grand. Then he asked me to meet him at the Waldorf for supper the next night, just the two of us. And there was an orchestra, of course. Even fancier than Newport.

"We drank champagne. One glass. It went right to my head. Was I even eighteen years old? Love at first sight, yes, he had brown eyes, like dark gemstones, and just as hard."

"Nana . . ."

She held her hand up, looking out to the Sound, seeing the old hotel.

"'I have a room,' he told me. 'I've got another bottle of champagne up there.'

"I said nothing. I just went along. I was a fool. I went along! I can still imagine looking out on the city and seeing the lights. And then he kissed me, and then he touched me. How could I let him!"

"But he had touched you when y'all were dancing."

"Not like that. Where no decent woman would have allowed."

"Oh, Nana, that was so long ago."

"Not to me, dear."

"Nobody cares about that kind of thing anymore."

"Rosey would have cared."

"You were dating somebody else, too?"

"We met later, at a New Year's Eve dance in Georgetown. I was visiting my girlfriend, Bernice, in D.C.. Rosey. He was handsome, exotic, of a different faith, but just like me, too, in so many ways, Jewish or Christian. My flyer who went off to the Philippines."

"Oh, this is all so romantic. I never knew!"

"Romantic? It was a terrible thing to be a prisoner, and such a young boy, such a handsome boy. Such a devoted . . ."

"Friend?"

"Husband, Angela."

"You had a husband before Lucky?"

"We were children."

"I'm twenty-two years old and you never told me this? I can't believe it! I don't even know his whole name!"

"I was even younger than you are now. We were married, and then he had to leave." Nana stopped talking. Sandpipers skittered by them, a ship's wave from the Sound throwing a skein of water onto the beach, then drawing it back.

"And he never came home," Angela said. "That's it, he just went to war and—"

"Stop!" Nana implored. "Just let him be."

Dear Bodhisattva Quan Am,

My name is Cam Nguyen and my father is devoted to you. He was born and raised in Vietnam, but I was born here in Mississippi. I live by myself with him. My mother died four years ago. She made ladies' hands beautiful. I never knew my big sister, Mai. You know her name. Daddy lights candles to her spirit all the time. She is with him more than me. I do not know why. She was born in Vietnam; maybe only you, as beautiful and calm as the mountainside, Daddy says, can take his message to her.

I am writing to you because Daddy does not listen to me when I talk to him. But he will listen to you. The girls at my school say Jesus talks to them. I don't think you speak like that. You are a woman and understand me and can say things in other ways. If Mama were here, I would talk to her.

Bodhisattva, I am afraid for Daddy when he goes on his boat for many days. He has a little statue of you there, too, where he burns incense and sets out an apple. "The seeds," he tells me, "tell a story about new life coming out of old." I am like the seed of that apple, but Daddy sees only the fruit. Mai has been gone from Daddy's life for many years, but he sees only her.

I am here, Daddy, in front of you. I am your American daughter, your Mississippi daughter. I cannot be anybody else.

When Cam finished her note, she went to her father and asked him for the truck keys. "I need to go to the drugstore," she said.

"Come back in twenty minutes," he said. "It will soon be ten o'clock. Be very careful."

She was over fifteen-and-a-half so her Mississippi intermediate license allowed her to drive until 10 P.M. In the truck, with the note folded in her pocket, she headed down Oak Street, past the pawnshop and Vietnamese restaurants and pool halls and filling stations, past the doughnut shop and the outlet mall with its gold jewelry and yogurt and CD shops, across I-10, and to the side road to the high school.

It was there on the dirt road heading off to the right, near the falling-in barn and trailer park, that she turned and slowed, until she passed the trailer with the Rebel flag window curtains and turned into the shell parking area of the Buddhist Temple.

Quan Am, thirty feet tall, rose before the small wood frame Temple, visible by the streetlamp. The monk's car was not there. Cam was alone.

In the pale light she stepped out of the truck and approached the towering figure whose right hand was held up in a sign of the Buddha and whose left held a down-turned pitcher of water. She pressed her hands together and bowed, then took out her note and set it at the Bodhisattva's feet. She struck a match, touched it to the paper, and sent her missive, as ashes and smoke, toward the serene, knowing gaze.

FOUR

Surrender

Frank strategized their dates like an art, a Dixie Chicks concert at the Biloxi Coliseum, boiled crabs and beer at the Friendship House, a James Bond movie, a boat ride. Angela told him that men she'd gone out with had typically called last minute, mostly to hang out at Rudy's. "I'm impressed with your planning," she said, "of course, I don't *officially* date military, like I said."

He laughed and said, "Nothing official about us."

"I did mention you to Nana."

"When can I meet her?"

"When I know it'll stick, at least for a while."

"You already heading out the door?"

"You'll meet her soon enough."

When they sat in his car looking out at lighthouses across the Sound, and the oldies station played Dylan's "Lay, Lady, Lay," she leaned over and kissed him. As she sang along quietly, he fantasized about her lying across the big brass bed. The way she pressed against him, he knew she was willing. But the time for that was not right either.

As November unfolded, she entered his mind at every turn, as he did his five-mile run at dawn wearing a rucksack, then a hundred push-ups and fifty chin-ups; pored over "Severe Convective Storms" and "Meteorological Measurement Systems" in weather class; spent two hours on computers studying forecasting. Angela, Angela, wove through it all. The courses that awaited him, some at other bases—field training, water survival skills—would demand physical stamina. Mental discipline above all was essential. *Coela Bellatora* was the motto, he told Angela.

"Weather Warriors. Mud to sun."

"I'll go for the sun part," Angela said.

He tried to approach faith in their conversations, finding out she'd had little churchgoing as a kid—her mother had her baptized in the Presbyterian Church to please Nana—but that was about it.

"Religion's fine," she said. "Just don't let anybody preach to me about it."

In fellowship meetings he had shared his story a hundred times. He would wait until the time was right to reveal it to Angela.

On his free time, when he went to Biloxi Beach to walk and pray, he knew that the Lord had given him a very special kind of faith journey. He liked to trace it in his mind.

Growing up at Sunrise Baptist in Marks, he'd sat in the front pew with his mother and sister as Daddy preached. When he was baptized at age nine, he could not imagine anyone but the Reverend Frank Semmes dunking him into the baptismal pool. He was brought back up into a father's as well as pastor's embrace.

In his teens he began to realize he was also on display, a "PK," a "preacher's kid," held to a higher standard of behavior, watched by all. The men in their starched suits, the ladies in prim dresses—they looked on at his family as if it were they who sat in judgment. And he gave them all much judging to do.

By the time he'd gotten his driver's license, the girls became his vice, his insides turning over with yearning from the glance of a slender blond or black-haired darling as mysterious as night.

When his buddies began to pass around flasks of sour mash whiskey, it was like a struck match to a fuse. One swig, another, and he was a goner. The devil could come in a dress and heels, or blue jeans and sandals, no matter. Burying himself, half drunk, against the flesh of a hot babe was all he wanted.

"No son of mine's going to be running the roads, stinking of whiskey and whores," his daddy told him. "No, not my son."

"Jesus turned the water to wine," he'd spoken back.

His father raised his hand to slap him but held his rage and simply said: "You're a foolish boy. Wine, wine? 'Oinos' is the word in Greek, grape juice. Not booze, not whiskey! Jesus was no saloon keeper. You've heard me preach on that, if you were even listening. Study your Bible, study!"

Lord knows he had tried.

He had sworn off liquor and started poring over Bible verses until he could not see straight.

He listened closely as his father preached on Matthew 28: 16–20: "Therefore go and make disciples of all nations, baptizing them in the name of the Father and of the Son and of the Holy Spirit, and teaching them to obey everything I have commanded you." It was the Great Commission, Jesus's directive after leaving the tomb before ascending to Heaven.

To Honduras, Ecuador, the Philippines, and West Africa, Sunrise congregants and others flocked as missionaires, fulfilling that mandate. Frank took up the charge, too, traveling with a group to the Dominican Republic, building houses in the morning, at night taking part in showing the Jesus film and clapping with joy as sinners answered the call. He was a model PK.

He headed to Kentucky Faith College. The road signs to bourbon distilleries were like invitations to Gehenna, but the ministry would be his path. He had not yet heard the calling to pastor a flock, but when he did, he would be ready.

But the calling came from a redheaded teaching assistant in Bible class who made his body race with desire. When he was kicked out of the school, Daddy said, "God help you," and sent him to live with Big Frank. If anything, a grandfather who had survived the brutalities of the war, a POW who had come to faith by the hardest war could show him the righteous path.

It did not take Frank long to discover his grandfather was hardly churchgoing reverential. But the old man tolerated no foolishness either. He sent Frank to scrape boat barnacles at the dry dock. While grinding at the port side of a barnacled hull, he met Brother Tim, chipping away on the starboard.

Forever after, they would describe their meeting as two halves creating a whole.

Frank had told Tim his story; Tim told him about Victory Brotherhood. "Jesus," Tim said, "is the God of second chances. Victory Brotherhood is his church."

At Victory, Frank had walked into a sanctuary of broken men and women, the homeless, the alcoholic and drug dependent, the feeble and the poor. Here were no deacons in freshly starched white shirts and black coats and ladies in somber Sunday dress *tsk-tsking* at his failings, but the pious of all backgrounds in worn jeans and threadbare suits from mission store racks.

Brother Tim had led him down to the beach one night and told him of "the key to true faith," that "each of us has his own key, we have to know what it is, the lock, the door." When Frank had looked up at the sky over the Sound, the clouds parted, showing a cavalcade of stars blown by the wind, heat lightning brightening all Biloxi before the heavens plunged into starry velvet again.

The words of Mark 13: 25-26 rose before him: "The stars of heaven shall fall, and the powers that are in heaven shall be shaken. And then shall they see the Son of man coming in the clouds with great power and glory."

He had dropped to his knees and wept.

It was a breezy Friday evening when he walked with Angela down to the spot and he began to tell her about Brother Tim.

"Right here," he said, "is where I fell to my knees."

"Oh."

"The stars and the sky, the wind and the clouds, the storms. My key," he said. "The weather."

She looked out at the Sound, back at Frank. She seemed as distant as Ship Island.

"It's right here that I was truly saved."

"That's nice."

"Nice?"

"I just don't relate to it, Frank. It's not how I was raised."

"This is not about raising. This is about being, about becoming. That's what Brother Tim says."

She gathered a shawl around her neck. "I'm chilly," she said.

"Oh, Angela."

"I think I need to go in."

He left her alone at her apartment door. During their next two phone conversations she seemed distant, cool.

On Sunday in church he bowed his head and prayed on what to do. He received the answer. Afterward he drove to Coastal Arms and signed in as a visitor. Angela was with Nana in her room.

Nana perked up at his entrance; he charmed her with tales of the Air Force; he made her laugh with stories about Big Frank. When he got ready to go, he leaned over and Nana wrapped her arms tightly around his neck.

"You sure are a huggin' sweetheart," he told her.

When he stood back up, he could feel Angela's warmth pouring toward him again.

It was Angela's turn to meet family.

Big Frank was a slight man with a jut jaw, gnarled hands, and right leg gone below the knee. On the end of his dock, sitting in his chair with his prosthesis off and set to the side like an object he might have whittled, the eighty-one-year-old looked like a character out of a sea saga.

"Never seen something like this before, have you?" Big Frank said to Angela as they approached.

"Granddaddy," Frank said, "don't run her off yet!"

"Japs did it," Big Frank said to her. "I saw you pull up in that car." He motioned to Angela's Toyota in the drive. "I paid for that car."

"It's a different world, Granddaddy," Frank said.

Big Frank flashed a big grin at Angela. "You sure are pretty. Do I get a hug?" He held out his arms.

Angela leaned over and gave him a quick half hug and pat on the back.

"This is Angela," said Frank.

"We're already the best of friends," Big Frank said.

She tried to sneak a glance at the stump of his leg. Just above the knee it was capped off by a shiny orb as smooth as a thimble, and a latch.

"Go on, don't be shy," Big Frank said. "Take a good look. It's got 'Bataan' written on it."

"Pardon?" She stared right at it now.

"Bataan!" Big Frank said with orneriness.

"How're the mullet, Granddaddy?" Frank asked.

The old man looked over at the water. "They were running earlier."

"You like to fish?" Angela said.

"Throw a net," he said, nodding to a long skirt of netting hanging from a peg.

"That's hard, I'm impressed."

"I like her," Big Frank said, looking back at his grandson. He winked at Angela. "What's a pretty lady like you doing with the likes of him?"

"We met—" Angela began.

"At the base," Frank finished.

"Okay, then," Angela said. "You tell it."

"She was visiting a girlfriend of hers there, and we were having a drill."

"Yes," Angela said. "I picked him right out of the formation."

"Formation," Big Frank repeated. "You must come from military."

"My daddy was a Vietnam vet."

"Was? He passed?"

"Might just as well have," she said. "He was so damaged by the war, he never got right in the head again. He left my mother and went to upstate New York when I was still a kid."

"Hand me that," Big Frank said angrily. He nodded at the fake leg.

"Yes sir," said Frank, who reached for the prosthesis and gave it to his grandfather, who attached it and started to struggle up from the chair. Angela held out her hands, clutched his, and gave him a tug.

He lurched toward the peg where the net hung. She went to help him but he waved her away.

"You know," he said, lifting the net off the peg, "I can feel my leg even when it's not there. Phantom pain, they call it. How many times you ever hear me complain about it?" he asked Frank.

"Not once, Granddaddy."

"Now you've heard me talk about the Japs and what they did, and how brave our men were, and how some lost their minds not just their bodies—hell, what's nothing but a damn leg —but you never heard me say I couldn't be who I am, take care of my family, hold down a job, none of that 'cause of what I went through."

"No sir."

"Look out there at Back Bay." The bayou was serene, its glassy waters pushing up to pine trees on the opposite shore, the rush of traffic far away where it headed from Highway 90, crossing a bridge on the way to I-10. "How many shrimp boats you see?"

Angela counted aloud nine, moored in a shabby marina around the point from the High Chaparral Casino Hotel.

"Them's Vietnamese boats. Those folks suffered, too, you know. I can hear what they're saying sometimes on my CB radio I keep out here on the dock. I can hear 'em laughing, cussing, getting excited, but never no complaining."

"Granddady, you don't speak Vietnamese!"

"But I know bellyaching when I hear it!"

He lifted the net, slung it over his shoulder, and galumphed toward the edge of the dock.

"Mr. Semmes, careful, sir," Angela said.

"Your daddy had no right to throw you away 'cause of some made-up excuse about what happened to him overseas."

"It messed up his head, Granddaddy," said Frank. "All we can do is pray for him."

"Don't tell me about having your head messed with!" He began trembling, as though his heart were giving out, but he slid the net off his back, brought it around in front of him, gripped the hem with his left hand, and lifted it to his mouth. He put one of the weights that lined the hem between his teeth and clamped down on it like a horse taking a bit. He leaned his head back to straighten out kinks, then with his right hand, began to furl the net over his shoulder until he was half draped by the webbing.

He kept his gaze trained on the bay, motionless, like a heron ready to strike. He rocked back, letting the net swing behind him, then pushed forward, hurling it outward, letting go with his teeth and hands and watching it spin upward in a perfect circle, arc, and turn downward, becoming a maw on the water.

He dragged it up slowly, methodically, empty save for some strands of marsh grass and two baby crabs that, as he shook them loose, skittered joyfully over the side.

"You know," he said, "I've seen men prisoners to the goddamn Japs turn and pretend to try and escape just so they could get shot to death."

"Yes sir," said Angela.

"Seen Americans beat for no good reason at all just 'cause they were Americans."

She shook her head sadly.

"What you know about Bataan?"

"Not very much."

"It's a peninsula, west of Manila. Jungle and Japs. That's all it was when I was there. Just after Christmas 1941. MacArthur told the Japs, 'Come on in,' and moved us to Bataan. See the patch of woods over there?" He motioned to a thicket of pines across from the High Chaparral.

"Take that times a hundred times a thousand—jungle. Put yourself down in the middle of it with the enemy coming at you, hordes of them, and you fighting like hell to stay alive. Skinny Wainwright done it, made the biggest damn surrender in U.S. history. I remember the morning word came through. Next thing I know we were out on a road, Filipino and American, all of us. 'Don't slip. Don't fall. Don't let yourself look tired. You'll get a bullet in the head, a bayonet in the ribs.' I seen it all. I kept going, though, saw a man get shot just for stopping to put his head in a ditch trying to suck at some filthy water, and—"

"Granddaddy," said Frank. "Maybe you should try for mullet again."

"You ever hear tell," Big Frank went on, "of a place called Camp O'Donnell?"

"No sir," Angela said.

"Cabanatuan? Bilibid?"

"No sir."

"What do they teach y'all in school these days!"

"My grandmother was married to a man who was in the war," she said.

"Lucky," Frank said.

"Before Lucky. He died over there."

"You didn't tell me that," Frank said.

"You know where he was?" Big Frank asked.

"The Philippines is all I know. His name was Rosey."

"Maybe Italian?" said Big Frank.

"I think Jewish."

"Marks, Mississippi, was founded by the Jews," Frank said. "Daddy preached on that: Jesus, Son of David."

"Your turn to do the preaching?" Big Frank said impatiently.

"Granddaddy's still feuding with the Lord," Frank said to Angela.

"I'll show you a feud! I met God all right, met him in Japan. And this is what He told me: 'Don't matter how you pray, where you go to church, you're either good or a bastard,' pardon my French.

"And they were bastards! I can still see the one who took my leg. He was a big Jap, too, bigger than most you see. He used a hard stick and cracked me with it, over and over. I had to work with my leg beat up like that, and the sore got festered. The flies, the stink of it. If it was gonna be sawed off, I knew right then and there that, if I lived to make it home, I'd have them do it in the VA hospital.

"If I'd screamed and wailed and said I couldn't work, I know what the Japs would have done, carried me into a back room and strapped me down and sawed it off right there. I heard men scream when that happened. They pleaded, they wailed.

"Then, it would get quiet."

Big Frank got profoundly quiet, too. The silence was broken by a slap on the water. He sprang into action, making up the net, leaning back, rocking forward, spinning out the circle that sank quickly into the water. The shiny heads of mullet bumped against the sudden cage.

He hauled up his catch, opening the net to see the seven fish, like silver bullets about to explode, flopping and gyrating on the wood. He stared down at them. They stared back with their big, bug eyes, beginning to still.

He went from mullet to mullet, pushing them with his prosthetic foot to the end of the dock, then kicking them over. He watched as each one revived and, as though startled by the suddenness of water, zipped away.

"Come back soon," he said to Angela. "I love you, boy," he said to Frank.

"B-A-T-A-N."

Sitting in a coffee shop with her laptop across from the Sound, Angela typed the letters into Google. The question popped up, "Do you mean, 'Bataan'?"

She clicked.

"There are 12,487 matches for Bataan. Related searches: Bataan Death March, Prisoners of War, WWII Philippines."

She clicked on "Bataan Death March."

Across the screen opened a photograph of men beleaguered and gaunt, traveling along a road, their eyes looking not at the scene in front of them but down, as if focused on one objective: to walk.

"The Bataan Death March," said the text, "the forced march of 15,000 American soldiers and 60,000 Filipinos from Mariveles, on the southern tip of the Bataan peninsula, to Camp O'Donnell, 90 miles to the north. Along the route, at San Fernando, the prisoners were herded onto rail cars for passage to Capas, where they marched the remaining stretch to Camp O'Donnell, a former Filipino military base, converted to a prisoner camp by the Japanese."

She tapped "casualties":

Approximately 6,000 men lost their lives in the Bataan Death March, executed by Japanese guards en route. Slowing down, stumbling, dragging back in any way was considered an offense punishable by death. Once the survivors reached Camp O'Donnell, a facility constructed to hold 4,000 men, the more than 50,000 prisoners were subjected to starvation, dysentery, and infectious disease. Those who survived O'Donnell were shuttled to other prison camps for the duration of the war, among them Cabanatuan, Nichols Field, and Bilibid Prison in Manila or its surrounding areas. Up to nearly 2,000 of these men were ultimately incarcerated in unmarked Japanese freighters known as "Hellships," and taken to Moji, Japan and other ports to be used as slave labor for Japanese mining and industrial operations.

She looked up, at tour buses that lumbered toward the casinos at start of day, parking out front while tourists clambered off in the holiday sun, the men in red and green sports jackets, the women in Christmas sweaters adorned with jolly Saint Nick and dashing reindeer. Among them were groups, she knew, from foreign countries, including Japan, touring the American South. Sometimes, during free time, they crossed the street to this café for a leisurely tea. She grew embarrassed at the thought of one of them catching her with her nose in this virtual world of their ancestral atrocities. They bore no more responsibility for harming her people than she did for the ruination of the Native Americans by the white man. Or were they all guilty?

There were Indian mounds not far from here, and Biloxi itself, Pascagoula, and Mobile a couple of hours down the highway, had taken their names from native tribes. The chambers of commerce could speak of the French past, and celebrate Mardi Gras, blending it with old Dixie flag waving, but the names of their towns spoke first and foremost of the original owners. How distant that time was, though. She was no oppressor.

But Big Frank bore the memory of the atrocities on his body. The elders of some of the very casino-goers who had traveled over the Pacific Ocean to arrive at the Gulf Coast might have committed them. When Big Frank was gone, would those memories—the phantom leg that never stopped aching—disappear altogether?

She thought of the Japanese businessman from the week before, ordering sake—the casino was shrewd enough to stock it—and pumping silver dollars into a slot machine. When she brought him a shot of the

Japanese liquor, he asked for two more, smiled, nodded, and handed her a $50 bill. "There's no charge," she said.

"For you," he said. "Tip."

"Thank you, sir. I hope you're having a nice stay in Biloxi."

"We are on tour of American South," he had told her. "We hear the jazz last night in New Orleans. This Dixieland, it swings! Tomorrow we visit the plantation houses." He grinned. *"Gone with the Wind!"*

As a child, she had heard a story that she hoped the Japanese businessman had never learned. It was about a Japanese exchange student in Baton Rouge named Hattori who had been invited to a Halloween party and decided to go as John Travolta. Angela imagined him as Tony, from *Saturday Night Fever,* with platform shoes, slicked-back hair, a white disco suit. Hattori had gotten lost, wandering with a friend through a Baton Rouge neighborhood looking for his friend's house. When he knocked on the wrong door, a man answered, told them they had the wrong address, then closed the door. A moment later, the man appeared in his carport with a .44 Magnum and told the boys, "Freeze."

Had Hattori thought the man said, "Please?" He had stepped toward him.

"Don't come any closer!"

"We are here for the party."

The man fired. Hattori crumpled to the ground.

She knew that Japan had grieved long and loud for the boy, not fathoming a nation where ordinary folks kept firearms in their closets. The man who'd slain the youth paid damages to Hattori's family but was let off scot-free from punishment with the argument he had acted in what he believed was self-defense. It had all just been a sorrowful misunderstanding.

She had read an article on the recent tenth anniversary of the shooting that said the Japanese had nursed a lingering fear of the Deep South, and for years it had impacted their travel to Louisiana and the Gulf Coast. Now that incident could have happened as long ago as the senseless violence wreaked on Big Frank.

She began to click on other links, looking over the wealth of material: "Bataan, starvation"; "Bataan, executions"; "Bataan, Corregidor"; "Bataan, Cabanatuan"; "Bataan, Oryoku Maru."

She found one that said, "Bataan and Corregidor Families Association," and clicked.

My name is Roslyn James and I am looking for information about my grandfather, Cpl. Ray James, who died on the Bataan Death March. If you knew him, please contact me.

My great-uncle, Carl Rose, who was in the 4th Marines, disappeared after being taken as a prisoner to the Arisan Maru. If you know what happened to him, any details, please fax or e-mail.

My father was taken captive and sold for slave labor to the Mitsubishi Corp. for a mining operations near Moji, Japan. We never received his remains. I want to make a scrapbook about his life for my children. If you were in the war with him, please contact me.

My husband, who sent me his last message in 1943—a POW card, through the office of the Imperial Japanese, never came home. His name was Capt. Jack Steinhardt. He was very handsome. We were married only one year. If you knew him, write to me with your memories.

Angela looked at the dates alongside the thread of messages. The last one was as recent as last week.

How many people walking by the café, or into the casino, trailed the sadness of someone gone? How many, no matter the time that had passed, lived with the absence as if it had been set into motion yesterday? She felt a wave lift her, a sensation of floating over a rolling sea of loss.

She peered into the screen, finding the box that said, "Post your message or query."

She typed out: "My name is Angela, I live on the Mississippi coast, and I am looking for information about a soldier nicknamed Rosey, that's the only name I have right now. He was married to my grandmother. He was in the Philippines. And he never came home."

It is New Year's Eve, at a party on base, and the deejay is keeping the rec hall jumping. The lights are low; the room is crowded. In less than an hour it will be 2003.

The deejay puts on Faith Hill's "The Way You Love Me," and Frank takes Angela's hand. The tempo is just fast enough to begin a slow swing but easy enough for him to pull her toward him and sway together.

Over the weeks he has been ardent enough—sweeping her up in bear hugs, kissing her until her lips become chapped—but measured, too, Angela has realized, as if the rest of their bodies have been off-limits. As he brings her to him on the dance floor, she senses his heat and perspiration, smells his aftershave of sandalwood. She feels his whole body straining toward her, but holding back.

Between dances they share talk with Frank's fellow airmen about the dismantling of the Taliban in Operation Enduring Freedom, of the smart bombs that have hunted the lair of Osama bin Laden and will eventually outwit him, of the necessity of stopping Saddam in his tracks, and of the groundswell of support in Washington for doing so. He tells her about a man he helped at his store in Ocean Springs, Mississippi, one summer, Buck Raheem, a Muslim and Iraqi, who prays for the Americans to liberate his people.

She repeats her concern, saying that she is skeptical. She remembers how her dad railed against Uncle Sam for sending young Americans into Vietnam, the blood that was spilled, the quagmire the war became, and for no good reason. "'Quagmire,' yes, that was the word he used," she says. "He's been a jerk to me, yes, but I'm still thinking it must have been Vietnam that made him that way, no matter what Big Frank says."

"It won't happen to me, Angela. And no matter what, I could never be that way to you."

During a break in the music, they step outside. "In summers when I'd visit Granddaddy, he'd sometimes bring me here," he says. "This is like home."

He puts his arm over her shoulder against the Gulf Coast chill, and they stroll out past the barracks, by the cafeteria and base store, past the weather station and Billy Mitchell Field, where the C-130 Herculeses rest like primitive beasts in hibernation. "Fifty-third Weather Squadron—Hurricane Hunters," he says. "Maybe I'll ride with them one day. Hurricanes, cyclones, tsunamis, floods, droughts, twisters, tornadoes. I hate what heavy weather does to people. But I love being in it, too."

"It can be strangely beautiful," she says, "but it terrifies me even more."

"I'll give you shelter," he says, and she thinks of General Wheeler reassuring Francie Holcombe at Coastal Arms.

They pass a 1940s fighter plane on a pedestal, wings banked, with a plaque: "USAF F-84 Thunderjet."

"There's a load of history here," he says. "The Tuskegee Airmen did some training at the base. Heroes. Back in the sixties they trained some Vietnamese pilots here, part of trying to get those poor folks to take over their own fight. Heroes, too. Now the runways are kind of short for the new fighter jets, and who knows if we'll survive the base closings—of course, the big ones will be there forever, Hurlburt, Lackland, Sheppard, the rest, I did basic at Maxwell—but this is where I belong. I'd like to get back here one day to teach, when I'm old. Thirty, forty. See that name up there?"

She looks up at a street sign: "Hap Arnold Drive."

"Hap learned to fly from the Wright brothers. Is that cool, or what? He was a five-star general, head of the Air Corps during the Second World War, a member of the Joint Chiefs of Staff. No wonder they called him 'Hap.' For 'happy.' Who wouldn't be?"

She hears the party music resume, a rousing tune with airmen and dates singing along, their hubbub drifting across the airfield.

Beyond the base, along Back Bay, a car's headbeams move crookedly down the road through an intersection near the bridge.

"My mother lost her life"—she stops walking, raises her hand, and points across the way—"right about there."

"You've never told me exactly what happened."

"Those car lights, they make me think of it."

"It was a drunk driver? Oh, Angela."

She shakes her head. "No, it was a big summer storm that knocked out all the traffic lights, and it was her turn to go through the intersection."

"Dear God," he says.

"This imbecile came racing through."

"Was it late in the summer? August? It was the start of Tropical Storm Helene?"

"Yeah."

"The summer I was fifteen, I was here visiting Big Frank, and he was taking me to a fish fry at the VFW, but we couldn't get there, this big accident tying up the road. We got out and went to see if we could do something, help somebody who needed a ride. We were wearing these yellow rain slickers, I remember now, yellow slickers, and we got close enough to see it. The car was yellow."

"My mom had a yellow VW."

"The Lord has strange ways."

She reaches over and puts her hand over his mouth. "Don't talk to me about the Lord."

He nods.

"You saw my mom," she whispers. She moves her hand away.

"I didn't mean . . ."

"I know."

They continue on, arriving at the small, brick houses of the officers. He gestures to her, leads her into a side garage. He looks under a mat and finds a key. "Captain Reggie, a disciple of Brother Tim's, we go to Victory together. He's out of town." He slips in the key, they enter. Frank goes into the living room and opens the sliding doors leading out to the lawn that sweeps down to Back Bay.

His breath is coming faster, in rising puffs of fog. She leans through the fog and kisses him.

"You went to help," she says.

"There was nothing we could do! Like Big Frank says, it breaks your heart."

She undoes his top two shirt buttons, puts her hand on his heart. She slides it lower.

"I can't," he says.

"What do you mean?"

He hesitates. "Not until I marry. I made a vow."

"You've *never*?"

"Yes, lots, plenty of times. But that was then. Another me. A crazy me."

She lets out a laugh. "Crazy now, I think. I was wondering why you hadn't tried, really tried. I didn't think you wanted me!"

"I do. Oh, how I do!"

A volley of firecrackers erupts. Across the water M80s, set off in trash bins, sound like an attack.

"If we do invade," he says suddenly, "if we do go after Saddam, I told them I want to go."

"Frank."

"If I die, it's God's will."

"Don't talk like that!"

"I want to do it for Big Frank. I want to do it for you. That's what's important, not this."

He reaches into his shirt pocket and pulls out a picture of himself in his dress uniform to give to her—a strong, smooth-faced young man in a blue Air Force suit, chevrons visible at his shoulders. She wonders if Nana's aviator looked like this.

She touches the picture, then places her hands on the sides of his face. "Nothing's going to happen to you!"

The curve of his neck is dark and warm, and when she nuzzles there, she takes in his scent of sandalwood. When they go into the house and lie on the couch by the den windows, she arches to his touch, until, shutting her eyes, she feels his hands all over her, their clothes slipping off, his skin against hers like a shock.

"Let's just lie together," he says, his breath pulsing against her as hot and damp as a horse's.

"Okay," she murmurs, feeling herself turn to honey beneath him.

He whispers to her that he has "protection." "I still have one, you know, in my wallet, it's still good—but the right thing to do is wait."

"Yeah," she says, floating with the weight of him against her.

In the distance they hear a throng of voices counting down, "Five! Four! Three! Two! One!" And then comes a blast of horns, and the Biloxi sky is filled with rat-a-tat-tats and showers of red and gold light.

"Or should I?" he says, reaching for his wallet and readying himself, poised above her trembling, his single, aching syllable—"Yes?"—running like electricity through her.

"Yes."

FIVE

Foreign Correspondence

Along Oak Street, by the Vietnamese Catholic Church with its pagoda roof and statue of Mary like a Bodhisattva near the koi pond, Cam biked through the Saturday afternoon sunshine. She'd played piano at Coastal Arms that morning while Daddy headed to his shrimpboat to work on the engine. As she cycled along, she passed two teenage girls in jeans and T-shirts logo'd with Benneton and Abercrombie, and a wizened old woman in a rice paddy hat, one of the conical, straw numbers sold, along with dried noodles and Vietnamese-dubbed Chinese videos, in Trai Huong Market. How she wished for a car, a red Mustang like Carrie O'Connor from St. Benedict's, or a bright blue Saturn like Marie Schwartz, who had Cam's same piano teacher, a shiny rocket ship to take her to realms she could hardly reach on her bicycle. Daddy let her drive his peeling truck on rare occasions, but he was not even willing to upgrade the sound system from cassette tapes to CD. When the Vietnamese and Laotian guys, with their tricked-up cars, had their drag races along the county highway, she yearned to have any kind of wheels at all, even a boxy little Chevy.

A postcard had just come in the mail that showed Ho Chi Minh City—Daddy insisted on still calling it Saigon—and she knew her father would be eager for the greeting from his brother, who had stayed in Vietnam and now had a thriving shoe store. The architecture of the buildings looked strange to her—she had never traveled there—although she had seen images of her homeland countless times on the Internet when clicking on its news, weather, or sports for Daddy.

She approached the docks with the giant, steel-hulled shrimp boats moored closest to the High Chaparral. With their huge refrigeration units, the steel boats, largely owned by long-time American shrimpers, were able to go out for weeks on end, deep into the Gulf of Mexico. The smaller, wooden boats, like *Miss Mai*, many owned by Vietnamese, went out for a few days at most, though her father and cousin Thanh pushed way out into the unpredictable Gulf when state waters were closed for shrimping in winter and spring.

She cycled down the wooden planks to where the *Miss Mai* was lashed to its pilings and shouted out, "You've got mail!"

Daddy appeared from the engine room, smudged with oil. "I must speak with you."

She handed him the postcard, and he pressed it to his chest. Then he gazed at Cam with sadness. "Who is trying to do this to me!"

"Do what, Daddy?"

"It is the Rebel men in the trailer."

"What do you mean?"

"A policeman called our house this morning when you were gone, someone made a report, they said we are burning paper. They gave the license plate of our truck. What do you know about this!?"

"I don't know anything. Why *would* I know anything?" Her heart churned.

"Have you been smoking cigarettes near the temple?"

"No sir."

"Cam, have you been smoking marijuana there!?"

"Daddy, what do you think I am, a drug addict?"

Only the second time she had been to visit Quan Am, to send her letter in ashes toward the Bodhisattva's wise countenance, the flame had caught the pine straw and skittered toward the fence dividing the temple from the trailer park. She had hurried to stomp it out, then sped away in the truck.

"The Rebel men in the trailer," he fumed. "I will find out their names and go to them!"

"What if they have a gun?"

Phi produced a long, curved knife from beneath a coil of rope, but a police car turned by the docks. He stashed the knife away, peered out at the squad car. The cop saw him, waved, kept driving.

He leapt off the boat, hurried up the walk, and called out, "Policeman, sir. I need your help."

The car slowed, circled back, crunching over the oyster shell parking area.

Cam recognized him from St. Benedict's. How could she forget Joseph Donahue leaping toward the basketball goal, swishing the ball into the hoop to win against Gulf Pines Military Academy. Lanky, lean, short black hair curly like a little boy's, he'd been a senior when she was a freshman and was older than that since he'd lost a year of school when his family moved from out West. She had thrilled to his prowess on the court and loved how his neck and forehead had glistened with sweat beneath the gym lights. She had always figured him to become a teacher or a coach, not a cop.

Joseph parked, rolled down his window, and listened as Phi said he wanted to file a complaint against the men who lived next to the temple, for harassing him. "Can you do this for me?" he asked the policeman.

Joseph turned off his engine and got out of the car. "It was me, sir, who received the complaint this morning when it was phoned in, burning paper in the city limits, a routine misdemeanor if there's no permit. Call was anonymous. Still, we have to check everything out. Procedure."

"They want to hurt me and my family!" Phi said. "They say I catch their shimp."

"Probably just some crackpots."

"I will make them pay for what they try to do to me!"

"I can't advise you on this, sir. You can always get yourself a lawyer, if it's something more."

"I have no money for a lawyer."

"There's a legal aid office near the Singing River Mall in Pascagoula, and you can check with them." He looked up. "Cam?"

She could not believe that he knew her name. They had conversed only once, in the lunchroom, when he sat next to her by accident, and they had chatted about the rain and basketball and summer jobs.

"Yes, Joseph, right?"

"That's right. Call me Joe. St. Benedict's, I graduated last year."

She pushed her hand through her hair to free any tangles.

"I met a man at the casino," Phi said. "A lawyer named Goldman, at the poker table. Legal aid, he was in legal aid. I remember now. He gave me his card. I will call him."

"That's up to you, sir."

"I work hard, Officer Donahue. No man can take away from me what I have done! I will show them who I am."

"Yes sir," said the policeman. "We have to check everything out. Could be just a mix-up." He glanced over at Cam. "So what are you up to these days?"

"Going to school," she said sheepishly, "playing piano, helping my dad with stuff."

"Biloxi's a good place, you know," Joe said. "Nice folks, friendly, stay out of trouble for the most part." He cleared his throat. "How's this? *Jow. Kweah kohng?*"

"Very good! Hello, how are you?"

"We got so many Vietnamese on my beat, I figured I'd learn to say a few things. *Goh theyn la yi,*" he said.

"My name is Cam," she answered. She felt Daddy scrutinizing her.

"*Cahm unh,*" Joe said.

"Thank you, Joe. *Kohng sao doh.*"

"What's that?" Joe asked.

"We go now," Phi said.

"It means," Cam said, "you're welcome."

"*Kohng sao doh* to you, too," Joe said eagerly. "Mr. Nguyen, you ever got a problem, just give a holler."

"We are okay," Phi said. "We go back to our boat. Cam?" he said sternly.

"Yes sir, Daddy."

"*Jow*," said Joe, getting into his car.

"*Jow*, Joe." She watched him roll away, her heart giving a little jump when he waved at her one last time through the squad car's sunshiny window.

On a gauzy gray Sunday afternoon in early February, Angela arrived at the coffee shop across from the Sound. She took her laptop out of her backpack and checked her e-mail.

She was startled to see a message from a stranger, Flyboy6@ithaca. rr.com, with the subject line: "Bataan."

She clicked.

> Dear Angela.
>
> My name is Stan Trainor, and I am a retired newspaper editor living in Ithaca, New York. During the war I was a writer for *Stars and Stripes*, and knew a soldier in the air patrol named Rose, a flyer, from somewhere in the heartland. I never knew what happened to him, but I got to know him some at the airfield in Manila, which is where the Manila airport is now. He was a nice man, an honorable man, and a good soldier. I lost track of him after Christmas of '41, MacArthur gave Manila to the Japanese, and most were removed to Bataan, but I went on assignment to the Solomon Islands. Rose was a brave man, and he died with honor. He was a hero, and you can always be proud of your grandfather.
>
> Stan Trainor
>
> P.S. If you ever find yourself up this way and want to talk about the war, I am eager to do so. I have five grandchildren, and three great-grands, and none could care less.

Angela felt the floor lift and move, as if she were being transported across the café.

"My grandfather was Lucky," she whispered.

The new message icon popped on. Was the old Army journalist staring through the screen at her?

From: JRRoma@via.it. She opened it.

Dear Miss Angela,

I received your request for information about the man I presume was your great-grandfather or other ancestor. I fought with the U.S. Army in North Africa—I was in Operation Torch—a long way from the horrid jungles of the Far East, but I did my basic training at Fort Benning, Ga., and there was a fine young man from Arkansas, Rosenski, he could not wait to go overseas after what the Germans did to his people on September 1, 1939. I had thought he was stationed in Pearl Harbor. I am happy to know that he survived the attack that will never be forgotten in all history. I feel certain that he got a few of the enemy, made them suffer, before he was captured and brutally tortured. Combat is Hell, but it is honorable Hell. Torture reserves a special place in Hell for those who commit the heinous acts. I returned to Italy after the war, where I had met a lovely girl, Stella, whose brother was a proud Partisan. We were married 52 years, one month, and one day. She died in my arms. We have lived our lives, all of us, free to choose, to worship, to have a say, because of men like Rosenski. He did not die in vain.

Sincerely,
Jonathan Riley, professor emeritus, American Studies, University of Rome

She thanked the men for their e-mails, put "Rose" and "Rosinski" and "Philippines" and "WWII" in a search engine, and received over ten thousand links, but nothing high up in the choices to suggest a close hit.

Then, before signing off, she checked the basket marked "Spam," and among the promotions for erotic pleasure devices and antidepressive pills and get-rich-quick schemes was a message from Bigboy4@ bataan.org. She clicked.

> A Jewish kid from Alabama gave me a drink of water when we were on the Bataan death march and saved my life and a Jap guard saw us and ran to us shouting. He grabbed a different soldier by mistake—they couldn't tell us apart—and beat him to the ground and put his boot against his head and his rifle against his temple and pulled the trigger. The soldier's name was Rosenbush, the one who gave me the water, and God spared his life because he had saved mine. He cried like a baby because of what had happened as we marched. We never found out the name of the man who was killed. Rosenbush said a prayer in Hebrew for the dead man. We were together all the way to Camp O'Donnell, but got separated there. I think about him all the time. I have nightmares still. I am an old man in them, as I am now, but Rosenbush and the other are still young, no older than that day.
>
> Sincerely,
> Jeremy Rivers, 1162 Grand Concourse, 6R, Bronx, NY

She saved the letters on her hard drive and looked out toward the Sound. The images began to interplay and merge in her mind: the young soldier Rosinski at Fort Benning remembered by a professor in

Italy; the flyer Rose in Manila who suffered such abuse; the man on the death march, Rosenbush, giving water to a stranger, saved by the hand of fate while another was sacrificed.

When Frank and Angela made love, he lost himself in her full, soft contours. At her apartment, in a bungalow at Bay St. Louis, on a buddy's sloop off Petite Bois Island, he felt the intoxication of her body against him. Unlike other women he'd gone for, she was not especially buff, toned, or athletic. But when they lay together and she enfolded him with her easy warmth, he felt she could carry him aloft.

When she excitedly told him about the letters concerning Rosey, he voted for letter three and said he could imagine himself risking his life to give another man water. When she talked about the e-mails again, and yet again, and that she had written back to each of them, he warned her "to be careful."

"What do you mean?" she said.

"All kinds of crackpots go on the Web."

"These old guys?"

"I see some strange things."

"I think I can take care of myself."

"I'm just saying."

They celebrated with champagne when he got a promotion in rank—the bump in pay made him feel flush with funds—and talked about an overnight to New Orleans. But no matter her ardor, he sensed she was still not completely part of his world.

He could tell by how quiet she became when he talked too long about his future in the service,or how she seemed self-conscious when he reached out clutching her hands in a restaurant to say grace before a meal. She did not squeeze his fingers in return.

"The Bible tells us to pray without ceasing," he said.

"I don't like to make a show," she said.

"She's not that into God," he told Brother Tim, "but she makes me feel closer to the Lord. Weird, isn't it."

"I can sense that she's good for you, Frank," Tim said. "That storm inside of you, it has not yet fully subsided. She provides the calm."

"I want her to hear you," he said.

"Bring her to Victory Brotherhood when she's ready," Tim said.

"How will I know?"

"Don't push her. You'll know."

Meeting up on Biloxi Beach, Frank's heart did a somersault when he saw Angela waiting for him, kites dipping and swooping around her, Frisbee players tossing bright saucers, migrant workers chattering in Spanish throwing fishing lines into the shallows. In the distance the Cotton Gin stood like a dormant Oz.

A clear image rose before him of the two of them, hand in hand, in a pew. He had seen his mother and father like that, his friends and their new wives like that. Sunday mornings he ached to have Angela by his side. This was the moment.

They took off their shoes and strolled along the surf, and he recounted scenes of the wild life he had led before—"the crazy me"—a glimpse of his time at Kentucky Faith and how the story of the Prodigal Son best told his tale. His walk with Jesus had taken an unlikely path—"They all seem unlikely," Brother Tim had said, "then inevitable"—but a powerful one, too.

"I guess you could also call it just growing up," Angela said.

"Look at this." He held out his hands, as though balancing the atmosphere in his palms. "Amazing grace."

"You know, Frank, when I told you about those letters, you really weren't that interested, were you?"

"Of course I was."

"You didn't even want me to be in touch with them!"

"I was just trying to protect you."

"Oh, please. You don't care about any of it; you don't want to hear about anybody else's heroism."

"How can you say I don't care? And I've been damn attentive to Nana, too."

"Oh," she mimicked him, "you sure are a huggin' sweetheart.' Sweet-talkin' Granny to get the girl."

"Come with me to Victory Brotherhood," he said.

"It's all about you. Patriotic, churchgoing Frank."

"I want you to experience what I experience. It's beautiful, Angela."

"Just drop it."

"God put us together," he said.

"Then he's got a great sense of humor."

"Listen to me. The president's going to give word soon about Saddam. I know he is. This is about something bigger than you and me. Service before self."

"You used that line on me before," she shot back. "I'm not some casino whore, you know. That's why you couldn't tell Big Frank where you really met me. I should never have slept with you. You and your Jesus."

"You haven't even met Brother Tim."

"Weirdos come in the casino every day."

"Pray with me!"

"Forget the whole thing," she said, turning and walking away.

He started to race after, but felt hot around his neck. "Go live Nana's life," he shouted at her back.

"Fuck off, Sergeant."

He realized he was standing near the place on the beach where he had knelt with Brother Tim. The indentations of his knees had remained there for days, he recalled, as if immune to the tides. Now at the spot were a couple of crushed paper cups and a hot dog wrapper tangled in sea grass.

Seething, he kicked at the littered sand. "Shit," he said.

Propped up on her pillows in bed, Nana welcomes Angela into the room. On the side table is a jar of cold cream, and Angela unscrews the lid, swipes two fingers through it, and dabs it on Nana's cheeks, chin, and forehead. "How you doing?" Angela asks as Nana feels her granddaughter rub the cool, rose-scented lotion into her skin.

"I feel better," Nana says, "just to be rubbed. Everybody does."

"I remember going with you and Lucky to the beach, and he'd put sunscreen on your back. I can still see him moving his hand over your shoulders."

"It seems like he's been gone so long," Nana says. "You know the way he used to come in the door, put his hat on the hall tree—he wore a hat long after it was out of fashion, he didn't care, he had his own sense of everything—put his hat there and saunter over and give me a kiss? I don't mean just a little peck, a little nothing"—she made a *mwoh* in the air with her lips—"but something any starlet would have been happy with.

"He was a good engineer, and he always came home from the office with some detail about a bridge they were building or repairing. Bridges were his specialty, of course. We never crossed one without his saying, 'Without this, we'd still be stuck on the other side, feel its sense of certainty.' Just like him, he never changed his stripes, never let me down, and when your mother was treated so horribly, I mean horribly, by your father, Lucky was there. The Lord is my Rock and Redeemer, but Lucky was my rock, too. And when we lost her, it was Lucky who got me through."

"Yes, Nana. Look." She takes a silver dollar out of her purse and holds it to the lamp. "Lucky gave it to me. My fourteenth birthday."

"It's so bright."

"I polish it sometimes. I'll never spend it."

"If you do, make sure it's for something very special."

"You can't ever get anything for a dollar."

"You can't?" Nana said, feeling anxious all of a sudden.

"Maybe in 1943, but hardly now."

"Oh?"

"Nana?"

"Yes?" She gazes at the sweet young woman. Her name is Angela, that's right, her granddaughter, Angela.

"Nana, I got some letters today, some e-mails. Letters about Rosey."

Nana scoots up higher on the pillows. Rosey she knows. "Yes?"

Nana hears about the march, and the water, and the guard and his boot and bayonet, and then hears the shot and Rosey's prayer. She is standing next to Rosey in a sanctuary, and he is saying that prayer, grieving for his grandfather, the Kaddish he calls it, the mourner's prayer, and she is the Virginia Presbyterian in the minyan of Southern Jews, and the strangeness of the language, the Biblical exhortations, sadden and thrill her, and she knows she will never let him go.

She holds her hand up. "Not Alabama, Georgia. Not Rosenbush, Rosengarten. German, for rose garden. Come here."

She brings Angela close and says, "Bless you. He could still be alive."

SIX

Out of the Blue

Sunday night passed, Monday and Tuesday, and by Wednesday the first call from Frank came. Angela didn't answer the phone, just watched defiantly as his name showed on caller ID. She'd finally deleted Max from her caller list; in another week or two she'd scroll down to Frank's number and do the same. He called again. She did not answer. He left no messages.

On her Cotton Gin shift she flirted with a senior from Cornell named Aaron, who was on a Southern road trip with his buddies, answering his questions about where to party late at night, then saying, yes, she might just be at Rudy's, too, that evening. At the bar at 11 P.M., buzzed with her third beer when Aaron arrived, she took to the dance floor right away with him. He was tall and cerebral and cool, maybe a Jew, even better an atheist. They did not quiz each other, which was fine by her. Going back to his motel room, she let him kiss her like a hungry wolf. She did not push his hand away when he moved it under her T-shirt. She went home, hoping to see him again the next day, knowing just when Frank went for his run and where they could stand in his path, making out. When she went to Aaron's motel room and knocked on the door, a cleaning lady opened it, saying, "Checked out."

Friday was her birthday, and after work, before going to see Nana, she sat on a bench facing the Sound to collect herself. When visiting her grandmother, she needed to be wearing a smile.

Her phone rang.

"Hey, Dad," she said, punching the speaker button.

"Happy birthday," he said.

"Thank you."

Silence.

"How's my Angie? Work? Love? Wassup?"

"Wassup?"

"I get that from Donnie. He's graduating from fourth grade this May. I know he'd like to have you here."

"He doesn't even know who I am."

"Tell you what. Birthday gift—let me go in half on the plane ticket. Dee Dee wants to get to know you better, too."

"I can't believe you married another woman named Dorothy."

"She goes by Dee Dee, Angie. She respects the memory of your mother."

"Dad, I haven't been 'Angie' since tenth grade."

"You think I married Dee Dee to hurt you? She's tried, she's really tried."

"What about Tuesday?"

"Tuesday was a bitch. She was mean to you, awful, I know. Why do you think I left her?"

"Because she slept with the golf coach? Yeah?"

"Good from bad. I got custody of Dylan. He looks up to you, Angie. Asks about you all the time."

"Work's fine," she said.

He did not ask what kind of work she was doing.

"What's that noise?" he said.

"Seagulls."

A silence fell again, this time seeming to stretch for a full minute, only the squawk of gulls filling the empty space between Biloxi and Rochester, New York.

"Who's the lucky guy in your life now?" he asked with determined cheeriness.

"Betwixt and between."

"You've got plenty of time, don't worry."

"I'm not worried. The last guy was out of Keesler," she said. "It's fine."

"Oh, Angie. What do you expect from the rah-rah types."

"And he was a born-again Christian, too," she went on, getting ever more annoyed that her father could just drop into her life out of nowhere and presume he could be a dad again.

"A Bible thumper! Damn! You are reacting."

"What do you mean?"

"Dee Dee said you might go opposite to me. Freudian or something, she's a psychologist."

"She teaches Pilates!"

"She's got me doing them, too." He chuckled. "Can you believe it?"

"At least Frank has character," she said. "*Something* he's passionate about."

"So did Nixon and Kissinger."

"That was your war, Dad. Your problem. You don't have to let it wreck you forever."

"I was spit on."

"It's not like you lost a leg!"

"Spit on and ridiculed."

"And you turned around and spit on Mom, and you do the same to me."

"You'll regret every word of this," he said ruefully. "You'll grow up one day. I call to wish you happy twenty-second but you're still fourteen."

"I'm twenty-three, and you only call on my birthday. Don't ruin it next year."

"Of course, of course, I met your mother when she was twenty-three."

"Good-bye," she said.

"I was going to get the kids on the phone and we were going to sing to you."

"See ya."

She held the phone up to the sky for the wheeling gulls to express their agitation.

At Coastal Arms she entered to find the residents listening to Cam at the piano, but Nana was waiting in her room. As soon as she entered, Maria Torres appeared with two brownies for them, one with a lit candle. "*Feliz cumpleaños*, Angela."

"That's happy birthday," said Nana.

Angela made a wish that Nana could get one year younger in exchange for every year Angela aged. She closed her eyes and blew hard enough to extinquish a hundred flames.

They sat by the window. Angela got out Nana's pink polish and began to apply it to Nana's fingernails.

"So," Nana said, "did you hear from your father?"

Nana's memory could still be sharp; maybe a piece of her birthday wish was already coming true.

She nodded as she touched the bristles to a nail. "I told him not to call me next year."

"He could at least pretend to be a decent father."

"If I could just forget Mom and Dad fighting. I know they must have been happy once, but I never saw that part. Some nice memories would be great to have."

"Don was never happy," said Nana. "He wouldn't know happy. I told Dorothy that, but thank the Lord, there was one thing wonderful to come of it all. You. My birthday girl."

Nana reached up with her free hand and touched her soft palm against Angela's cheek.

"Thank you."

"Is your boyfriend taking you out tonight?"

"I'm done with guys, my romantic life's over."

"Pishposh. He seemed like a nice boy to me." Nana lifted her painted fingers and blew against them. "He was a good hugger, too."

"You have a weakness for men in uniforms," Angela said.

"They have a weakness for me."

"You never give up, do you, Nana? A coquette 'til the end of time."

"I'm just old on the outside," she said. "I've been loved."

"It's not that simple, you know."

"It's not that complicated either."

"It seems like all I do with boyfriends is fight. Like it's all I know how to do."

"Well, you don't want to be a little Milquetoast either."

"A what?"

"These days," said Nana, setting out her other hand for nail treatment, "you call it, 'a wimp.'"

"Oh, Nana. What a trip you can be." She dipped the brush in and turned her attention to Nana's other hand.

"Rosey wrote me poems," Nana said like a bragging high schooler. "Can you beat that?"

She simply instructed, "Bring me the teak box. Do not open it."

"Yes, ma'am."

At Nana's storage room next morning, Angela moved the two sets of golf clubs propped in the corner, parted the ball gowns preserved in plastic cleaner bags, and peered into boxes marked "Parlor," "Kitchen," and "Living Room"—all the artifacts of the vanished life led by Nana and Lucky at their former house on the Sound—until she spied the box. She reached into the mothball depths and lifted it up. The latch was loose.

If she did not want Angela to open it, why did she tempt her so?

Inside were groups of letters stacked like freshly ironed handkerchiefs, bound with red yarn.

She shut the box, carried it to her car, and stashed it in the trunk, heading for her shift at the Cotton Gin, but work would not start for nearly an hour. She turned into a beach lot, parked, and got out. She looked at the trunk. "No," she told herself.

After walking to the sand and taking off her shoes, she decided to return and throw them in the trunk. The teakwood box sat there, burnished brown-gold.

She reached for the box, heard Nana's voice chiding her, stood up, reached down again. *What can it hurt? She'll probably have me read them out to her anyway.* She took out the box and carried it to the beach, sitting on a big rock.

She found collections of letters from her mother, from Lucky, from friends of Nana's.

On the bottom, under a medal and a ribbon, was a small batch with

"Robert Rosengarten" on the return.

She took them out and slipped one out of the envelope:

> Dearest Christiane,
>> *If I fly ten thousand miles without you,*
>> *Making journeys far and wide,*
>> *Over forests green and oceans blue,*
>> *I conjure you by my side.*
>> *Your golden hair and starlet eyes,*
>> *Can keep me from all harm,*
>> *I make my journey through heavenly skies,*
>> *But heaven is you on my arm.*
>
> Rosey

She folded away the letter and looked up at the pale blue sky. "Lord have mercy," she whispered.

She opened the second. At the top it said, "San Francisco, California."

> Dearest Christiane,
>
> I landed safely in San Francisco yesterday for refueling and engine maintenance and am scheduled to start another leg of the Midway route tomorrow. The formation of Warhawks making their way west is a powerful sight. I love to look at the American landscape rolling by beneath me—the Rocky Mountains are a spectacle to behold—and know this picture would thrill you, too.
>
> This is my first time to be in San Francisco, and when some of us headed into town to look around, we got quite a workout on the steep hills. You would love the historic houses and views. There's a bench with a view of the new Golden Gate Bridge. When we are

here together, I will sit you down on that bench and we can enjoy looking out at this architectural marvel.

"In San Francisco together?" you ask. My beloved Christiane, I am excited to tell you that some of the officers stationed in the Philippines for many months have the chance to take a short leave and return here for a rendezvous with their gals. That's just how quiet it is over there. Like I said, there's no need to worry. We can look forward to that reunion with happy hearts.

I think of your lovely face, your exquisite eyes. Your tender embrace. Christiane Rosengarten. I like the sound of that. I like the sound of Mrs. Robert Rosengarten even better. Mostly I like the sound of your voice in my thoughts saying "I love you," and I repeat the words in turn.

P.S. I started this verse, which I hope will make you smile.

> *Over the vast Pacific*
> *On wings to Manila soon,*
> *My course will be steady,*
> *Lovesick beneath the moon*

Love,
Rosey

The next letter was from Manila, and the next one, too, and as Angela turned through them, she noted how rumpled they were, the envelopes wrinkled as though they had been opened and closed a thousand times. Had Nana reread these in the years she was married to Lucky? Looked at them even after Lucky was gone?

Lovesick beneath the moon

Who wrote sentiments like that anymore? She took out the next letter, pressed her nose to the page. There was a faint scent. Impossible after all these decades. She sniffed harder: a delicate, far-off aroma of a spice. She looked around. There was no one near her on the beach. She detected silt in the bottom of the envelope. She opened it wide and saw shavings of bark, ground-up wood, like pepper. She poured it out into her palm. The fragrance opened.

Cinnamon.

There was a short note inside:

> My Dearest Christiane,
>
>   You always told me that my shaving lotion carried a touch of cinnamon. This is from the forest outside my barracks.
>
> Keep me close—
> Rosey

Angela breathed in and laid her face against his.

Frank remembered the feeling of seeing the teaching assistant, her hair like hypnotic fire against the evening window, three days a week. Always the same scene: class was done; he was walking down the hall; she was alone, sitting in a rocker, looking out toward the creek bank.

He felt the pull he could not resist, just as he did now heading to the Cotton Gin. The flask of whiskey he had chugged in the parking lot made the building tilt.

"Don't go in," he talked to himself then as now.

She had always looked up when he passed, smiled, waved. This time she said, "Hey."

"Hey," he said.

She waved him in. "I liked what you had to say about First Corinthians," she said.

"PK," he said.

"Preachers kids don't always know their Bible."

"It was either know it or get the strap," he said.

"Well, that's Christian," she said and shook her head. "I don't mean to disrespect your daddy, but come on!"

"He wasn't that bad. I guess I gave him other reasons, too," he said, trying not to glance at her bosom; her dress was low-cut, her cleavage promising a soft bed to rest his head on.

"You're looking at me, aren't you?" she said.

He bowed his head and closed his eyes. "Forgive me, Lord," he said.

"No forgiveness needed. That's why God made me this way," she said.

He felt her hand under his chin, lifting him back up. He opened his eyes. She was standing in front of him, his exact height. Her eyes were green and she smelled of peppermint.

"Want to walk along Limestone Creek?" she said, motioning out the window to the wooded stream behind campus.

He shrugged; his blood was a drum line pounding through him.

"I could talk to you about Malachi," he said. "I've been reading it again. Short book, big message."

"Like you?" she said, grinning. She had some lipstick on her teeth.

He could not shake that Kentucky dusk as he entered the Cotton Gin at sunset now, the garish lights creating a round-the-clock present outside of time. The redhead's appeal had pulled him onward, the abyss awaiting, just as Angela was doing.

He caught a glimpse of himself in the shiny side of an electronic bingo machine: a compact, brutish young man with a scowl on his face, shoulders hunched forward, determined to self-explode. "Turn around and leave," he instructed himself. The devil did not take orders.

Darkness settled in the trees as they made their way there while she gesticulated broadly and spoke of Malachi's prophesy of the Prince of Peace. "Among you shall be hypocrites," she said, "but God will not allow shame to fall upon them. They are children of the Lord, too."

"I don't remember that passage."

"It's mine," she said. "You do like the way God made me, don't you?"

They had reached a cove, hidden.

"Yes, ma'am."

"You're adorable," she said, drawing him to her and planting a big, red lipstick kiss full on his mouth. His whole body went tingling.

She produced the joint from behind her ear, bringing it out like a magic trick, flicked a lighter, and touched it to the end of the rolled paper. She sucked, held the smoke, let it curl from her lips. She handed it to Frank. He took it in, felt the sweet heat in his lungs, breathed out.

There was a bead of sweat on her shoulder, like a pearl. He leaned over and kissed it away.

She turned to him.

Back and forth they passed the joint until she kissed him again, then pulled away and lay down on her back. In a flash he was on top of her, yanking up her dress, and then he heard the voices—two students, seeing them, one he knew, a youth minister—and she was jumping up, shouting, "Get off me! Get off me!"

The college set the blame on them both, but did not call outside authorities. The teaching assistant was fired; Frank, expelled. His father came to pick him up. He remembered the feeling of slinking out of the administration building and into his father's car. Fellow students watched him with pity, as if they were spectators at the banishment of Adam from Eden. The PK, covered in shame.

He moved through the Cotton Gin, took a shot of whiskey from one waitress; pilfered a second shot off the tray of another. He went to the bar and ordered a beer and chugged it.

When Angela passed by him the first time, he said nothing, sunk into the spinning orbit. On the second pass he reached out and grabbed her forearm. "I'm not a hypocrite!"

"Ow! Let me go!"

"I love you!"

"Let go of my arm, Frank."

He let go. "I shouldn't have been like that to you on the beach. I don't know what came over me."

"You're so damn high-and-mighty. God and war. You know it all."

"I want you."

She backed away. "You're out of your mind."

He stumbled toward her.

"You're drunk."

"Angela," he said loudly.

"Sir"—a stony security guard towered over him —"we're going to have to ask you to leave."

Frank glared up at him. "You think you're tough? I'll be laying my ass on the line for you in Iraq while you're bullying folks here at this money trap."

The guard lifted his walkie-talkie.

"He's a friend of mine," said Angela. "He's had too much to drink. Please, Frank, just leave. We can talk later, I promise."

Frank got up in the guard's face. The man did not budge, saying with surprising composure, "I was in Desert Storm. You do not, sir, wish for us to call the cops in this afternoon or the Air Force boys will bust you good. "

"You're lying. You haven't been anywhere but here for the last ten years."

"Frank!"

"That's it. You don't deserve to wear a uniform." The guard put the receiver to his mouth. "Got a live wire near 4-A. Need some backup."

There was another commotion behind Angela, ladies jumping up from their slots and shouting at a man who was stumbling his way, visibly drunk, along the aisle.

"Where is the man Goldman?" the man was shouting. He was slight, lean, Vietnamese. "You know Goldman. The lawyer. He was here."

"Who's *he*?" said Frank.

"It was you," the man said to Angela. "You gave us a drink. The lawyer, I met him here. I am an American! The Rebel men in the trailer lie about me again. No one can fuck with me! He will help me!"

"Watch your mouth," Frank railed, overtaken by the crazy Frank now. Jesus had left the room; he was on his own.

The Vietnamese man swung out at him, and they fell to a heap on the floor. Frank felt himself snatched up suddenly by a bouncer the size of an Ole Miss linebacker. A second enforcer hauled up the other guy.

His military career was surely over. Charged with disorderly conduct, assault and battery, he would walk from the base, stripped, in shame.

He caught the word "police."

As he was being led to a side door and into a small room, the Vietnamese man beside him, he heard the floor manager telling Angela she was fired, that it was the last time she could bring this kind of commotion into the Cotton Gin with all her jealous boyfriends.

"And you ain't even that hot," the supervisor said.

"I'm already out of here, jerk face," she said, and stormed out, leaving Frank, and the Cotton Gin, behind.

Back at her apartment, pulling out a tub of ice cream, she flopped on the couch, ate chocolate swirl, and sought refuge in the letters.

It had been Nana's life, she realized, not her own, that was filled with passion.

> Dearest Christiane,
>
> After two weeks in Manila, we are settled at the air base, showing the flag, letting the Japs know that if they rattle their swords we will be here to defend our freedoms. Gen. MacArthur has brought in squadrons of B-17s, too. You should see those Flying Fortresses, they'd give anybody second thoughts about threatening American interests.
>
> Let me tell you what this island is like to fly over. Volcanoes and palm trees, blue water and rocky beaches, for miles and miles. In the volcanoes are cratered lakes that look like glimmering eyes in the bright sunlight. You asked me once before, when we visited Arlington, how man can be so cruel as to engage in war, why humanity can act that way. Looking down on this serene landscape, as quiet as the hills of my boyhood Georgia, I feel your question is truer than ever. I have no answers.

For your peace of mind I thank God we are not in this war. But if duty calls, you know that I am at the ready. Every fiber of my being is prepared for the noble fight. In Europe, I would do anything to defend you and the people I love against the tyrant Hitler. Over here, Tojo does not scare me at all. If need be, I will meet the Japs in the skies, and we will prevail.

My beloved Christiane, although many days have passed since I held you in my arms, it could have been this very morning, so vivid is the picture of you in my mind, reaching out to me as I was leaving. Oh, for just ten more minutes. When I come home, we will have all the time in the world together, forever.

Angela picked up another, dated October 1941. She read aloud:

The maple leaves will be turning where you are, although there is no season here but dry or rainy. No matter how far I stray from my own religion, the Day of Atonement is one I can never deny. Last week the chaplain called a service for the Jewish men, and we assembled for prayers, and I asked forgiveness for all my sins. I did not eat or drink all day. You once told me I should fast on our special prayer day, as you called it. Once again I thank God for bringing you to me. You take me closer to Him.

Love,
Rosey

Reading the letters, she curled on the bed and drifted to sleep, feeling like Nana must have felt, airborne and romantic, lifted from her small room to the vastness of Pacific Islands. Frank was, thankfully, far far away.

In the morning she woke holding the letter and read of rice fields and thick forests and thatched huts seen from far above.

She thought of Lucky, how he loved to eat roast beef and baked potatoes and sit with Nana on the den sofa watching the Florida Seminoles—his home state football team. He had served in the war, too, as a supply sergeant in Italy, arriving two weeks before VE day. They had all gone in that generation, and come home waving the flag forever. How many still did, hanging Old Glory out over porches in Mississippi houses, especially since September 11. Although she had grown up with her father saying, after Vietnam, he would rather burn than wave it.

Lucky and her dad—how often they had faced each other down over "American pride." She remembered when Lucky talked about Grenada and what American forces must do there, and her father had said any U.S. excursion onto foreign soil was to push the agenda of Uncle Sam with no regard for the native peoples. Lucky had left the room fuming. She had gone and stood by him, and he had told her never to show disrespect to the nation her grandfather and so many others had valiantly fought for.

Since then, whenever she saw an American flag—in front of schools, post offices, and VFW lodges, often next to Mississippi's Confederate-inspired state flag—she thought of Lucky.

Rosey had died for his flag. So different they had been, she thought. Lucky, who loved to golf and perform magic tricks for her friends, would not have even read a poem so much as written one. But they had shared devotion to a nation; to a woman.

On the edge of her bed, holding the letters still, Angela looked at the swirls of Rosey's handwriting, blue ink seeped into onionskin paper, finding its way right to her.

Frank called, called again. He left messages of remorse, yearning, love. He said that casino security had kept the drunken squabble an in-house matter, plying him and the Vietnamese man with coffee to sober them up, then escorting them out of the complex. He told her he heard "the s.o.b. manager" firing her. He had some savings; he could help tide her over if she needed.

She opened the door to go to the employment agency and found an
envelope with a sheet of paper inside. His script was large, boxy, like a
junior high kid's.

> Dear Angela,
>   I am a big, fatheaded ass. Thank you for helping
> remind me to be humble. I do not know everything,
> even though I sometimes act like I do. I do know if
> you give me one more chance, I can show you I can be
> a better man. Someone who deserves you.

She folded it up, put it back in the envelope, later took it out again.
By now, she had memorized the message.

When her girlfriends from the Cotton Gin met up with her at Rudy's
to boost her morale, she did not want to talk about work, only Frank.

After listing everything about him that was wrong for her—he was
bossy, self-righteous, had an explosive temper, was a know-it-all—she
heard Brandy ask if he had a good heart.

"He's a cheerleader for all kinds of good things, I'll tell you that—
church, the armed forces, even family—but it comes out all wrong.
Doesn't do me much good if he beats me over the head with it."

"Men his age," said Quenesha, "still got a long way to go."

"Does he make you feel good?" Brandy asked.

Angela felt herself blush. She brushed back her hair, remembering
how he had reached over and pushed it back when they rode the ferry.

"Mm-hmm," Brandy said, "I figured he did."

The next day she called him, whispering "Damn you" before he answered, but when he did, simply admitting, "Okay, one more chance. I
guess I haven't been the easiest girlfriend either."

"I like the sound of that word," he said. "'Girlfriend.'"

He invited her to go with him to an airstrip just outside town at two
o'clock Sunday.

"I'm not jumping out of any plane!" she warned.

"No, I will. You'll be at the controls."

"Frank!"

He laughed. "You'll be okay."

When Frank showed up, she let him take her by the hand as they went to his car. Fifteen minutes later they were at an airstrip at the edge of town with a sign "Home to Harrison County Soaring Club." Sleek, bright-colored sailplanes with narrow bodies and long wing-spans stood in a row.

"We're going in one of those?"

A grizzled man in a backward baseball cap ambled across the tar-mac, waved at Frank, and attached a long cord to the tail of a tow plane. He affixed the other end of the cord to the nose of a glider.

"It's safer than the ride out here," Frank said, parking and coaxing her onto the runway. "I promise." He reached the red-winged aircraft, which looked to Angela like it was made of balsa wood. "Gorgeous, isn't it," Frank said, "a Schweizer two-seater." The Plexiglas cockpit cover was turned up. Frank climbed in, strapped on his safety harness, and patted the seat alongside. He grinned, the boy with the perfect teeth and easy charm she had first met in the Cotton Gin.

"Never."

"C'mon." He reached out to her. "It's a rush."

"Why am I doing this?" She hopped in, narrowly wedged into the seat alongside him.

He attached her harness belt and kissed her on the cheek. "You'll see why."

The tow plane began to hum, then roll, pulling them along.

"Don't be scared," Frank said.

"Just pay attention to what you're doing," she said anxiously.

They were moving swiftly over the runway tethered to the tow plane, the asphalt singing beneath them.

"The first time I ever went up in one of these," said Frank, "my first solo flight, I wasn't but sixteen. My knees were shaking."

Angela watched the tow plane lift off and seconds later they were tugged upward, her stomach playing catch-up, and they were rising over the high school, which became a set of blocks, and a little house on stilts next to what weirdly looked like a tiny Buddha figure and a

gas station with a sign advertising $1.98/gallon. Attached to the pro-
peller-droning mother ship by the slender umbilical cord, they went
higher. A pine forest became a bolt of green cloth, a red dirt road a hair
ribbon.

"Hold on!" Frank said. He reached down and pulled a switch.

She felt a thump as the tow cord was released and became a stringy
tail behind the tow plane. which banked and shot away, heading back
to the airstrip, leaving them, propellerless, to the fate of the skies.

They were up on their own, in the blue silence.

"My God," she whispered.

"Like angel wings, isn't it?" said Frank. He moved the controls and
they climbed higher. The wind made a soft whooshing over the wings.

"What keeps us up?"

"Faith." He grinned. "And those." He nodded down to a concrete
parking lot. "Anyplace that gives off heat."

"What do you mean?"

"It's called thermals," he explained. "Heat rises, simple as that. We
catch them, the thermals, that is, and that's what"—he turned to the
left and passed over the top of a church with a bright tin roof, and they
rose—"does that."

"How do we get down, though?"

"Down?" He shook his head. "Damn, I forgot to learn that."

She pinched him on the arm. "Funny funny."

He tapped the controls. "It's a lot easier than flying, not much in-
strumentation to worry about. Flying excites me, soaring mellows me."

"And casinos make you go ballistic," she teased.

He eyed her and grinned. "I knew you'd get into this. I can tell you're
relaxed."

"I shouldn't be," she said. "But . . . *wow.*"

After flying parallel to the shore, over the lush treetops and long,
gray heat strip of I-10, Frank brought them around, and they soared
over the shiny bubble of a water tower, a line of doll house antebellum homes, and the boxy toys of the Cotton Gin, Casino Fantasy, and
High Chaparral. Pirates Plunder was a galleon made from a model kit.

On the Mississippi Sound, stretched out like a blue cloth, were white accents of sailboats. Far beyond, in a curve of bright gold, was Ship Island.

They floated out over the Sound, inside a watercolor composition.

"I got to talk with your Vietnamese friend when we were cooling off," Frank said.

"I don't even know him."

"Well, y'all have one thing in common. You hate the Japanese."

"I never said I hated the Japanese," Angela said.

"Like Rosey, like Big Frank, the Japs gave him hell, too. His name is Phi. He told me his people are from Cholon, a Chinese section outside of Saigon. The Japanese were brutal to his grandparents before they moved to Vietnam. He told me the whole story."

Shades of blue gave way to tints of green, brushes of aqua.

"What was he going on about at the Cotton Gin?"

"Some rednecks whose butts he wanted to kick who've been giving him grief because he's Asian and can haul up more shrimp than they can 'cause he busts a gut. He was looking for a lawyer he'd met at the poker tables who was going to do it the red-blooded American way— sue their pants off. I vouched for him."

"What do you mean?"

"I told them he'd fought against the Vietcong—he had, and was a patriot. He'd stood up for us, we could stand up for him. Whatever leniency I got, I wanted to make sure he got it, too. No cops, no way."

"That's nice, Frank. You did a good thing."

"I'm not such an SOB," he said.

"You play one pretty good sometimes. Just don't be so high-and-mighty about your God. I know there's something, I just don't know what, who, exactly. Not yet."

"Not yet," he repeated.

"I hope," she said, "you're right."

They continued on in silence, the streaming of air over the cockpit, the glimmering island growing closer.

"The Bible fills me," he said, "it teaches me. Out here"—he clasped her hand—"I think of what Jesus said at the Sermon on the Mount. Matthew 5: 'Rejoice and be glad for your reward is great in Heaven.'"

"I'm not ready to go there just yet," she said.

"Think of what it must be like," he went on. "The stillness, the silence, the beauty of it as far as you can see. Course you can't 'see,' not like we can, but it's all around you, you're part of it, and there's this light."

"Sort of like your island out there?"

"Yes. We can't reach it now, though."

"Thermals," she said.

"Yes, we'd never get enough lift to get back." He pulled on the controls, and they began to circle back toward the shore.

"I don't know if I believe it," she said.

"You don't think we're children of God? I once heard a military aircraft designer use the term 'the carbon displacement unit.' That's the human in the cockpit. Is that all you think we are? Carbon displacement units?"

"I believe in Heaven! But I don't know if it's like you describe it. I'm not even sure I'd ever want it exactly like that."

"What could be better than that?"

A puff of cloud was overhead. On the surface of the Sound the wake of ski boats made silver fans.

"I think of a moment I felt really wonderful," Angela reflected, "really special, and it's always with somebody I love. Like with Nana on the beach—it all looks so small from here, but it's all we know, all I know—and I was with her and she was telling me about when she was young, and how she went to the Waldorf Astoria in New York City to go dancing, and, Frank, she drank too much champagne—my Nana was tipsy!—and then she told me about Rosey. I can't imagine anything more wonderful than spending a moment like that with Nana. Heaven could just be that, a lot of great moments with the people you love. God knows there are so many sad ones. Oh, how I miss my Mama sometimes, all the time—but maybe I could have those too—moments like . . ."

"Yes?"

"Well, this one, too."

Before them, a gift, the seascape unfurled, and beyond the coastal development, the outlet stores and the fields and the airstrip, were the piney Southern woods again.

Frank lifted her hand and kissed it, then turned to her. "Marry me, Angela."

"What!"

"Marry me. Make this wonderful moment last for years and years."

"You want a church wife, you know you do."

"We'll make our own church. Up here."

"I can't just marry you. Not just like that."

"Why not?"

"Well, first of all, we haven't been seeing each other very long, and second of all, we're too young, and it's just all—out of the blue."

"We're in the blue."

"Nothing's real up here is what you mean."

"Is this real?"

"What?"

"When I saw those towers come down on 9/11, Angela, I told myself then and there, 'Don't waste a moment. Who knows when you'll walk into a room one day and vanish the next.' It's like the rapture—when it will come, no one knows, but it will come. And then we'll be gone from this place. But it can happen for bad reasons, too."

"That's no reason to rush off to the altar."

"How long did your parents date before they got married?"

"Two years."

"Well, there you go. Do you love me?"

"I don't even know what love is. Maybe, well, okay, a little. Yes. I feel I do."

"Then marry me, or think about it. Say you'll think about it."

"I'll think about it. Yes, Frank, I will."

He brought them back deftly, smoothly, gently touching down.

On the way back to her apartment they played the radio, and she sang along to Crystal Gayle and old Janis Joplin, and prize above all, Dylan's "Like a Rolling Stone." The whole day was proving a run of luck.

She imagined them as husband and wife, a tow-haired little Frank between them.

She went to check her cell phone messages, but realized she had left in such haste that she'd forgotten it on the table. When she arrived home, her answering machine was blinking.

She pressed the playback button.

"Angela, this is Fred Nelson at Coastal Arms. Your grandmother has walked out on her own again, and we are sending out a search party to find her. Please call us immediately."

She played the next:

"Angela, Fred Nelson again. Thank God we found your grandmother. She's back in her room, and Nurse Torres is cleaning her up. She's fine, she's safe, she got a little muddy but all is well."

The third:

"Hello, Angela, Fred Nelson again. Please call me to arrange a visit as soon as possible. We need to discuss Mrs. Fields's situation."

At their office the next afternoon, Angela was told by Director Nelson that Coastal Arms was "not the ideal place for someone, hard to accept, who's descending into dementia."

"I'm so sorry. Mrs. Fields has been such a wonderful part of our community," he said. "We're a family, that's our philosophy, and we live by it. But this is only assisted living." He recommended other options along the coast. "The best of care," he said. "The proper care."

"Do you have any idea of what this woman has been through in her life?" Angela said.

"There are liability issues, too," he explained.

"The losses she suffered," Angela pressed. "For our country? For me, for *you*?"

"We're sorry, Angela, we'll do everything we can to help with the transition."

"I can take care of her myself."

"You can't do it on your own."

"I can try."

"We love your Nana."

"Dammit, she'll just come live with me."

PART II

Feet Planted, Sand Caving

SEVEN

Over the Threshold

On a stretch of Virginia Beach near where Nana had grown up, dunes soared tall as a schoolhouse. During a driving trip with Nana and Lucky to Washington, D.C., when Angela had been a kid, Nana had insisted on a detour to that beach and an overnight at an ocean-side motel. Early morning, Nana had led Angela onto the dunes and showed her a childhood game of her own. They had stood on the grainy ledge, planting their feet, as waves rushed onto the beach and ate at the towering sands. Who could keep her footing the longest as the sand crumbled and they were pulled down—eruptions of laughter, shrieks of joy—into the roiling surf?

Those sensations came back to Angela as she drove the Mississippi coast, looking at possible alternatives for Nana's residence. When she had announced to her grandmother she wanted her to move in, Nana had refused, saying she preferred to stay at Coastal Arms.

"It's time to leave there," Angela said.

"Not for me."

"It's not up to your standards. You can do better."

"You think so?" Nana asked meekly, looking off as though uncertain where she was at all.

In case she couldn't convince her, Angela headed to D'Iberville to see one nursing home the director had recommended, then Gautier to another. Like Coastal Arms, both were clean and bright, with colorful awnings and smiling staff. As she was shown around, the aides stopped, hallway to hallway, to press security codes for entry and exit. "Is this a dangerous neighborhood?" Angela asked halfheartedly, dreading the real answer.

"These locks are not to keep intruders out," said a kindly nurse, "but to keep our patients in. Protecting them is an important part of the care we give."

Heading home, she thought of their lives as those dunes on long-ago Virginia Beach. Digging in as they might, trying to ward off collapse, the sand was giving way.

She mulled over options while working temp jobs, not yet finding full-time work.

"I loved my granddaddy 'til he lived with us," said a girl handing out flyers with her at a car show, "then I hated him, too, I mean, I felt bad, because I still loved him, but he kind of disgusted me, he got so old, and Daddy had to bathe him, I looked once, God, you wouldn't believe what happens to an old guy."

"My granna lived with us," said a bleach-blond cashier at a hotel where Angela was hostess for a convention, "and she kept her nose in everybody's business. I could hardly have a boyfriend without her asking if we were 'doing it' or not, and she *didn't* approve."

Could Angela even handle Nana as roommate?

When she met up with Frank near the Biloxi Lighthouse and she turned over her plight—"Should I really let Nana live with me? Can I handle it? Is it fair to Nana?"—he put his hands on her shoulders and looked into her with his deep, brown eyes.

"One of the hardest things I ever did in my life was go to jump school," he said. "I told you about how, when I was a kid, I read about Dodson, jumping with his weather gear on D-Day. What I didn't tell you is that I was petrified of what might happen to me if I jumped. I'd lie awake, thinking. What if I can't do it? What if I get to the open hatch of the plane, it's my turn, I look down, and then I freeze. My knees shake, my legs buckle, my stomach churns. I can't."

"It didn't bother you when the time really came, did it?" she asked.

"Hell it didn't. I was there, chute packed, door open, toes on the threshold of here and nowhere, wind whipping my clothes. I prayed, yes, I prayed, but even that didn't get me to cross over. Do you know what did? I thought of all the men and women who'd come before me, what they'd done, how they'd sacrificed, the moments they'd faced something that put fear into their bones—coming to America, or fighting in a battle, or having courage in the face of death—and I took a little piece of that courage and made it my own. Take a little piece of your Nana's courage. Make that yours, Angela."

"Will you be there if I fall?"

He opened his arms as if to catch her.

Taking Nana to a lunch buffet at Pirates Plunder, she appealed to her grandmother: "It's what Mama would have wanted. You and me. It'll be like Mama's right between us."

"Whatever you want to do, my Angel," she finally relented. "I'm yours."

Nana instructed attorney Flowers to put Angela on as cosigner for her checking account. Nana was still flush, but the cost of Coastal Arms, supplemental insurance to Medicare, and prescription drugs had drawn down her nest egg considerably.

Angela pinched off some of those funds to swap her one-bedroom rental for a pricier two-bedroom in the same complex, and to hire Maria Torres of Coastal Arms to work for Nana in her off-hours. She made a purchase, too—Coastal Arms's old piano, as the home had just secured a new one, though she had yet to transport it, another expense.

On the day they were packing up at Coastal Arms, and Nana was saying good-bye to the other residents—"I'll come visit," said General Wheeler, and gave her a rascally wink—Angela ran into Cam coming in the door, piano music under her arm. "I'll pay you five dollars an hour to play for Nana at our house," Angela offered impulsively.

Cam beamed.

"Three afternoons a week," she added.

"My Daddy . . ."

"I'll talk to him if you need."

When Angela put Nana in the front seat of her car, with her belongings piled up in the backseat, she imagined them going off on a road trip, to a place where she was a child again, and Nana and Lucky would be there, too, and she'd curl up on the couch between them watching old movies.

After they arrived at her apartment, they unpacked Nana's bags and settled in to drink tea and watch *Jeopardy* while roasting a chicken in the oven.

To her surprise Frank arrived in his car with two friends from the base following him in a truck. He announced, "Housewarming gift!"

Frank and his buddies, heaving and grunting, lifted the piano out of the truck and rolled it into the living room, positioning it by the window. His friends took off. Frank settled on the couch next to them.

Angela and her family were home.

Even after tuning, the piano still had a few off-notes and one B-flat that sounded with a thunk, but Cam lost herself in the canopy of music when she serenaded her audience of one, who nodded and clapped then drifted off to sleep. Daddy had okayed the arrangement, realizing he'd already met Frank and Angela at the Cotton Gin in that chaotic way, and he welcomed the pocket cash for his daughter with his shrimping business down, hurt by cheap Asian imports. "They are bastards who do this, and their shrimp are this small"—he held out his little finger—"and the Americans are bastards who let this happen."

He railed about the shrimp and kept on about the men who lived in the trailer park—though the matter was seemingly dropped after a conversation with lawyer Goldman—and after heading to the casino in the evenings, he returned drunk and knelt at his little shrine in homage to Mai and Kieu. When Cam helped him into his bedroom, he looked at her blearily, and said yet again, "This is no place for you, a young girl, alone with your father. Your aunt, your cousins, in New Orleans, that is where you should be. To meet a nice Vietnamese boy."

"I want to live with you, Daddy," she said, remembering her mother's words to her—"Take care of your father"—"until I meet the man I will spend my life with."

"At eighteen," he said, "at eighteen, you can live with your cousins then, and they will introduce you to that man. And you can go to college, too, it is my dream for you, my prayer to the Bodhisattva, that you will go to college and be a good wife and mother."

But she had already met that man.

Angela had checked out from the library the score of *West Side Story*, and as Cam played the romantic tunes "Maria" and "Tonight," she envisioned herself with her shining policeman. In his uniform Joe stood tall, gentle, and strong, and she clutched his arm.

Since the morning he had stopped to talk to Daddy in his squad car, she had watched police cruisers wondering if he was behind the wheel.

Had he thought about her? He had noticed her back in high school; she knew that much now. Did he favor Asian girls? She knew from her girlfriend Cecilia that some Western boys did.

"Cam," Nana said suddenly. "Do you have a boyfriend?"

Cam shook her head, continuing to play. "No ma'am."

She glanced over at Nana, whose eyes were fixed on her. Did she have special powers to read her mind?

Nana went on: "You're a pretty young lady. I bet there must be some nice Chinese boy who would like to take you to the movies."

"I'm Vietnamese, but my family's background is Chinese. So that would be okay."

"What about an American boy?"

"Well," she said, keeping up the music's tempo, "I guess that would be, well, okay. Daddy might not like it, though."

She finished the yearning melody of "Tonight" and stopped playing, turning to Nana on the bench. "Can I tell you a secret?"

Nana clapped her hands together. "I love secrets."

"There is one boy I like."

"Tell me, tell me."

"He doesn't know I like him, though."

"Well, that's not a big problem."

"It's not?"

"Do you know the expression 'You catch more flies with honey'?"

"No ma'am."

"When I was your age, I didn't have to work too hard at it, but"—she smiled coquettishly—"you always meet men who have to be, shall I say, given a little nudge. Because they're not paying attention to begin with."

"Joe's his name."

"Does Joe go to your school?"

"He graduated already."

"Good. Rosey was a little older than me, too."

"He's . . ."

"Go on."

"A policeman now."

"Rosey, in his uniform, so smart." Nana stood up now and went to the door. She opened it and peered out. "Did you hear something?"

Keep playing. Miss Angela had instructed her, over and over: *Keep playing.*

She hit the keys, the strains of "Moon River" rising through the apartment.

Nana stepped out onto the walk.

"Mrs. Fields? Nana?"

"Hello!" she heard Nana call out.

"He's in here, Nana."

Nana quickly stepped back in, looked about, and flopped onto the sofa. "He'll come back. Answer the door if I don't hear it."

"Yes ma'am."

Nana closed her eyes and began to snooze. Cam covered her with the melodies of happy show tunes until Angela returned.

What Nana and Cam talked about, Angela did not know, but when she returned, time and again after Cam's hour-long recital, Nana sent her off with a conspiratorial "That's just for us now."

Maria Torres was good for fifteen to twenty hours of work a week and fixed Southern food and Latin fare, too, in a way that everyone liked. Maria's daughter Jane—"Nobody calls me Juana here," Maria reported her daughter had protested—had joined up with the Mississippi National Guard and was in a transport unit stationed in Kuwait.

"She called me last night by phone, it was coming to me by a satellite," said Maria as she readied Nana for dinner, tucking in a napkin under her chin. "'*Mi madre*,' she said, '*te amo*. I love you. I will not be able to call again soon.' '*Preciosa*,' I told her, 'you are keeping us safe, and God will keep you safe.'"

Up the sides of her apartment building walls, along the boulevards, stretching over lawns, the azaleas turned the Gulf Coast March into a soft riot of color. Even the green-and-gray fatigues, and dress blues, of the airmen looked heightened by the shades of red that burst across Keesler. As Angela visited Frank there, she tried to imagine herself as a military wife. She knew the list of bases where they might spend their lives—from Fort Lewis, Washington, to Fort Carson, Colorado, to Fort Campbell, Kentucky, to Hurlburt Field, Florida—would prove an itinerant existence. Nowhere could be as serene and floral as the Mississippi coast. In a rash moment she imagined herself joining up, too. But she had her battle to commandeer—caring for Nana.

And as the president amassed troops in Kuwait and gave Saddam one warning, then another, she continued to have doubts about a preemptive strike. When Frank said again, "What if we'd stopped Hitler before it was too late," she stopped arguing. She did not sympathize with tyrants. But could she be as certain as Frank in his vote of confidence for his commander in chief? His passion, his certainty—yes, that's what she had told her tormented father—helped convince her it must be true.

He had been right about Nana, after all—cross the threshold, step out into the void, take your strength from those who were brave before you. Already she would not trade the time Nana had lived with her— their chicken dinners in front of the TV, their visits together to the nail salon, Nana wandering with her through dress sales at the mall—for any treasure in the world.

When she woke up early one morning to watch the first assault on Baghdad on TV—the precision bombs lighting up the sky like Independence Day fireworks over the Cotton Gin—she called Frank at the base, but all circuits were busy.

Then her phone had rung and it was Frank, shouting, "They got him! They think they got him!"

"What . . ."

"Saddam," he shouted. "Two Nighthawks blasted him right in his bunker. This will be the shortest damn war, hell, I wanted to be there for it, but who knew it wouldn't last twenty-four hours."

And by that evening, with Cam sitting on the couch next to Nana, having stayed on after her piano time, and Maria Torres on their side, they watched the American tanks roll through the desert, and saw the wasteland of sand and shattered stone, and everyone except Nana cheered. The newscasters were saying that the earlier reports that Saddam had been killed or wounded were unsubstantiated, that he may have fled to Iran, or was hiding in a cave, but that the Iraqi people, with Saddam dead or alive, would be welcoming the Americans with flowers.

"Are you okay?" Cam asked Nana.

"Would you like some hot tea?" asked Maria. "This would make you feel better?"

Nana brushed them away, then leaned her head against Angela's shoulder and closed her eyes.

A few nights later, as the embedded reporters pointed to blasted sites in Baghdad and small towns nearby, Nana was sleeping but Angela was still awake, hypnotized by the rolling footage of the war coming into their Biloxi living room. She thought she saw, among the camouflaged troops, a familiar face. The American soldier moved in and out of the alleys.

What was he doing there? She saw him up close now.

She had read in the *Sun-Herald* about a local woman who had glimpsed her son in the Army in Iraq while she was watching CNN. But wouldn't Rosey be old? Of course, like Nana, but time had not aged him. He was vital, bold, swift, rushing across the dry sand road, M16 at his side.

"Nana!" she tried to shout. "You'll be so happy," but when she went to wake Nana, she could not find her. Was this even her living room?

She was in a hallway now, searching for her: "Nana? Come, look, on the TV. Come, look."

The news camera zoomed close on him now. "I want to say hello to my family in Biloxi, Mississippi," he said. "I love you, my darling, we'll be home soon."

"Rosey!" she shouted at the screen. "Rosey, Rosey! Say Nana's name, say it. Christiane. She needs to hear your voice! Rosey!!!"

She looked around. There was Nana beside her on the couch, sleeping. The TV combat churned on. She started to move, but felt a crick in her neck: "*Was I asleep?*"

"Nana, Nana!"

Her grandmother opened her eyes slowly and peered at her. A thin smile curled on her lips.

"What would I do without you, my Angel?" she said.

A tap-tap came at the door. "It's me."

Frank was there, wide awake, bristling with energy.

"Your light was on," he said, "I can't sleep. I can't keep watching this. There's a huge sandstorm going on, it's making hell for the infrared sensors, for the optical reconnaissance, for the laser-guided bombs. It's coming right from Saudi Arabia, we can see it on the system at the base. I can't do any damn thing about it here. I want to be there, Angela."

"Let me get her into her bed and we'll talk," Angela said.

But Frank walked over to Nana, bent down, and lifted her up, cradling her in his arms. He stepped into her bedroom, and Angela hurried behind, turning back the covers.

In the living room, alone together, with the pictures of Baghdad rolling across the TV screen, she turned to him and said, "I don't need to think about it anymore. I don't want to think at all. I just want, I do want, to be your wife."

Outside Victory Brotherhood is a marker that reads, "The back wall of this building, originally Lutheran Church of the Redeemer, was all that was left standing after Hurricane Camille in 1969. With this testament to God's grace in its midst, Hope Assemblies of God built a new house of worship here in 1973, retaining the original wall. In 1995, Victory Brotherhood assumed ownership of this hallowed sanctuary."

Inside, by the pews garlanded with white azaleas, Angela, in a simple white gown, moves ceremoniously up the aisle to the "Wedding March" played by Cam on the church's piano. In the front row, Nana, in a light blue dress, hums loudly to Cam's music, having listened to her practice it over the last two weeks. Nobody minds. Maria Torres, attending to Nana, gently strokes her hand.

With no father to escort her—Angela's heartfelt note to him announcing her marriage was answered with a terse, "I'm sorry we can't be there, congratulations, Dad, DeeDee, Donnie, Dylan," and a twenty-five-year savings bond for $100—she walks alone, holding a picture of Lucky, then handing it to Nana as she reaches the pulpit.

Brother Tim welcomes family and friends, then turns the pulpit over to Rev. Franklin Semmes of Marks, who says the day is joyous for him as a father of the groom, and as a son of God. As Angela hears Little Frank talk about the power of Jesus, and the power of love, and that God is love, she looks at her Frank, and he gazes back at her, beaming. She sees him again on the boat to Ship Island, face golden in the sun. She had wanted him all for herself, she knows, thinking back, right then.

Brother Tim takes over again for the vows, and after they say their "I do's," and kiss, Angela feels herself lifted out of the chapel with her husband, taken by the heat that comes up through her body, his body, the thermals that bear them aloft.

They are set back down again at their party in the back room of the Biloxi Steakhouse, the three-piece combo playing a danceable mix of country rock and up-tempo blues, and the room, to Angela, is deliciously swirling.

"Nana?" she says.

Big Frank has invited Nana onto the floor, and the couple do a festive and clumsy two-step as Big Frank pivots slowly on his peg leg and Nana throws her head back and laughs and says to Cam, "See what I told you?"

A policeman doing double duty as a security guard eases in to watch, and when Frank, between dances, goes over to him to ask if everything is okay, the policeman shakes his hand, saying, "Congratulations," and waves to Cam.

Cam comes over. "Anybody giving your dad any grief?" the cop asks.

Cam shakes her head.

"Well," says Frank, "just come on in."

Cam introduces Joe, offers him punch, and they sit at a corner table, talking.

Before starting off on their honeymoon, Angela throws her bouquet behind her. Cam catches it, but hands it to Nana.

The newlyweds walk across the street to the Cotton Gin. Brandy and the other cocktail servers have pooled their tips and rented them a room as a wedding gift. Just like in the movies, Frank lifts Angela over the threshold, carrying her as tenderly as he has carried Nana and laying her down on the bed, then sweeps her up in an embrace meant only for a bride.

They make first married love with the lights of Biloxi Harbor glimmering below, and second married love with the first light rising over the Deer Island trees, and again, with the TV turned low, but forgotten.

"One day," Frank says, "I want to take you to the Philippines. We'll go to all those damn places, take a video, bring it home for Granddad and Nana. Corregidor. Bataan. Manila. We'll go there and live like kings, and show how our families survived, how nobody can ever keep us down."

In the afternoon, as they share Bloody Marys from room service, the TV quietly humming, they watch as the people of Iraq throw ropes around a statue of their deposed ruler and yank him down to pieces on the ground with cheers and upraised fists.

Frank is right there beside her, but also, Angela knows, now far away.

EIGHT

Hidden Voices

Dear Bodhisattva,

My mother told me that you are much wiser than we are, and sometimes we do not know that the answer to our question has been given. Speak to the Bodhisattva, my mother said, and she will not speak back but will tell you what you need to know. I never knew what she meant by that. Now I think I know.

I asked for Daddy to see me, to hear me, and not just the memory of my sister. This is the answer. There is someone else now to hear me—Joe.

He is so handsome. He has black hair with little curls. He is twenty years old, and a policeman. Daddy was five years older than mother when they married. I have only talked to him a few times, but he hears me.

Bodhisattva, Daddy would be very angry with me if he knew about Joe. He wants me to marry a Vietnamese or Chinese boy, you know all these things in your wisdom. Can you tell me what to do in your special way of giving an answer?

She folded up the letter and took off on her bicycle down Oak Street. When she zipped across the highway and down the road by the school shuttered for summer, she saw the Bodhisattva standing tall, her beatific eyes downcast, her left hand holding the pitcher that forever poured water, her right hand up in mystic gesture—palm out, thumb to index finger in a circle. How beautiful she was, how welcoming in her tranquil gaze. Cam rolled to a stop at the temple and set her bicycle against a railing.

She approached the wise goddess.

A disembodied voice, soft and low, addressed her: "Cam Nguyen."

"Yes?"

"Why do you come here all alone?"

The question lingered in the rose trellis behind the Bodhisattva.

Cam bowed her head. "To tell you something, Bodhisattva. To give you a letter."

She looked back up.

"Place it there," the voice instructed. "I will read it."

Starlings coursed from behind the roses and swooped deliriously over the temple.

Cam stepped forward, put the letter down, took out the matches, and struck one. She touched it to the letter, which curled red like a lotus flower.

"Child, what are you doing?"

From behind Quan Am stepped Monk Thich Thien Thai in his saffron robes, bald-headed and round-faced.

Cam pressed her hands together, bowed.

"This is the way you offer your supplications?"

"To the Bodhisattva, yes, Monk," she said.

He laughed, his round face as beatific as a shining boy's.

"This is bad of me?" she said.

"Look and you will see, listen and you will hear. If you want an answer, you will receive an answer. It does not matter how you ask your question."

He made a short bow, and headed to the temple, climbing the steps to its front door. At the landing, before entering, he called down: "Remind your father we still have many pledges to be met."

"Don't tell him you saw me come here," she implored. "Please, Monk."

"This is good you are here." He disappeared in the door.

She stood in front of Quan Am and closed her eyes. "Please, Bodhisattva, forgive me if I have offended you, but I no longer care about Daddy. I only want the love of Joe."

In response she heard another voice: "So you're the firebug?"

She opened them to see Joe standing at the edge of the temple grounds.

"Thank you, Bodhisattva," she whispered.

"They've been waiting for this," he said, nodding toward the trailer park. "I think they had the precinct number on speed dial."

"Am I under arrest?"

"Yeah, that your bike? Come on and I'll throw it in the trunk. I'm taking you in."

He opened the back door of his cruiser and Cam climbed in, and he went around and cranked up the car. The police scanner crackled, and Cam heard the reports of the crises that plagued their little town—a call to EMS from a man suffering from asthma, a teen scuffle near the seashell emporium. And one firebug, she knew, at the Buddhist Temple. She awaited news of her transgression, the happiest criminal in Biloxi just to be captive in Joe's car.

Around the bend from the temple he pulled over and patted the front seat. "Just climb over."

"I thought you were taking me in!"

"Lord of God, you think I'm crazy? I have to keep up appearances, you know."

She bounded over the seat and plopped down on the passenger side, and he headed off again.

"This has been my morning," Joe said as the car made its way through corridors of pine. "One domestic dispute—a man socked his wife in the eye—two speeding tickets, one of them DUI, an old man complaining about his neighbor's playing rock 'n' roll too loud, and"— he grinned—"a Vietnamese pyromaniac. I just figure it's some Buddhist thing, like Catholics burning incense."

"A Buddhist thing," she repeated, and laughed.

"I didn't mean to offend you," he said.

"No, no, it was cute."

"Cute, well, I'll be." He grinned.

"Do you have dimples?" she asked. "I never knew you had dimples."

"I don't smile too much."

"You're not happy?"

"It's not what I'm paid to do."

"Come to think of it, Joe, you seemed pretty serious in high school, too. Officer Joe," she added.

"Come off it now. Joe."

Those dimples again.

"You seemed pretty serious, too," he said. "I always figured it was because you were really involved in your music, you know, your piano."

"I can't believe that you even knew I played."

"First time I ever laid eyes on you was the Christmas concert. You were playing 'Silent Night.' It was beautiful. You were beautiful."

She felt herself tremble. "I was fourteen!"

"I wasn't counting."

"I watched you playing basketball," she said.

"I knew that, too. You weren't at every game, 'cause I'd glance around for you."

As the squad car rolled along a back road, Cam felt the power of authority. As other cars approached, they slowed, worried about the speed limit; as old-timers raking pine straw in front yards looked up, they stood still and stared, wondering who the law was after. One man got up from his porch rocker and ducked into his front door.

She knew she should ask where they were going, but she did not care. She was with him; that was all that mattered. And that was where she was supposed to be.

"You know what I was always wondering?" Joe said as they turned off the county road onto a bumpy, unpaved lane. "Why you being of your Vietnamese religion and all, you were coming to St. Benedict's."

"For the same reasons I do everything," she said. "Daddy."

"He seems like the strict kind, old world, and all that."

She nodded. "Definitely."

"I know he felt burned up plenty when I saw him that day at the dock. I could understand it. He's got a lot of pride."

"He works so hard," she said. "He's got the smell of seafood in his skin. That's what an aunt of mine in East New Orleans says."

"So why St. Benedict's?"

"So I wouldn't be around any bad boys at the regular high school. He's seen some of the Vietnamese kids get hooked up in gangs, seen the girls pulled into it, too. And he's afraid of blacks."

"Crips, Bloods, Asian Tongs, we've got them all, he's right. Sometimes you'd think this place was Detroit, L.A., or Brooklyn."

They rode in silence for several minutes, listening to the scratchy voices on the scanner. A report came of a missing child near Tecumseh Lake.

"Don't you, like, have to go protect anybody?" she asked.

"Well, I'm looking out for you." He turned onto a rutted, red clay lane. "Oh, just joshing you. My shift's over." The car bumped and rocked as they passed alongside a stream. "Only one thing I don't know," he said. "And that's how I got to be so lucky as to get the call today about you."

"Quan Am," she said.

"What's that mean?"

"Think of her like the Virgin Mary."

She looked over at a sprawling, dilapidated wooden house with a screened porch and antlers over the front door. "Where are we?"

"We call it Fly Creek," he said. "Our hunting camp. Let's have a drink."

They got out and went into the lodge. A buck head hung over the fireplace, its taxidermy eyes in glassy stare. A wide mouth bass twisted against a backdrop of wood near the kitchen window. Cam scanned the snapshots of hunters with camouflage paint on their faces proudly holding lifeless turkeys or squatting next to slaughtered bucks.

In one picture she recognized Joe, his face smeared with dark red paint. She stepped close and peered at it.

"My first buck," he said, coming up behind her and putting his hands on her shoulders. "You smear his blood on your face. It's ritual."

He turned her to him but did not draw her any closer. His face was red, blushing hard. "How old are you exactly?" he asked.

"About sixteen."

She was pulled toward him as in ages-old ritual and received his softest, sweetest first kiss.

Marriage, day in and out the first weeks, the initial months, provided all the happiness Angela could possibly hope for.

Frank out to the base, Mrs. Torres in to sit with Nana, Angela out to her temp jobs, Cam in to play piano, everyone together when possible for dinner—the rhythms of the home were sweet and sustaining. The domestic round was gentler and just plain more fun than she had ever guessed it could be growing up amid her parents' slash-and-burn marriage.

Nana even had a gentleman caller, General Wheeler. Twice a week, Mrs. Torres was hired by his family to chauffeur him to the VFW, and once they stopped by for him to say hello to Nana. Angela did not know what the two talked about sitting in Nana's room, sipping sweet tea. She heard laughter, godsend enough.

After Frank completed his courses in combat weather and extreme weather at Keesler, he was sent to Hurlburt Air Force Base. Rather than move as a family, they decided to stay put, with Frank taking the monotonous, two-and-a-half-hour drive east to Mary Esther, Florida, and bunking there until his days off. When he showed up at their Biloxi apartment, no matter the hour, they enjoyed honeymoon nights again. He put his name on the wait list for a two-bedroom apartment at Hurlburt, and brought home apartment listings for Fort Walton, the beachside town near the base. But the Mississippi coast, for the time being, was their life.

Angela had been alone with Nana when she saw the president on May first step onto the deck of the U.S.S. *Abraham Lincoln* and announce the end of major combat operations in Iraq, a banner proclaiming, "Mission Accomplished." Her heart had spun like a glowing top: what need would there be for Frank, or any other serviceman or woman, to arrive there now outside of a peacekeeping role? She watched the insanity of department store and museum looters, but there was no role for an Air Force weatherman in curbing all that. Her head was dizzy with names—Sunni, Shiite, Kurd; General Franks, Lieutenant General Sanchez, General Abizaid; Abu Musab al-Zarqawi, Muqtada al-Sadr—but the only name in her central nervous system was Frank.

She found a website, www.spousebuzz.com, introduced herself online as a "newbie," and read the blogs and comments from military spouses, mostly wives, detailing endless scenarios of husbands in different branches of service. One woman described the shipping out to Iraq of her husband's Army Reserve unit in Alabama as "an afternoon full of cheer and tears." Another, in Delaware, said she had gone with her husband to the local airport waiting for a plane to transport his unit to Kuwait; they waited and waited, went home, then got the call again two hours later. "It was like a big cluster f***," she had typed out. "Nobody knew what was happening. We parted from each other kind of in a bad mood. God forgive me."

She read a series of exchanges between wives on the annoyances of relocation, base to base, and another among spouses of the growing number of wounded. The U.N. headquarters in Baghdad was bombed. Basra erupted in riots. These events found their way onto the blogs, the TV, the newspapers; they had never felt so close as they did now.

She read Nana some of the entries and said she was thinking about going to the "milspouse" meeting at Keesler, just to meet some of the other spouses.

"We've got our own milspouse club," said Nana. "You be the president."

"What will you be?" asked Angela, laughing.

"Social director. Let's have a party now."

"Nana?" she asked.

"Hmm?" Nana was heading into the kitchen, reaching into the cabinet for wineglasses.

"How would you feel about moving to Florida, say, Fort Walton Beach, that area?"

Nana turned, as though stricken, barely able to talk.

Angela leapt up and went to her. "Are you okay? Say something!"

"I'm just"—Nana took a deep breath and exhaled slowly—"Florida's where they send the old folks!"

"Nana! What's gotten into you?"

"I like"—she sniffled—"living here with you."

"I didn't mean we were sending you off to Florida! I meant move there with me and Frank. That's where his base is."

"Oh," she said flatly, clearly not yet appeased. She reached for the wineglasses again and brought down two. "Your place is with your husband. It'll be"—she opened the refrigerator, the familiar Nana again, and brought out a bottle of grape juice—"okay." She peered at the label, unable to find her glasses. "Is this a good vintage?"

"Excellent," said Angela.

"To the milspouses," said Nana, clinking her glass against her granddaughter's then taking a sip. "It tastes like Manischewitz."

"What's that?"

"Jewish wine. They drink it at the Passover."

"Tell me about Rosey being Jewish and all."

Nana nodded.

"Was that difficult?"

"Not for us."

"So everybody was happy?"

"My mother and father, no, to tell you the truth. But we never got far enough to see if they really meant it."

"Meant what?"

"That if we had children, we should have them christened, or else. Rosey's mother and father said if we had children, we dare *not* have them christened. Or else."

"Else what?"

Nana made a thumbs-down gesture. "To the dogs with you."

"So y'all were like Romeo and Juliet?"

Nana poured another half glass of grape juice. She touched it to her lips, then put it down. "What about my things?"

"What about your things?"

"If we move to Florida."

"Don't worry. We'll pack you up. Let's get back to the story of you and Rosey."

"My Victorian sofa," Nana started in, "my claw-foot table, my Dhurry rugs, my Tiffany lamp, my president's rocker, my Limoges, my—"

"You got rid of that stuff a long time ago, Nana, or put it all in storage."

"It's all at my house!"

"What house?"

"Are you drunk already? The house where we live!"

"We live here," she said, hearing the despair in her own voice.

"*You* live here; I'm just visiting. Right?"

"Right, Nana," Angela said softly.

"If I move," Nana said plaintively, "how will Rosey know where to find me?"

Angela watched her grandmother's face closely, looking still for a hint, a sign that she was kidding. But she knew already Nana wasn't. She started to try and reason with her, but just said, "Let's watch TV."

"Do we have any chips?"

With snacks on the side table, they sat on the couch, Angela channel surfing to avoid anything about the war, and came to the movie channel. They sank into a vintage replay of *Show Boat*. Soon Nana put her head on Angela's shoulder and fell fast asleep. Night came down. They were bathed by the light of the TV screen.

Meet Me in St. Louis came on next, and Angela watched doe-eyed Judy Garland singing grandly on a trolley car, but her ears, like a wild animal's, picked up the turning of Frank's jeep into the parking lot and his footsteps at the front door.

He entered, and with Nana curled up on the couch snoring, the couple tiptoed like sneaky kids into the bedroom, pushed the door closed, and ferociously stripped each other naked and fell into bed, Frank on his back, Angela straddling him.

"I don't want to ever grow old, Frank," she said desperately, leaning down to receive his kisses on her mouth, on her breasts, then with him whispering into her ear, "I won't let you," feeling the rush of him pushing into her. As she rode him with the night sweeping through her, his body rising through hers, she felt tears run down her face.

He reached up and traced them. "Are you sad?"

"It's just I'm so happy," she said.

Afterward she lay curled against him, recognizing how she fit perfectly into the curve of his waist, the turn of his hip, the sprawl of his arm. They were two creatures comprising one.

"I'll never let you go," he said.

As Angela drives through town in mid-September, 9/11 having come around again with second anniversary commemorations, she thinks of how they walked the grounds of Keesler on New Year's Eve and Frank made two wishes—to teach at the base one day, and to ride with the Hurricane Hunters. As if the ghost of Hap Arnold had been listening, his wishes have already been answered. He has made it clear to her that, if the chance arises, he will exploit his talents in a war zone, Iraq or Afghanistan, and "live up to the model of Rosey and Big Frank," but that, in the meantime, he can take a special assignment to teach introductory weather skills at the base: his test scores had been the highest of his class.

And after only a week back at Keesler, Captain Reggie has phoned to invite him to ride along as an observer on a flight with the 503rd Wing. Hurricane Isabel, which started out as a tropical wave off the coast of Africa but intensified to a behemoth over the Atlantic, is taking aim at the coast of the Carolinas.

The giant plane with Frank joining the crew has lumbered into the sky this morning, and Angela can still hear its roar beyond the pines. The projectile of steel in the Gulf Coast sky has become a sliver of silver, then a glimmer, a dot in the back of her eye. She imagines Frank looking down at the green-brown Mississippi Sound changing to blue-green Gulf waters and soon deep blue oceanic depths.

The first time she heard of the Hurricane Hunters, she had been twelve, on a Girl Scout field trip; her mom was leader. One of the airmen had told them that the C-130, used for the day-long forays into the eye of a storm, was called the *Hercules* because of its massive strength. He showed the Scouts a dropsonde, the piece of equipment—"It's as big as a toaster oven," she remembers him saying—dropped to the ocean with the storm swirling around. "It sends us back all the vital information."

The Scouts had seen a short film about how the airplane approached the screaming storm, pushing through series of rain bands, the *Hercules* like a toy buffeted by ferocious winds, finally punching through into the calm center.

As a Scout, she understood when the hunter told them he had signed up to fly into the chaos of storms in order "to help people learn about the natural disaster," but also, he admitted, for the "excitement of the chase." At the time, "excitement" made perfect sense.

Now she wonders why someone would want to hunt hurricanes at all except to find that still place inside? Angela envisions Frank in the eye, floating there, the dropsonde hurtling down, slowed by the opening of its tiny parachute, its whirligig insides churning and clicking, measuring wind velocity, barometric pressure, temperature, plummeting to the ocean surface, sending back data to the plane's computer.

She drives to the dry cleaners, drops by a new casino to leave an application, heads to the store to get the makings of dinner.

The afternoon rolls on and becomes eerily quiet. On the radio a report on Isabel says its winds are clocked at 130 mph, its trajectory taking it in the direction of Cape Hatteras. She tries to shake the image of Frank inside that tiny plane—the glimmer of silver, the dot at the back of her eye—smashing the far side of the eye wall as the *Hercules* bursts into the swirling winds again. She feels the shaking of the plane; her hands on the steering wheel are shaking.

Is this the intersection where her mother had been rammed?

"How did I let myself drive this way?"

She sees again her mother in her yellow VW, easing through the intersection where the wind whips the trees and the dead lights swing like a madwoman's necklaces. From the left a truck comes barreling with a teenager behind the wheel, singing to music, high on beer, a murderer who's tapping a drumbeat on the dashboard.

Her cell phone rings. She glances down: Mrs. Torres.

A horn blares and she slams on the brakes, her Corolla fishtailing across the middle of the intersection.

"Lady!" a man shouts through his window. "You crazy? You high? You ran that light and almost got us both killed!"

"I'm sorry," she calls out and pulls over to see if he wants to confront her, call the police, but he drives on muttering.

She phones back Mrs. Torres, who says she has to leave early to go to the Greyhound station to welcome a friend of her daughter's just back from Iraq. Cam has offered to come play piano an additional session.

"*I need you, Frank,*" she thinks, and glances up at the sky.

When she pulls into the parking lot of her apartment complex, she can see Nana through the window, a man next to her on the couch, but it is not Frank. Near them Cam is bending at the piano. He leans forward, a lean, black-haired youth, laughing and clapping, then settling back.

A voice calls out sternly from behind her in the parking lot: "Good evening, Mrs. Semmes."

Phi Nguyen walks toward her swiftly, looking down.

"Mr. Nguyen, how are you? I can give Cam a ride home if she needs."

"I am not here for that reason."

"Cam's such a fine young lady. She is giving my grandmother so much more by her friendship than even her beautiful music."

"Mrs. Semmes, may I speak to your husband."

"He is not here. Is there something I can help you with? And please, call me Angela."

"Mrs. Semmes, this is for me to say to your husband, but I will say to you. I do not wish for Cam to paint her face and curl her hair at your house. She is only a child."

"Oh, Mr. Nguyen"—she has to suppress a laugh—"that's just my Nana."

"Tell Mrs. Nana for me," he says briskly, looking up now.

"Yes, of course."

"My wife was a beautiful lady. Her hands were perfect. She had a shop for lady's fingernails."

"I know all about this. Cam told me. She loved to go there with her."

"In Vietnam she was a teacher of little children. She learned the nails here, like so many from my country. It gave her headaches, the smells. The smells in her . . ." He taps his chest.

"Her lungs?" she says.

"Yes, her lungs."

"Did that"—she hesitates—"hurt her?"

He nods. "I smell like fish," Phi says. "Like the boat. Cam tells me this. But this does not kill me."

"I'm so sorry."

"Cam is all I have."

"I understand. I lost my mother at about the age Cam did."

"Then you do understand." He adds, "My Mai."

"Pardon?"

"Mai, she is my daughter, too."

"Oh, yes, Cam told us about her sister. So sad."

The door to the apartment opens and the young man appears. Cam comes up behind him. She bends toward him to kiss but gives a quick glance over at Nana and instead reaches out and shakes his hand.

"Cam!" her father shouts as the man disappears into the shadows, then walks to the other side of the complex to get his car.

Cam looks with bewilderment at her father.

"I have seen that boy! Who is he?"

Cam says nothing.

"Who is that boy?" he shouts but does not step toward her, does not move at all, as though he is afraid she might vanish like a hunted deer.

Slowly she answers, "His name is Joe."

"The policeman?" says her father. Angela can hear his sharp intake of breath. "Tell Cam I will be in the car. Good night, Mrs. Semmes."

When she enters the apartment, Cam is gathering up her music. "Your husband called," she says. "He'll be in about two in the morning. He couldn't get through to your cell."

"Thank you, Lord," breathes Angela. She adds aloud: "No friends, please, when you're here with Nana."

"Yes *ma'am*." As Cam steps to the door, her face changes to an icy mask; she walks on in silence toward her father.

"It's my house," Nana calls out behind her, "and you have guests here anytime you want."

The envelope from Brooklyn, New York, arrived a few days later with a typed letter and some black-and-white photos of soldiers inside:

> Dear Angela,
>
> I got your address from Jeremy Rivers, who told me he came across your request about your relation on the Internet. I missed the computer revolution by a decade or two, so I will have to write this by hand.
>
> I am Rabbi Jerry Silverman, retired from Congregation Beth Elohim in the Park Slope neighborhood of Brooklyn. Fifty-three years ago I was a chaplain with the Army Air Corps stationed in the Philippines. It was there among the Jewish servicemen that I met the man I believe you have been searching for. Jeremy Rivers recalls this man to be Rosenbush from Alabama, but I remember him as Rosengarten, maybe from Louisiana.
>
> I do know, and we are both in agreement, that his nickname was Rosey, thus it must be the same person. It was an unusual moniker for a man to be sure. But many of the men from the South especially went by boyhood nicknames, so I thought nothing of it. Maybe it will be the very fact about his life that rescues him from being forgotten, that and what is clearly your own loving determination to make that memory whole. "We live on in the minds of those who remember us," says the prayer. I wanted so much to help you when I heard you wanted to keep alive the memory of

this noble man. They were all noble. They all made a sacrifice. They all paid a price. That we should remember them is the least we can do in return, our way of honoring them.

I have three pictures in my mind of your Rosey, and one real one, too. (I will explain the pictures in this mailing in a moment. They are copies. You do not have to return them.)

The first mental image of your Rosey is one that lifts the heart. On Yom Kippur the Jewish servicemen were allowed the day off to pray and fast. While the sense of religious observance varies a great deal among the men—and I believe Rosey was not traditional, perhaps even knew little Hebrew, this was sometimes the case with the men from the small towns in the Midwest and South—all the Jewish men took the opportunity to have free time, whether they worshipped or not.

Among those who did worship, and who did fast, was Rosey. I remember this quite well because I was walking across the air base in the afternoon and I found him, sitting alone, writing. He asked me, "Rabbi, am I allowed to write on Yom Kippur?"

"The day is to be set aside to cease from work," I answered him.

He told me he was writing a poem. I thought of the great Jewish poet of World War I, Siegfried Sassoon, although we were not at war at that time. I thought to myself, maybe this young man from Louisiana (perhaps Arkansas) could be a great poet, too.

"It is," I said to him, "your own form of prayer, your own form of atonement."

That night the commanding officer let us sit apart at the mess hall and have wine and bread to break the fast (our cups of Philippine wine did not last long as we ended up sharing them with all the other soldiers on the base! "I like your holidays," I remember one soldier saying.)

That Yom Kippur of 1941 was the last we would observe in such a fashion.

I became a prisoner, too. My chaplain status did me little good, but I was there to hold their hands, to listen to the prayers, of men of any faith. Once the Japanese saw that I was a kind of holy man, a priest of some kind, I believe they gave me some measure of respect. They did not let me go, but they let me alone.

It was for that reason, I believe, that when I saw Rosey again, I was not taken with him or the other captives. Two years had passed by then and I had seen none of the men from the first High Holy Day service. I was in a work crew of prisoners near the Manila dock where shipload after shipload of men—who knew what branch of military they were in, they were like sticks in tattered rags—were marched onto Japanese freighters. *Oryoku Maru, Arisan Maru, Noto Maru.* "Maru"—the word, in Japanese, meant circle. But they were not meant to circle the globe and return to Subic Bay. They were going straight to hell.

Angela, I do not know what you may have learned about these freighters known as the Hellships, but they were aptly named. Your Rosey, may his memory be for blessing, was taken onto the *Oryoku Maru.*

There was no indication there were POWs aboard. The laws of the Geneva Convention were as nothing. What the Nazis were doing to the Jews in Dachau, Bergen-Belsen, and Auschwitz, the Japanese Imperial Army were doing to American and Philippine soldiers in Subic Bay, although it seemed there was little they could do they had not done already.

Rosey disappeared into the hold of the ship. As the *Oryoku Maru* pulled away, my heart this time was weighed down as though by an anchor.

I said Kaddish for all of the men. I said the prayer of mourning so often during the war that it cracked my lips. But I kept, in my mind's eye, the third picture of Rosey, the one of memory of him beneath the trees with his little notebook, knowing he had written verses to herald the beauty of life and all God's creatures, at the same time as the war ravaged and destroyed so much of it.

The fourth picture, the actual one, you will find in the envelope. That is me, as a young rabbi—I am second from left, the one with the big ears and prematurely receding hairline. (Hair long gone now!!) Second from right is Rosey.

May the Lord guard thy going out and they coming in, from this time forth and for ever, Angela. That is from Psalm 121, the benediction of the Sabbath service, which you may well know. And two more words: "Shalom. Peace."

Sincerely,
Rabbi Emeritus Jerry Silverman
Temple Beth Elohim, Brooklyn, New York

Second man from the right. The slender frame, the dark eyes, the rich lips, like an artist's drawing of a Mediterranean youth, the prayer book clutched in his hands. She brought the photograph closer to look and put her finger on Rosey's hand with the book, as if she could feel its rough binding.

"Captain Rosengarten," she whispered. "Rosey."

As she heard Nana calling from the next room, she slipped the photo back in its envelope, folded the letter, and put it all into the larger envelope. On the back of the envelope she saw an additional note from the rabbi: "P.S. Already sealed this up. FYI, I recall Rosey had a brother down South who played sports. Baseball?"

"My Angel!"

"Coming, Nana."

She tucked the mailing away.

NINE

Farewell

After eight months of marriage, Angela was still learning the different aspects of her husband. There was his "I'll pray on it" part, where he wrestled with matters of right and wrong, from whether to tell Big Frank to hire a male nurse to help him with personal matters (Big Frank kicked him out of the house with his prosthetic leg when he finally brought it up), to questioning if drinking three beers on his nights off was too much or just being sociable. There was his "I'm here for you" self, when he held Angela all night in postcoital tenderness, then rose early to help Nana up, fixed breakfast for everyone, and left extra cash on the dresser for Angela to buy "something cool and sexy." There was his anxious mood, when he worried about "money we didn't have to spend," and looked twice at any man who looked at Angela even once when they went out to the High Chaparral buffet on Tuesday nights.

The part of Frank she could still not yet figure out how to respond to, how to accommodate, was when he came home in the evenings and said, "I'm not cut out for this."

"What?" she said, knowing full well his answer.

"The 'Chair Force,'" he said. "I'm about to jump out of my skin."

"Oh, Frank, you're an excellent teacher."

"It's making me fat." He turned on the TV and watched images of soldiers on Fox News. He turned it off, then went and listened to his Walkman. She heard him singing along, quietly, to Dylan's "I Believe in You."

Sundays she started going with him to Victory Brotherhood, up-lifted by his sense of uplift. Brother Tim was eloquent, a good story-teller, and enjoyed recalling the time he had been scraping barnacles off a boat and met Frank. When she watched the congregants wave their hands in the air, was surrounded by joyous clapping to the praise music band—drums, electric piano, and bass—she felt happy for her husband. The message of Jesus Christ still did not stir her in the same way. Frank, she knew, was convinced it would one day. So be it.

After church one fall Sunday, when they went to the Shed in Ocean Springs to eat barbecued ribs and hear blues music, she had an in-stinct of what he was going to say. They were sitting side by side at one of the picnic tables of the open-air restaurant. He put his arm around her, kissed her on the cheek, then said he'd gotten word to do training at an Army base in Arizona. The program was for Air Force weather specialists to learn Army culture. At the end of the training he'd be at-tached to an Army division heading to a battle zone. "The classroom's just not for me," he whispered. "Not yet anyways. It'll be perfect for when we're raising our family."

"When will you be back?" she said anxiously.

"Five weeks, maybe six."

"And how long then before you go . . ." She motioned to the distance.

He shrugged. "No telling. Maybe we'll be done by then. Maybe it'll all be over."

"It's what you want, I know."

"It's who you married."

"It's who I married," she said.

Then he was away, and on Thanksgiving she took Nana to the Pi-rates Plunder holiday buffet and ate in silence while text-messaging Frank "miss u, luv u" three times, and come Christmas, with Mrs. Tor-res staying with Nana a couple of days, she flew to Airzona to spend twenty-four hours of Frank's leave time making love to him in a small motel room outside Fort Huachuca. New Year's 2004 she drove along the outskirts of Keesler and gazed out at the hangars and airfields. In the distance the oaks bowed somnolently down to Back Bay, lonesome already. He's only gone several weeks, Angela thought. *"How will I survive when he's away months on end?"*

She tried not to watch anything about the war, but the worn and grizzled face of Saddam, who'd been rooted out of a hole in the ground, looked back from every TV channel and magazine cover at the grocery store checkout line, and she held her breath—maybe this meant the end of it all. But she saw something about an attack at Red Cross headquarters, a Chinook helicopter shot out of the air, a march of Shiites on behalf of a holy man, Ayatollah al-Sistani, demanding control for the Shiites, and she wondered how much longer it could all go on. She heard a discussion on a TV news panel about the wisdom of having prosecuted the war at all given the fact that weapons of mass destruction were still nowhere to be found. She started to ask Frank about these criticisms when he called her, but backed away. Their time together was too precious—his conviction too strong—to start what would only amount, when he got home, to a dinner table feud. The hours were not enough to risk spending even one of them, when together, turned from each other in a cold, yawning bed.

She set herself the task of finding out more of Rosey's story from Nana—Frank began asking her about it—but her grandmother gave out only bits and pieces of the story. She looked at Rabbi Silverman's letter again and searched the name *"Oryoku Maru"* on her laptop. She read that 1,619 men had been taken aboard the ship as prisoners in December 1944. Fewer than 300 had survived.

She hit a link to a journalist from long ago by the name of George Weller, who'd written a series of articles about the Hellships in 1945 as a correspondent for the Chicago Daily News Foreign Service. The articles were shown in photocopy, as if it were nearly sixty years earlier and the headlines screamed the news: "Horrors of Jap Prison Ship Told," and "Suffocating Yanks Go Mad on Jap Ship."

She read Weller's narrative of the *Oryoku Maru*: "As the first faint light crept down through the parted planks of the hatches the men in the holds looked about them. Some of the men were in a stupor, a few were dead, a few were mad. . . . It was hot. The labored working of hundreds of lungs had expelled moisture which clung to the sides of the bulkheads in great drops. Men tried to scrape off this moisture and drink it. . . . Their fingers seemed long and thin. The ends were wrinkled as though they had been soaked a long time in hot water. But their throats were sand-paper dry."

Hadn't Rosey been captured just after the war started? He had spent nearly three years in POW camps, she realized, before being herded onto the *Oryoku Maru*.

But the *Oryoku Maru*, the website said, had been sunk by U.S. warplanes that mistook it as enemy transport since it contained no markings of a POW ship. The soldiers tried to swim to land and escape but were recaptured and taken back to Manila, where they were crowded together at a town called Olongapo, awaiting removal to other prison ships. Had Rosey been transferred to one of those? The *Arisan Maru*? The *Enoura Maru*? Had he swum to land unseen, and stolen off through the Philippine jungle?

A shudder moved through her. She sat up, thinking of Nana's fantasy: "*He could still be alive!*"

But what would have prevented him from making his whereabouts known as soon as the war was over? Wouldn't he have done anything to see his beloved Christiane again?

There was no proof he was forever gone but the decades.

No. She shook her head. It was impossible. It was *crazy* to imagine him still thriving somewhere. But was Nana crazy to think so? When they sat together on the couch watching TV, or played a game of gin rummy—even while scrambling the decades in her mind, Nana could keep perfectly straight her hearts and clubs—Angela looked at her with new appreciation.

When Frank got back home for a two-week respite before heading to the Middle East, it was her time to tell him, even as he was packing his duffel, "I'll never let you go."

For all the times that Frank had visited New Orleans over the years, he felt different in the city now. In twenty-four hours he would be headed to Sheppard Air Force Base in Wichita Falls, then on to Kuwait. As he looked at the statue of Andrew Jackson, then the cross atop St. Louis Cathedral, which seemed to sit on the general's shoulder, he felt a deeper connection than ever before to his misssion as a combatant for his nation, a warrior for his faith. "Photo op!" he said, and squared Angela in the viewfinder before the statue. Her ringlets of brown hair, full bosom, loose-fitting blouse. "You look beautiful," he said. *Click.* Chiseled in the monument to the hero who had saved New Orleans from the Brits was the oath: "The union shall and must be preserved."

"Time for raw oysters," Angela said.

"Ah, you think I need those? With you?"

She looked at him, puzzled.

"Big Frank always told me they make a man, you know . . ." He patted just below his belt. "At the ready."

"What a line!"

He added: "And strong."

"No," she said, coming toward him and draping her arms over his shoulders, "you don't need them. But"—she kissed him tantalizingly—"they're fun to eat."

"Sounds good to me!" He reached in his pocket for their room key.

"No, not *yet.* We've got all day. Let's explore."

Mardi Gras was not until the end of February this year, but the New Orleans French Quarter was already swinging—purple-green-gold banners draped over doorways, drunken girls on hotel balconies yanking up their shirts in exchange for beads.

The blessings of a wife, Frank thought, standing taller with Angela at his side. No good-time gal out for a love fix with a passing dude. The young man who had ever let himself be taken in by that allure was, like so much else, the Frank of long ago. By the Royal Street antique shops, by the goateed gallery owners smoking cigs in doorways, past the praline stores with endless loops of Dixieland jazz, they made their way, a wedded couple. In God's infinite wisdom He had created the bond of marriage. They were designated, for all time, to watch each other's backs.

They roosted at Café du Monde, where a Vietnamese waiter brought them beignets and chicory coffee, and a Japanese student in a Tulane sweatshirt was at the next table talking excitedly on a cell phone about hearing old-time New Orleans rocker Dr. John.

Old wars, yesteryear's antagonists, all come together, he realized, around powdered doughnuts and coffee strong enough to jump-start a riverboat engine. One day Sunnis, Shiites, and Southerners might do the same.

"Hey, you," Angela said and leaned over the table. "C'mere."

He leaned forward, thinking she meant to kiss him. Instead, she gave a puff and a cloud of beignet powder swirled up toward his face.

"Why . . ." He blew a cloud back at her. "Now *this*," he said, "is war."

"That they could all be this way," she said.

"Angela? Hey."

Frank looked up to see a tall young man with a scruffy beard peering down, smiling.

"Remember me? Aaron. From Cornell. My buddies and I . . ."

"The road trippers," Angela said. "Wow. You've got a great memory. My husband, Frank."

"Good to meet you, man."

Frank put out his hand to shake. The guy reached out and slapped palms. Arrogant.

"I graduated last year and took a job here as an architect. Cool houses in this town. Sorry to disturb you. Congratulations, you guys." He bounded off.

"Weird," Angela said, and proceeded to blow more beignet powder across the table.

"You guys?" Frank brushed his hand through the sugary cloud. "Where'd that joker come from?"

"Just some nerd with a gang of his Yankee friends at the Cotton Gin, doing their Southern *thang*. They asked me, like, a million questions about where to go."

"I bet they did."

"Let's walk by the river," she said.

"Sure." They got up. "Sure," he repeated.

They walked along the Mississippi, watching the tourist paddle wheelers easing by like nineteenth-century dreams. "Mark Twain!" she said. "We learned about how he got his name in Miss Nancy's class, ninth grade."

"Congratulations?"

"What?"

"What's his name said congratulations."

"Because we got married, I guess."

"He obviously knew you'd been single," he came back at her. "Sounds like you gave him a whole damn lot of Southern road trip information."

"Okay, okay. You and I had that fight. I bumped into him at Rudy's. We danced. That's all."

He had an image of the sruffy college boy pawing at his wife. It would be a long rotation for him in the Middle East.

"Frank," she beseeched. "Frank!" She stopped walking, turned to him, and threw her arms around him and squeezed. "You're the only man in my life and always will be. Nobody else exists!"

He felt himself relax. "Okay." He let out a laugh. "Okay. You see, you should have just let me take you to our hotel room!"

But the mood had passed. He would regain it quickly enough. Get back on an even keel—that's what they had to do. The hours he had left were already peeling away.

He nodded toward the aquarium, and they headed that way.

They entered and gazed upward at its transparent walkways, where manta rays moved overhead on sluggish wings, redfish meandered, and sheepshead drifted by in parallels. They climbed the steps to the shark tank, and looked in at the dark behemoths cutting through the tank: feeding time.

"Oh, look!" said Angela.

From behind by one large shark, a smaller one emerged. "It's a baby!"

Frank stood close to the glass.

"The other night they ran an updated special about the 9/11 babies," he said. "You and Nana were asleep. It really choked me up."

"Which one do you mean?" She began to wag her finger at the little shark, trying to catch its attention. It turned in her direction, but streaked by in dumb disregard.

"The one about the babies born after September eleventh. To the fathers who were killed in the Towers. Angela?"

"Hmm?"

"I've been thinking."

"That's always a good sign," she teased.

"What about *us*?"

"What *about* us?"

"Children are a blessing."

She turned away from the tank. "I never said I didn't want children. Oh, Frank, you're coming home, you know! 'Ever after.' And we'll have a little Frank and maybe even a little Angela, too, in that ever after!"

"What about now?"

"Me?" She touched her belly with her fingertips.

"No, the stripper on Bourbon. Of course, you!"

"But a mama's like"—she gestured to the huge shark cutting fiercely through the water—"like that, big and protective, watching out."

"The way you take care of Nana," he said, "wow, it's something, Angela. If you're not a nurturer, I don't know who is. You'll be a great mother, like yours was."

"I want more time just to be your wife!"

They turned to go out of the aquarium, passing the inanimate sea turtles, the weird ribbon fish, and surreal pompano. "And you're leaving tomorrow morning," she said.

"We'll be together this afternoon."

"It doesn't happen that easily, Frank."

"It's your time, isn't it?"

She shrugged. "I wasn't keeping track."

"Remember when I called you from the drugstore twelve days and six hours ago and asked if you wanted me to pick up anything and you asked me to get, you know . . ."

"You've been charting my cycle? What am I, a weather system?" She shook her head and laughed. "But guess what, Staff Sergeant Semmes, it's not that precise."

"All I'm asking is that we don't do anything to keep it from happening." They arrived at Canal Street. "God will take care of the rest."

They crossed Canal, by the grand stores with their cast iron facades and funky music shops with posters of new wave rockers next to photos of zydeco bands. Toward the river was a casino that here, by contrast to those along the Mississippi coast, seemed lost in the urban landscape.

Mixed into the usual run of folks Frank saw every day on the Mississippi coast—groups of tourist in leisure suits toting cameras, middle-aged ladies with shopping bags, teens black and white in low-slung gangsta pants—were men in turbans, yarmulkes, heads shaved or with dreadlocks, and women in side-slit skirts or tight blouses exposing butterfly tattoos on lower backs. Through the everyday carnival wove a young couple with a little girl in a backpack; passing close by, the little girl showed big, dark eyes at Frank and Angela.

He heard her say the magic words: "Let's do it."

"Really, okay?"

She nodded.

He gave a leap and pushed his fists into the air like Rocky training for a fight on the streets of Philadelphia.

On the other side of Canal, walking uptown, Frank spoke excitedly of how the United States was winning the war on terror, that Saddam was in jail, and that "if it weren't for our sacrifices in Iraq, you might see al-Qaeda coming over that levee one day. I won't have our child coming into a world with those kinds of threats."

They arrived at Lee Circle, where the statue of the Confederate general presided over a hectic traffic round and rumbling trolleys.

"This way," he said. Large, boxlike buildings crowded in on them. "See?"

He pointed to the camouflaged wall of the largest of the buildings. Against its green-brown side was printed in big white letters, "D-Day Museum."

They entered, seeing the amphibious Higgins boats in the lobby like motionless fish in the aquarium. In the exhibition hall were giant images of Normandy and touch screens showing the plans of attack, the endless loop of old newsreels with images of men parachuting to the beaches, the graphics with yellow, red, and green arrows indicating the assaults.

"This was the beginning, when you think about it, in our modern times. So simple, so basic, good versus evil."

She nodded.

"Just to have been part of that," he said. "To have been in uniform then. I think of Big Frank. Of Rosey."

She took his hand and squeezed it. "Thank you," she said. "Look." She lowered her voice. "All the old men."

They drifted about, singly or with grandchildren at their sides, on walkers or in wheelchairs, bald-headed or silver-haired, around each of their necks a yellow tag with the words "WWII Veteran," and in the eyes of each man a faraway look. More than sixty years had passed since some of the men had stormed the French coast that early summer morning, on the lines or behind them, or far away but part of it, like Frank was part of his war, their war, the one they were all engaged in now.

Above them, in giant portraits, loomed some of the adversaries: General Dwight D. Eisenhower and Field Marshal Bernard Montgomery; Field Marshals Erwin Rommel and Gerd von Rundstedt. Beneath their fierce gazes, brought down only by time, the old warriors milled about musing and nodding and telling their grandchildren their piece of the day. She heard the names of the beaches repeatedly: "Utah," "Gold," "Juno," "Sword," "Omaha."

"You men are heroes," Frank addressed a cluster of yellow-tagged men.

"Thank you, son."

"Staff Sergeant Frank Semmes, U.S. Air Force," he said, reaching out to shake a vet's hand. "And this is my wife, Angela."

"I'm Oliver Walker. I was with the 101st Airborne."

"What y'all did," said Frank, "was amazing, it was brave. If it hadn't been for all of you, we might not be standing here in freedom today."

"Are you active?"

"In battlefield weather."

"June fourth was supposed to be the day," said Walker, "but weather pushed it to the sixth."

"I know, sir," said Frank.

"We had a clear dawn when we did go in," said Walker. He gestured to the colored arrows on a wall map showing the Normandy beach assaults that had begun hours before the dawn. "The planning was contingent on knowing it."

"I've studied the conditions of that assault extensively," Frank said.

"It was a dry day," the old vet said, "little wind."

"Low humidity, yes sir," said Frank.

"Not like down here in June," said another, who introduced himself as Hiram Branch from Pensacola, an Army vet in the liberating forces of Bergen-Belsen.

"We're stopping the next Hitler," said Frank. "We got him where we want him. Now we just need to finish rounding up his henchmen."

A few other men had stepped over to listen.

"I'm heading out tomorrow," Frank said, letting his words reverberate in the air.

The men pushed closer.

"Sheppard Air Force Base first," he went on, "then to Kuwait. I'll be in Iraq, I figure, before the month is out. Attached to an Army unit."

A few of the men clapped.

The concentration camp liberator spoke up: "I hope the cowboy knows what he's doing."

"What the hell you mean?" said the 101st Airborne vet.

"The president," said the liberator.

"I know *who* you mean."

"It was Osama who attacked us is what *I* mean. Haven't we gone after the wrong man?"

"You going to tell this proud sergeant he's not a patriot?"

A younger man in a blue jean jacket pushed up to the front. "I was in 'Nam. It's being a patriot to question."

"It's not my job to question," said Frank.

"We all should!"

It was Angela who had spoken the words.

Frank looked at her in silence, his eyes narrowing. "You're not," he said now, leading the way out of the exhibit, "behind me all the way."

"Of course I'm behind you."

"Of all times to show me up!"

He moved away, glowering, mute now before the displays.

"I didn't say I questioned *you*," she said, going up to his side. "I was talking about questioning, in general. Isn't that one of the things"— she gestured to the breadth of the museum and the veterans milling about—"they fought for, too?"

"They fought to win."

"Of course, but what did they achieve, Frank?"

"Victory."

"Yes, and in victory—"

"The defeat of evil. And that's what I'm part of. And even if I weren't, even if the whole thing was a sham . . ."

"Then what?"

"I'd want to be there because I am a patriot, good, bad, right, wrong. It's called duty, Angela. Service before self. That's the watchword. I thought you admired that."

"I do, I admire you. But you might question, that's all I'm saying."

"No!"

They arrived at the entrance to a new wing of the museum, the Pacific Theater, with sweeping displays of Okinawa, Peleliu, Iwo Jima. She walked up to an enlargement of men on the Bataan Death March, a blowup of a picture she'd seen on the Internet. Was there somewhere, in that cadre of beaten-down, trundling soldiers, a Georgia Jew who was about to risk his life to give another man a sip of water? And next to him, a nameless soldier who would pay the price by taking a bullet in his head?

"I love you, Frank."

"You don't want to question that, too?"

"You're being impossible!" She turned and left the museum.

Outside, on Julia Street, he trailed behind her, past art galleries where couples browsed arm in arm and cafés where lovers bent head to head in cozy conversation. It could be so easy, he thought, if he had chosen a civilian life, become a teacher or accountant, or perpetual student, an ordinary guy whose most pressing concerns might be saving enough money to take his wife on a Caribbean cruise. Or if he'd chosen a churchgoing, pro-military girl who was happy just to work all day, have sex all night, and make babies without pondering the damn prospects of it all.

Angela had stopped, lingering in front of a store window, pretending to be interested in curios inside a shop.

He spoke at her back: "Do I have to be killed to be a hero? If Rosey had come back alive, would he be just another tired World War II vet dragging his grandkids around the D-Day Museum? Maybe you'd have been one of those kids, and you'd be, like, 'I don't want to hear it again.'"

"Like the way you still are with Big Frank?"

"God dammit, Angela, you don't give me a fucking inch of credit. Nothing I say, nothing I do, makes a point, even when I have a good one. Okay, you're probably smarter than me. Word smart. You win. Here"—he reached in his pocket and fished out the car keys—"take 'em. I'll catch a taxi to the airport."

"Oh, Frank."

In silence they continued back to the Quarter, stopping into Acme Oyster Bar, where they sat at the counter downing raw oysters with hot sauce and drinking beer, saying little outside of commending the food and half watching a basketball game on the TV over the bar.

As they were paying their check, Frank said sadly, "I wanted to get you a present, but the shops are closed. What a day."

Outside, the dusk hours gave way to the evening; French Quarter gas lamps flared.

"Being with you is all the present I want," she said, trying to get him to soften, he knew, but he still felt remote, still injured.

And the hours were grinding away.

She kissed him; he responded, but coolly.

On the way back to their hotel, they passed a corner bar where a cover band was banging out a foot-stomping "Will the Circle Be Unbroken." Frank stopped to peek in. The place was filled with young people, swigging beer and dancing and singing along. The band started into "Bad, Bad Leroy Brown," and Frank took out his wallet and paid the cover.

"Boilermaker," he shouted to the bartender over the din. Angela opted for a ginger ale.

After downing his bourbon shot, guzzling a mug of beer, and calling out for another round, he pushed onto the dance floor and Angela followed. He began to dance loose-limbed, turning his head from side to side, like a man halfway between ecstatic ritual and trying to put himself out of misery. Still gyrating to the music, he grabbed his second round off the bar, made quick work of it, then ordered another. The band shifted into "Proud Mary."

Frank went to the middle of the floor, rocking from side to side, spinning his hands, and suddenly dancing with a girl with short blond hair, a blue micro-mini, and multiple earrings.

Frank danced back to her.

"So what was that all about?" Angela yelled at him through the cacophony of music and a hundred drunken sing-alongs.

"I'm on the team," he shouted back. "I believe in it. You know that about me."

"Oh, Frank," she said as she pulled him close and he put his face into her neck. "I do." He felt his legs give way as she propped him up, repeating, "I do." They stumbled out of the bar as she implored him, "Don't drink so damn much; don't get so carried away. We were just talking. You don't have to be like this."

"Ridiculous. I'm not being any way at all."

By the time they arrived back at their room, he zigzagged to the bed, kicking off his clothes and opening his arms for Angela.

Pressed against him, naked, the length of her ample body sending eletricity through his, he tried to make love to her but could not sustain his arousal. He fell asleep, woke up, and tried again, but the liquor had done its work. Nothing. He prayed, but no use.

When they awoke with the sun pounding on the pillows, he barely had time to put on his fatigues, grab up his rucksack, and have Angela drive him to the New Orleans Airport for the first leg of his journey to meet up with his outfit.

As the last boarding call was made, they held each other tight near the security gate, kissed fire, made chaste love through their touch, poured yearning into each other's eyes, then he was on his way.

She waited for word, and when it came soon—"I arrived safely, I miss you terribly, I love you"—she let out a deep breath and thanked God and prayed he would be safe in every moment waking and sleeping.

How had she sent him off so abruptly? Drinking too late in the evening, and all too turned around and woozy, the two of them collapsing into bed as the clock spun mercilessly fast to his moment of departure.

But he had sounded good on the phone, clear and close, and so soon he had called. Not at all like he was far away. She had slipped a letter to him to read—"You are with me every moment, and I am with you"— and she imagined him unfolding the page and taking in her words and fashioning his own.

Yet how far away he was, too, leaving her like this just as she always knew he would, but it seemed at the wrong time. She was empty, her body moving through its monthly cycle with no miracle of life under way, no blending of them both. She was just in her early twenties, had many years still to become a mother. But how wonderful it would be to devote herself to the life inside her while he was gone. How lucky it would have been to have him out of the house when her belly grew fast and her ankles swelled and she upchucked from morning sickness. (That's what girlfriends were for!) And when he returned, what a prize she would have to show, and would he, could he, ever wish to leave home again?

A young woman let herself in the doorway now, said, "Hello, what a pretty bright smile," and took her seat at the piano, playing "Stardust."

Christiane began to hum along. "We heard from him," she said suddenly. "So far, so good. He called on the telephone."

"Yes ma'am."

"His voice so clear. Keep an eye out for the postman. I know he'll be writing soon."

She lost herself in the song the girl played. Cam was her name, she remembered it now, and Christiane thought of the warm place beneath his neck, the smell of his aftershave—that hint of cinnamon—and the orchestra music as he reached down and undid her nightgown and she felt his smooth, muscular shoulders, his skin creamy as a child's, his olive complexion glowing in the light from the foyer, his face against hers, his lips burning against her own.

PART III

The Roaring Wave

TEN

Counting the Days

Waiting. In her apartment on the third floor of a Georgetown apartment building. Waiting, as she watched the capital turn to soldiers everywhere, guards doing rounds by the White House, the Washington Monument, the Pentagon. Waiting, gazing out the window, pouring a glass of red wine into the silver goblet that she'd given Rosey and that he'd drunk from the night before leaving, the feeling of blessed sleep enclosing her like a narcotic. Waking early always, with the sun hammering the pillow just like it had that morning, checking to make sure that his shoes she'd polished had no veil of dust over them—polish, buff, snap!—or his shirts, which she'd washed and ironed and hung deep in the closet, were not odorous of mothballs. Dunk, lather, wring! Keep everything just as it was. Waiting.

"Why don't you come stay with us?" her mother had asked, down to Virginia, where the Atlantic swept onto the beach and the sound of it rocked her to sleep, not like the Mississippi Sound with its sonorous rising and falling of tides and where her granddaughter, bless her heart, rose and fell with the days, the weeks, that her groom was away. "We are praying for him every day."

The landlady downstairs in the basement apartment, the Polish storekeeper on the corner, her boss at Kress's, where she took a job after four months, and at the Red Cross, where she volunteered after work, all praying.

What could she say in her prayers that she offered, looking out the window as she looked now, over the parking lot of the apartment building beyond the Mississippi oaks with their moss like the shawls of widows lumbering their way toward the barren Sound? No, not Mississippi, where Angela had put up a map of the Middle East on the kitchen wall like a hurricane tracking chart and marked it with Frank's movements from Kuwait to Baghdad to a forward operating base north of Baghdad, where the time was 1943 not 2004 like the calendar lied, and where she knew what prayer to offer: "Dearest Lord, Watch over my husband who suffers in this war. Keep him safe in captivity, and keep his heart and mind free even if his body should be imprisoned. Let Rosey come back to me safely. And watch out for all the other soldiers, so many, and keep them from harm, and give peace to all of those who wait for them. Amen."

Had the radio, with its news of her and Rosey's war, been better than the television, with its news of Angela's and Frank's? When the images played over and again of prisoners kneeling before hooded terrorists who threatened to behead them and often did? The screen showed the violent extremists speaking their impossible language, the English subtitles telling their political demands. How could she have gone on if she had been able to see Rosey, brought low by his captors, rolling out in footage for all the world to see? But how had she gone on seeing nothing? Knowing nothing? Only hearing of the men shrunk to skin and bones in the prison camps, of the early morning darkness raids to liberate when remotely possible, of the violations of the POW codes of conduct, as though any sane conduct could be expected in the insanity of war?

She heard music out the window. The carousel. She had read her letters from Rosey at a bench near those slowly spinning horses, the National Mall spread out around her in fairyland green, the reflecting pool in its tranquility belying the turbulence of the world beyond. "Lovesick beneath the moon," she had repeated aloud, laughing, imagining him penning that before flying out from San Francisco. The letters. Where were they? Oh, yes, in the teakwood box. Weren't they under the bed at her house by the Sound? In them she had the whorls of Rosey's handwriting, testaments of his presence in a way all the cell phone calls between Frank and Angela, the fleeting "instant messages" on Angela's computer, could never match.

She peered out to the Mississippi sidewalk. An ice cream truck. Its recorded music played "Tie a Yellow Ribbon Round the Ole Oak Tree," so that she started humming it, thinking of the yellow ribbons on the oaks near the Biloxi Welcome Center tied by the Daughters of the Confederacy, but she was sitting on her bench on the National Mall watching the carousel, with its calliope whistles ringing out "Let Me Call You Sweetheart."

"Nana? Do you want me to play that song?"

"What?"

The Vietnamese girl, what was her name? Oh, Cam. "Yes, play that song." And the girl strange to her but also familiar with her correct posture and straight black hair and intense gaze riffled through a book of music until she found the one she was looking for, and "Tie a Yellow Ribbon" lilted through the apartment.

"No," she said, "this one," and began to hum, "Let Me Call You Sweetheart."

"I don't know that one."

Joe—that was his name, Cam's boyfriend, although she said they had stopped seeing each other weeks ago after her father demanded it, then started up again ever more slyly, then stopped, started, oh, the way of young love. The balmy spring had given way to the broiling summer that kept on well into the fall, and when she had warned Cam to wear a shirt that covered her midriff, the girl had explained to her that "it's cooler this way," and slipped a halter top out of a shopping bag and tried it on for Nana, with her belly exposed to the air, saying, "It's our secret, Nana, I know you like secrets. Daddy wouldn't approve. Joe, he . . . Joe . . ."

"Joe likes it," said Nana, and Cam had nodded. "Good. Besides, you're not wearing it for Daddy."

Joe, that was his name, too, Joe Orange. His hair just like his name, the color orange, and his scent like Florida citrus. The painted horses of the carousel bobbed up and down, and the mothers with their young children gripped the poles and smiled and waved and she waved back like she did now out the window. One month, four, eight, nine, enough to have a beautiful child, but Rosey locked away.

Those mothers on the carousel, their arms wrapped around their beaming kindergarteners, daddies away at war but able to write as Rosey had written her as long as he could, even enclosing a shaving of cinnamon bark from the Philippines. She kept a pinch of it in an envelope that she carried in her pocket; she opened it, breathed in his scent. What letters he would write her now if only he could, but the news of him came on preprinted cards from the International Red Cross.

"Pretty music, isn't it?"

A soldier, just behind her right shoulder. Tall, she could sense it.

"Yes," she said. Why had she spoken? A nod would have done just fine.

"I'm Joe," he said, stepping closer, in front of her now. "Joe Orange." She did not look up. "Mrs. Robert Rosengarten," she said.

"Where's your guy?" he asked.

"Please, Officer . . ."

"Lieutenant Orange. I work with the Joint Chiefs," he said. "A numbers cruncher."

"Really?" She looked up now: bright, orange hair, freckles, lean as a rural fencepost. "Do you have any way of knowing something about prisoners, something the average person doesn't know?"

"Oh, I'm sorry. Where is he?"

"The Philippines."

"I don't have any special access to files, but, well, I'll see if I can take a look."

She gave him Rosey's birth name, rank, company. He said he would meet her the next night with some information. Could they rendezvous at the Blue Note? "No," she said, "I'm a married woman."

"I'm a married man," he said. "My wife's in Knoxville. I don't mean any harm. I'll find you here tomorrow?"

She nodded.

When he arrived the next day, he said, "Cabanatuan, that's all I could find out just now. That's where he is."

"What is that?" she asked. "What does that mean? I've seen that name."

"It's a big camp near Manila. Lots of men, probably work details during the day. It's safer than the battlefield."

"Thank you."

"I'll find out more, there are some reports on it."

"I'll be here tomorrow."

"I can't get off during the day, but in the evening. I sure wouldn't want you to meet me out here, no telling what . . . The Blue Note, it's a good place to meet."

She could see his Adam's apple moving up and down in his throat, the faint red stubble of his whiskers. She had not studied another man's face so closely since taking her vows.

"I'll bring my girlfriend Bernice."

"It's a nice place," he said. "Bernice will enjoy it, too."

She called Bernice just once and, when there was no answer, took it as her okay to go ahead by herself. A public place. Information about Rosey. A mission any wife, in her agonizing situation, would under-take. She resolved to sit with him only briefly, if at all, and near the doorway, holding her handbag as if ready to spring up from the table at a moment's notice and head off on more important business.

Meeting her at the entrance, he gave her a peck on the cheek. Fresh. They had all gotten that way, the ones at home. What did a wedding ring even mean to them anymore?

"I know what you're going through," he said, showing her to a table, not near the entrance at all, but in the center, near the dance floor. "Please don't think me forward. We're all going through this together."

"What can you tell me?" she said. "What more do you know about Rosey?"

"Not a lot, but I'll tell you what I know." He raised his hand first to summon a waiter for a bottle of wine. "Red okay with you?"

"Just a taste," she said.

The wine arrived. She took a sip, another.

"He's safe," Lieutenant Orange said. "I believe he's safe. He's okay."

"What do you mean, 'safe'? He's not in . . ."

"He's in the camp, most definitely. But most are on a work detail. I looked over a list."

"What list?"

"A lot don't make it, you know. The diet, the work, the sun, infections, stomach sickness. Heartbreak. The Imperial Army sends a report. Just a list, that's all. Died of natural causes. That's what they all say."

"He's not on that list!"

He shook his head.

"Of course not," she said. "I would have been able to tell. His shirts, his shoes. I keep them ready, for when he's back."

"The war will be over soon," Lieutenant Orange said.

"You're a lieutenant," she said, "not a general."

"Your guy will come home, don't worry."

He poured her some more wine.

She sipped it. "At home I sit in a chair and listen to the big band hour," she said. "And I see us dancing. 'Stardust,' 'Bye Bye Blackbird,' 'You're Nobody 'Til Somebody Loves You.' And I can look out the window and see as far as the Philippines, and read his last letters to me, over and over, about our life together when he returns, the places we'll go, the family we'll have. We'll do all that. Me and Rosey. When he returns. When he returns."

Orange stood. "I could use a dance, too." He held out his hand to her. The band had begun playing "Tennessee Waltz."

"No," she said.

"It's my national anthem," he said. "In honor of Rosengarten."

There was no one here who knew her face, much less her name. All she saw were a thousand strangers in uniform, or their dates, or their wives, dolled up for a Saturday night on the town while the radio, forgotten at home for a few hours, crackled of the latest transgressions of Il Duce or Tojo or the Führer.

She went onto the floor with him and put one hand around his waist and the other up to meet his. He was taller than Rosey, bonier, too, his shoulders like cordwood, and he smelled not of aftershave with a hint of cinnamon but of tobacco, and whiskey. The music began to catch her up.

Why was she counting out the beats—*one two three, one two three*—as if the rhythm were not already deep in her feet and legs and hips from the time she was a little girl and her own Nana showed her how to waltz to the band shell music on their summer visits to Newport from Richmond. *One two three, one two three.*

She could sense that moment he pulled her a little closer, a quarter inch, a half, then right up so close to his chest that she wanted to lean right into him just to feel a man's warmth against her, but she kept herself apart and they danced, *one two three*, until the band changed the beat and began to play "Stardust."

"I need to sit down," she said, but he pretended not to hear, and she did not say it again.

Pressing up against him now, letting him kiss her gently on the lips, then deeply, fully, as they turned to the music, she was somewhere else, where there was no war, and no Rosey, and no Washington, D.C., and she felt his sex harden against her and did not pull away.

He stopped kissing her and spoke at her ear through the music, "I know Rosengarten's a Jew."

"You don't know anything about my husband," she said, standing back from him now, though he tried to pull her close again.

"I know that if Rosengarten didn't suffer as an American to the Japanese, he'd suffer as a Jew to the Germans."

"Leave me alone."

"You're not a Jew."

"I'm Mrs. Robert Rosengarten is what I am."

"Let's go to my place. We can be alone there."

"Stop playing that song, stop it, no more 'Stardust.'"

Cam looked up at her, nodded, and put her music away for that afternoon.

Each time Cam had gone to the hunting camp with Joe, she had let him kiss her in a new place, but always within limits of what she believed her mother would have thought proper. Lips, chin, neck, shoulders, even high on her back. As the Mississippi heat gave way to hunting season fall, and the far-off crack of hunting rifles was intended first for turkey, then deer, she felt Joe press ever closer, hotter, running his hands over her clothes, but never undressing her save for the top button on her blouse, then one more.

When he pushed her blouse off her shoulder this evening, she pulled it back up. "That gives me goose bumps," she said. Then she felt his hand on her waist. She let it linger there, safe enough.

Then he stroked her belly; she pulled away. He stepped closer, stroked her again. Her skin tingled. She relaxed.

She had seen the girls at the public schools with their tummies hanging out like young rock stars with shiny little studs, flickering come-on's. "*Touch me,*" they said.

"They are trash," Daddy had said.

Because she let Joe touch her there, did it mean she was trash? But wasn't he a policeman? Didn't he know what was right?

And didn't it feel good?

If only her mother had been able to tell her all she knew about boys and girls. "On Sunday," she had told Cam. "On Sunday we will take a picnic to the beach and have a talk," and she had imagined them sitting there together, talking about what she did not exactly know at age eleven, how a man and a woman came close and a baby was made. She knew how bees pollinated flowers, and that what happened in humans had something to do with pictures she had seen drawn on the wall of the ladies' room at the Biloxi seafood shack. But could that really be true? When she watched the dancers on MTV gyrating and grinding against each other, she had wondered if that's how it happened, the boy's place and the girl's rubbing, the man's seed somehow passing through.

That Thursday night before their picnic, her mother had not come home from the nail shop, having called Cam's father to say she was unboxing new polishes and emery boards and cuticle scissors from the supply house. An hour passed; another. When her father went to the nail shop to see if she was okay, he found her unmoving in a chair, a case of nail polish spilled out and cracked on the floor. By the Sunday they were to have had their picnic, her mother was an urn of ashes and her father was making plans to take her back to Vietnam. And Cam was destined to go live with her aunt in East New Orleans, where her girl cousins had told her about the birds and bees with expressions of "Isn't that gross," and "Can you believe it!"

When she had moved back in with her father in Biloxi after many weeks, to cook for him and keep the apartment straight and tidy the beds and keep watch over the house when he was on his boat, she had not been able to ask him anything at all.

How would her mother have explained what it meant for a man to become somebody else, like Joe seemed to be now, pressing hard against her while trying to kiss her farther down her chest? When she felt his hand move between her legs, she pushed him away. "No," she said.

"But I want you like that," Joe said.

"No," she said. "Not until I'm married."

"St. Benedict's taught you well," he said. "But guess what? That's not like the girls at St. Benedict's."

"It was my mother who taught me about that."

"Your mother," he said, kissing her collarbone, "must have been a beautiful Oriental lady."

"Vietnamese."

"Oh, Cam. I can't help myself."

She pushed him away firmly.

He grabbed her shoulder. "You don't understand," he said.

"No."

"You're incredible."

"Take me home."

"Don't be a tease."

"No."

"You don't understand," he repeated.

"Understand what, Joe?"

"That we probably will be."

"Be what?"

"Married."

She let him stand closer, melting inside. "I want to go to college," she said.

"College, yeah, I will, too. I'll start some night courses soon. The department will even pay for it."

"Daddy wants me to marry an Asian man. I told you that."

Joe put his index fingers against the sides of each of his eyes and pushed upward. "Will this do?"

"Stop it. Some of the boys at school once made fun of me like that."

"Tell me who they are."

"We were in junior high."

"I want to take care of you," he said. He put his hands back on her neck, squeezed a little.

"Owww . . ."

He dropped his hands, stepped back, raised a fist to his mouth, bit his knuckles, whispering aloud, "Hold on, Joe. Keep control."

"Joe!"

"Don't let this amazing babe make you lose your cool," he kept on. He stepped back toward her. "I could have been a *real* star in basketball, Cam, a superstar. I could have won a scholarship. It was control. Coach always said I had to be in better control." He took a deep breath, let it out slowly. His dark eyes became damp. "I'm in control now."

"You're hurting, aren't you?" she said.

He nodded. "Yes, but hurting me. I would never hurt you."

"Where do you hurt?" she asked.

"Here." He took her hand and placed it on his chest. "And . . ." Slowly, carefully, he took her hand and lowered it to his pants zipper.

She let it rest there.

"You do this to me," he said.

She answered nothing, shaking her head and pulling away from him, but he grabbed at her blouse, tearing a button.

"Stop, Joe!"

"I can't stop."

"Take me home."

She pivoted and started to head to the door, but he grabbed at her again, this time yanking her by the arm. She spun around and banged her face into the fireplace mantel. Her head flipped back like a rag doll's.

Blood poured from her lip, down her chin onto her pale blue silk shirt, and she felt at her mouth to find a loosened front tooth.

Joe was at her side with a towel, ice, hydrogen peroxide, saying it was a horrible accident and he would never forgive himself for grabbing at her like that. "You make me crazy, but I can't let that happen." He began to kiss her ever so gently, sweetly, on the forehead, the cheek. "I'll look out for you always," he said with aching tenderness.

Back in his car, he added, "You can't tell anybody what happened."

"What do I say to Daddy?"

"That it was somebody, a stranger, some men jumped you, pushed you down."

"Who? Where?"

"It doesn't matter. You didn't see them. Or say you fell."

"Joe, he'll know that I'm lying!"

"I'll be ruined! That can't happen to me; it can't happen to us. I'll make it right; I'll protect you forever." He slowed and pulled to the side of the road. Crickets pulsed in the woods. "I'll cherish you."

She leaned in to him as he stroked her face. To his touch she felt now like a sacred heirloom.

"It was an accident," she whispered. "I fell, from my bike."

Holding her close, he nodded.

She walks the sands of Biloxi Beach, her sandals slapping her heels, and hears Frank's boots crunching hard-packed Iraqi sands. She carries her groceries to her car across blacktop softened by bakehouse sun and feels Frank toting his equipment beneath blistering sun, his uniform drenched with sweat. She wakes to sun piercing the branches of loblolly pines and senses Frank rising to light fanning across desert expanse. Where she lies down, he puts his head on a cot. Where she walks, his shadow falls.

Fifty-six days, eighty-seven, one hundred and nineteen—the risings and settings of the sun are only markers of how long he has been away.

She has a sheaf of his e-mails printed out to reread, most a paragraph or two, telling about 120-degree heat, and sandstorms rising in long sleeves of grit, and full moons on clear nights that blast down light like meteors. When he writes of the date trees outside his base— he's first at a battered but extravagant, former palace of Saddam, with architecture befitting 1001 Arabian Nights, then at a makeshift facility near Baghdad, in the Sunni Triangle—she buys a bag of dates and chews on them slowly, near mystically, as she types in the names of the bases on the Internet. She reads of the "Triangle of Death," and in horror she darkens the screen. But she flips it back on and reads about Iskandariyah—his new base is close by, where he is attached to the Army 3rd Infantry—and of a suicide bombing at its Iraqi police academy where scores of Shia were killed, with blame wildly put at first on the Americans. But he writes of doves, too, their gentle cooing, when he is up at all hours taking weather readings in order to brief the Army helicopter pilots. That he has not had a lick of whiskey or beer since New Orleans—it is forbidden with U.S. military in Iraq, he explains to her—has kept his mind clear, too.

On his phone calls he is talkative, more eager to find out about home than to tell her more about his surroundings. He looks over their bank statements closely online, asking Angela about expenditures, but she is patient with his inquiries. During long hours alone it is only natural, she realizes, for him to fret about what she's spending.

From Iskandariyah he has kept track of the savage quartet to wreak havoc in Florida—Hurricanes Charley, Frances, Ivan, Jeanne—and during Ivan, called Angela repeatedly to give her updates on possible evacuation. His voice made her feel safe. When Ivan stayed east, savaging Mobile and Pensacola, but leaving Biloxi-Gulfport with nothing more than trucks full of rain, she felt Frank had willed her safety from halfway across the globe.

On Halloween, Angela checks her e-mail and sees a message for Nana: "A Halloween e-Card Has Been Sent to You from Iraq," and clicks to see an animated figure, a soldier in uniform holding a smiling pumpkin, blowing a kiss with the text: "Have a Sweet Halloween."

Then she sees another, addressed to her, and finds two happy ghosts dancing and holding a bucket inscribed, "You're a Treat."

Then she reads a third note, an e-mail from Frank, saying, "I have a confession to make. After our trip to New Orleans, I did question, and I love you for making me do that. I asked why are we here? And at first I could not discover the answer, but now I have. Every day I see something that gives us hope, that we can feel proud of. We have won the war and now we are winning the peace. A school for Iraqi children is being rebuilt, a mosque is having a wall put back. There are some here who do not like us, but most smile when we pass by. I am proud to wear the uniform of the U.S. Armed Forces."

He writes to her of how many are in the National Guard, the Army, the Marines, and how the Air Force, which carried the first Gulf War, is being used "strategically, but in numbers not so great in this one. Each one of us here is part of the worldwide fight against terrorism. I do question and I do choose." Southern boys, he says, "Dixie's girls, too," he adds, shoulder the burden more than folks from any other region.

She has been hired back at the Cotton Gin—the man who fired her is being sued for sexual harassment—and her second week back, the bartender Betty collapses in tears when she gets a call that her husband has been wounded in Fallujah by a cluster bomb. But he is in stable condition. He will, within several weeks, be transported stateside; then rehab will begin. Angela and Brionne and Quenesha and Brandy gather round Betty and help her to her car as if she had taken the shards of explosive in her own body.

Angela writes nothing to Frank of this incident.

A few days later, Quenesha's and Brionne's new husbands, both men in the National Guard Reserves, get shipped out. A friend of Quenesha's, Hector Blanco in Cotton Gin maintenance, has a wife who's already headed there. Angela and her coworkers call themselves the Gin Circle and share the goings-on in Iraq like it was just up the road.

That next evening, when a knock comes repeatedly at her door, she jumps, then laughs at her silly anxieties. It is only a UPS delivery. Return address: Buck Raheem, Ocean Springs, Miss. Inside is a note:

> Dear Mrs. Semmes.
>
> Frank is a brave young man. I have family in Iraq, some were victims of Saddam. What Frank and our other men and women there are doing is a great gift to us all. Accept this little gift as a token of my appreciation. I am sending one to Frank, too, at the address he gave me. Hopefully, you will be able to use them to stay close. I speak to my family often using it; the pictures are comforting. You are in my prayers.
>
> Sincerely,
> Buck Raheem

She takes out the computer and little camera and sets it up by the instructions, and in the morning gets a message from Frank to turn on the webcam. His image sharpens on the screen. He looks leaner, more angular, his deep brown eyes taking her in through the pixilations. She puts her hand out to touch him, taken aback to feel the cold skin of the monitor.

"You look beautiful," he says, his image changing a little more slowly than in real time, as though his movements were underwater.

"I love you, Frank."

"Love you, babe."

He vanishes.

She drives to the airfield where they had gone soaring, tuning the radio to WYYC country FM, where a Randy Travis song is on. Frank has taught her to appreciate the blues, but her heart still belongs to country. She gets out, all alone.

With the car windows down, the music pours into the Mississippi afternoon. She imagines herself standing outside a club with a band thumping away inside. She sways on both feet.

"Frank," she says.

She tilts her head. More softly she repeats, "Frank."

She closes her eyes and rocks side to side, turning her face into the crook of his neck.

Overhead, an aircraft slips through the blue, someone soaring, floating, watching over, as she dances.

ELEVEN

A Rising Wind

By how Joe cradled her—lifting her up lightly next to his police cruiser, carrying her through the doorway of the hunting camp—Cam knew he cared. When he laid her down on the Indian print spread of the beat-up sofa bed and kissed her on the forehead, she felt like his treasure. Gone was the rough Joe, the angry Joe. In his place was the attentive Joe, who went to the fireplace and got a blaze going to keep them toasty in the December night, lugged in a cooler from his trunk, and poured them a beer—her first-ever taste of the yeasty brew—and taking off his holster belt, settled down alongside her. Softly he drew his fingers down over her forehead, her neck, to the top button of her blouse, the next, the next, undoing them as he went, her body his map.

He explored farther, deeper than she had ever let him go, to her belly, the skin just below her belt, on down, until she gripped his forearm out of instinct—and he stopped. In the firelight she saw the happiness in his eyes. She eased her grip and gave him the slightest downward pressure on his wrist: keep on.

She held her breath like she did at the doctor's, but this felt immeasurably better, though scarier, too. His smile gave her courage.

A voice crackled outside the door.

"What's that!" she cried, sitting up.

"My scanner."

The voice intoned again: "Ten sixty-six. Ten sixty-six. Mayborn and Creek."

"We have to go?" she said anxiously.

"No, no," he said, easing her back down. "Suspicious persons call. It can hold. Probably a drunk."

"You are off-duty, aren't you?"

"Shh," he said.

They started where they'd left off, and this time she felt more relaxed. His rough palm low on her was already familiar. He was moving faster, tugging down her jeans, and the warmth of the fire on her legs felt good, and to keep from feeling nervous, she watched his blissful expression.

The scanner erupted again, and he began hurriedly undressing and was suddenly sprawled out on top of her, and when she said, "Wait, wait," he said, "We don't have much time," and when she said, "I don't want to get a baby," he said, "I love you," and when he tore into her and she grimaced, he said, "Oh, my God," and then he was done, calming down again, a cuddly teddy.

She ruffled his hair. He grinned.

"Ten seventy-one, ten seventy-one, Code 3."

"I'll be back," he said, jumping up. Shirt, pants, shoes, billy stick, gun—he was already heading out the door.

"Where are you going!"

"Ten seventy-one means shooting. Code 3 means I better get my ass in gear."

She was alone, the siren of his squad car whoop-whooping through the woods, and to the highway, and fading into the distance. The quietness rose. The hoot of owls, the saw of crickets—and something skittering across the roof, what was that?—replaced it. A pop! She turned to look: a spark from the fireplace.

"Bodhisattva," she entreated.

A whir overhead, a click. Tiny paws pattering. A branch scraped the roof like the tines of a rake. She held her breath, looked at the window, pulled the pillow over her head, then looked out again. Beads of water on the pane.

Did she feel different? Changed now that she had crossed the line all the girls talked about, fretted about, fantasized about, and never stopped doing once they had "gone all the way"?

Is this what her mother would have told her? That it took so little, she now realized, to make a man your own?

The winter drizzle became the sound of BBs poured over the tin. It was sleeting.

Had Joe locked the door behind him?

She thought to rise and check, but her clothes were on the floor in a sad heap, and she did not want to be naked even one moment walking across this fire-flickering room with its animal heads above the mantel and snapshots on the wall of men with blood smeared on their faces.

The mattress was wet; her thighs were sticky. She shifted to one side, brought the blanket up to her chin, and burrowed in farther.

She closed her eyes. Mai appeared to her.

She was a beaming girl, like in the photograph in Daddy's shrine, but she seemed much older, too, beckoning Cam to follow.

They wove through narrow streets crowded with fish markets and vegetable stands and people squatting in front of shops eating with chopsticks from wooden bowls. They wore hats like Mrs. Kwan on Oak Street but they were not in Biloxi; she knew the locale. They were in Cholon, her family's district outside Saigon. She looked up at the signs in front of shops—smart, neatly lettered Vietnamese script. Daddy's handicraft. He could not read well, but he could copy—words for "school," "doctor," "police," and scores of others she could not decipher, done in his precise way. He had an artist's soft, expressive hands; not yet a shrimper's nicked and calloused. They passed another building, a school for little children—people hurried by them on bicycles, motor scooters, voices rising—and she saw Mother through the window, inside, leaning down to the children, beginning to lead them toward the door.

There was a gunshot; another. The shooter was loose, no, two shooters, ten, dozens, the shop doors were opening, the school doors were opening, there were sirens—*whoop, whoop*—and soldiers running through the streets. *Pop!* A young woman crumpled. Helicopter blades beat the air overhead. *Tat-tat-tat.* An elder man fell.

"This way." Mai waved her on.

They arrived at the harbor, and her mother and father and grand-mother were there, too, and Daddy was handing cash to a gaunt man naked to the waist with a scar across his chest, and then they were crowded into a boat with a horde of others and Daddy was shouting to Mai, who jumped from the dock to join them, Cam following. The sun beat down as they pushed out from the harbor, and when Cam turned back, she saw the commotion on the land—people running, screaming, soldiers grabbing victims and pushing them to the ground, rifles raised, explosions erupting in government buildings and homes and temples, other boats crammed with escapees starting out from the docks, those left behind leaping out only to crash into the gunnels or fall short into the muck of the port.

They were on open water now, the South China Sea, and the breeze was uplifting. They were free, all together again. From his duffel Daddy brought out a statuette—Quan Am. A smile flickered on her countenance; her gaze was beatific. Mai reached out and touched her. Cam touched her. The tips of their fingers hummed.

Where did the first wave come from? It rolled beneath them like the shoulders of a leviathan until the sky, quickly darkening, got closer, closer still, the swirling clouds within reach, the next wave higher and another until they were on a carnival ride unhinged, rolling, bucking, rising, falling, the voices of the passengers ascending, beseeching Buddha, Quan Am, Jesus, the ancestors, the wind itself, and a wave larger than any before washed over the boat and Cam felt her face dampened, another wave and she was drenched, and Daddy began yelling louder than all the others and pointing to the towering waves, stripping off his pants and shoes and starting to go over the side.

Grandmother was gone.

But Mai went over first, and Cam looked over to see her sister swimming with the strength of a sea creature, a porpoise sliding in and out of the waves, her skin flashing when the heavens lit up. "Mai. *Mai . . . !*" Their voices merged.

"Mai!" she called and opened her arms, and her sister appeared, young but old, tireless but weary, hair black yet silvered, "Mai," and the piscine girl came up out of the waves and into her arms and Cam grasped her tightly, welcoming her, enveloping her.

Who was shaking her shoulder? She looked up. Joe.

"See?" he said. "Back already." He picked up her clothes and lobbed them at her. "Let's scram."

"Jingle Bells" had never sounded so tinny, the mannequin Santa so downcast on his sleigh in front of the mall. It was her first Christmas without Frank, and she felt like the sad, drooping tree in the corner of their apartment doing its tinselly best to stay festive.

She finally felt satisfied, at least, with the gifts she had sent him, writing out the APO numbers in black marker, putting "SSgt. Frank Semmes" in block letters, drawing a heart beneath her return address: antibacterial soap, mint-flavored Crest, a Mennen Speed Stick, a red and a white Polo shirt, a pair of Tommy Bahamas sandals, recent copies of *Field & Stream* and *Sports Illustrated*, CDs of the North Mississippi All-Stars, Keb Mo, Luke Wallin, and her favorites, Faith Hill and Bonnie Raitt, a Best of Dylan, DVDs of *Star Wars* and *Superman* and *Mission Impossible*, a 2005 "Triumphs of Aviation" calendar, a key chain with the motto "It's Ginning Time at the Cotton Gin," and a big "Behold, Jesus Is Born" card from Victory Brotherhood signed by Brother Tim and drawings from the third grade class at Biloxi Grammar, who'd adopted Frank as pen pal, her favorite a picture of a soldier riding an American flag like a magic carpet over pyramids below.

On Christmas Day, she got his e-mail thanking her for the "amazing presents, how I wish I could be opening them beneath our tree with you and Nana," and telling a story:

> Before dawn this Christmas morning I was taking a
> weather sighting, and went outside to look to the east.
> I have never been anywhere so close to Bethlehem on
> Christ's birthday. I saw a star, Angela. It was Jupiter,
> the Mighty Warrior planet, symbol of Christ's victory
> over Satan. I believed it to be the Star of Bethlehem

that rose that morning over two thousand years ago. I knelt and prayed. I thanked God for sending His Only Begotten Son. Then I heard footsteps and next to me I saw Pvt. Simon Pulaski from Chicago. "Can I join you?" he asked. I nodded.

I had led a prayer group one day last week and Pulaski had stood watching from a door. Pulaski was a mutt, as they say, when it came to church, he had a bunch of different religions in his family, and didn't believe much at all. That same night there was an RPG attack that did damage to our mess hall. (I knew you'd worry if I'd told you then, everything's okay.) Pulaski was pulling mess duty and it shook him up pretty bad. When he put his knees down onto the sand next to me this very dawn and said, "I don't really know how to pray anymore," I told him what Brother Tim had told me about the key. "Look to the Star over Bethlehem," I told him. Pulaski turned to the star then lowered his head and began to cry.

When Frank called that night, he wanted to tell her again about Pulaski, but she wanted to ask him more about the presents she'd sent, make him feel less lonely so far away.

"Did you take Nana to her church," he asked, "or go to Victory Brotherhood?"

"We didn't make it this morning, Nana was—"

"Oh." Silence. "Christmas isn't just about presents, you know."

"I thought you liked what I sent you."

"You could have put Nana in a wheelchair if she wasn't up for it. You never know."

"You sound so far away," she said. "Farther than the last time we talked. Did the shirts fit? I got medium. I didn't know if large was better."

"I haven't had a chance to try them on yet."

"Oh."

Another silence.

"I bought a present from you to me!" she said cheerily.

"I tried, Angela, to get something to you, but, you know, the mail here . . ."

"It's a party dress. You'll love it."

The emptiness on the line yawned immeasurably across the latitudes.

"Was it on sale?"

"No, silly, it's the spring line. Sale stuff's last year's. I look"—she whispered into the phone—"sexy in it."

"Stop doing that to me," he said.

She purred with pretend sultriness: "I can't help it, *handsome*."

"You've never called me that before."

"What's wrong with 'handsome'? You *are*."

"It's not what you call *me*!"

"Who else would I call it!"

A ringing nothingness, a noise that was the absence of even a pin drop.

"Frank? Are you still there?"

"It's just hard being away from you," he said softly. "Holidays and all. Just a few more months."

"A few more months," she said.

"Merry Christmas," he said.

"Merry Christmas."

On nights when she could not sleep, and Nana was up, too, roaming around the apartment, Angela would say, "Tell me about those days again of Rosey. About the men in uniform, and the songs, and everybody pitching in to do their part."

And Nana would tell her how she had waited, making her way down to the National Mall from her Georgetown apartment, looking up at the soaring white obelisk and the noble dome of the Capitol Building and the pristine gardens of the White House, where, in a cloistered room, shrouded by an arbor of roses, FDR was plotting the course of the world.

It was a late afternoon, with rain coming down and wind whipping up the Sound, that Nana began suddenly: "There was a carousel."

"What about it?"

"I used to sit on a bench there and read and write to Rosey. I even had an admirer who pestered me there—you know men—a redheaded boy from Tennessee who was from the Pentagon. I simply told him, 'I'm taken.'"

How Nana could still make her laugh. "I'm *taken.*" She paused. "Nana?"

"Yes, doll."

"He didn't turn your head even once?"

"Stop it," said Nana. "Stop it!"

"Stop what?"

"You know how hard it was, once he was gone. No word, Angela, no word. We couldn't write back and forth like now, it's so easy. 'Where is he?' I would ask. 'We believe he's been captured, Mrs. Rosengarten. We believe he is a prisoner of war.' I was supposed to see him in seventeen days. We were going to rendezvous in San Francisco, he had a leave."

Angela nodded.

"From the last time I heard his voice, I heard nothing . . . But this."

"What do you mean?"

"Hand me my purse."

From an inside zipper she slid out what looked like a yellowed card with typescript. At the top were the words "International Red Cross," and "Imperial Japanese Army":

1. I am interred at Philippine Military Prison Camp #2.

2. My health is—<u>excellent</u>; good; fair; poor.

3. I am—injured; sick in hospital; under treatment; <u>not under treatment</u>.

4. I am—improving; not improving; better; <u>well</u>.

5. Please see that—<u>my family is ok</u>.
6. Regarding family—<u>love to all</u>.
7. Please give my regards to—<u>all our friends</u>.

Nana reached for the paper, but Angela kept studying it. Nana pulled it from her hands and folded it back into the secret pocket of her purse.

"How did you get through it?" Angela asked.

"I kept his shirts on their hangers, his socks rolled in the drawer. His favorite dessert, lemon pie, in the icebox, his inkstand and paper dusted on the desk. When his shoes got dusty, I polished them. When the radio played big band numbers—Glenn Miller was his favorite—I turned it up loud, fixed myself up, and thought about him coming through the door."

"You still listen to Glenn Miller, Nana."

"You're right, my Angel. I still do."

"You were hearing it the other night, weren't you?"

She nodded. "I didn't break my vows, Angela. Never ever! I didn't."

"Nana! I'm not questioning you."

She opened her purse again and this time, from another compartment, took out a page with tiny writing on it, Nana's handwriting, clear and precise from years ago. "He loved this Psalm I copied from his Bible when we were first married."

Angela read aloud:

> *With wondrous works dost Thou answer us in righteousness, O God of our salvation;*
>
> *Thou the confidence of all the ends of the earth, and of the far distant seas;*
>
> *Who by Thy strength settest fast the mountains, who art girded about with might;*
>
> *Who stillest the roaring of the seas, the roaring of their waves, and the tumult of the peoples;*
>
> *So that they that dwell in the uttermost parts stand in awe of Thy signs;*

Thou makest the outgoings of the morning and evening to rejoice.

"Frank will come home," Nana said.

"And we'll keep on," Angela said.

They gasped at the knocking at the door, insistent, ominous, steady. Angela went and flung it open. "Cam, oh, why so mysterious?"

As though blown in by a rough wind, Cam entered, her hair in a tangle. "I can't tell anyone this," she said.

"Tell us," said Angela. "Whatever it is, you can tell us."

Cam shook her head, then sat down at the piano and began to play. It was from her classical repertoire, not the old show tunes and moonlight crooner songs that held and soothed Nana, but great, crashing passages of Beethoven.

"Cam?"

The girl tossed her head, playing deep into the music, and when she stopped and looked over at them, her face was wet, glistening. Like a little girl, she licked at the side of her lip, catching the tears, then wiped at her cheeks with the back of her hand.

"Poor child," said Nana, and pulled a tissue out of her purse.

She turned to Nana. "It's blue."

"What's blue? Your spirits? We all get blue sometimes."

"The test. From the drugstore. I've done it twice. How can it be? But I won't give it up. I'll never give it up. Mai, my sister. Her soul."

She laid her head down on the piano keys with a bang.

Cam could feel the shift of weather in her body, the sky brushed with blue going to indigo, the soft caress becoming a rush of air that set the lines of her father's shrimp boat snapping and made the house eaves moan. Into the first weeks of January, storms had ripped through north Mississippi and as far down as Hattiesburg—tornadoes. When the local news channel showed hot spots of red over south Mississippi locales, and school was canceled, she cycled to the dock where Daddy was securing his shrimp buckets and nets, and thought how he might take the news that she and Joe would be married, and then, that a grandchild was on the way. He loved babies, she knew that. She could see him light up during prayer service at the temple when a couple came in with a newborn. "Like the seeds of the apple," he said to her. "New life, starting from old."

On his boat he kept a dish with a piece of apple, a stick of incense, and a figurine of the Quan Am. Miniature, delicate, her little face no bigger than a baby spoon, the Bodhisattva still radiated calm as though the soaring statue behind the temple had given birth to a perfect replica.

Would her baby be a replica of herself, joined with Joe? Mai's eyes— delicate and dark—she knew them from Daddy's photograph in the shrine.

The wind rose.

"Daddy?"

"Stay back." He walked out to her.

"Can I help you?" she said.

He waved his hand at her. "Wait there." He opened the hold and stepped down into his small engine room.

From her shoulder tote she took out a piece of paper and pen.

> Dear Bodhisattva,
>
> As the ashes took my prayer to you, so I hope now the wind does, too. I have a secret life inside my belly, and even Joe does not know. I love my baby. She will be the cutest doll.
>
> Bodhisattva, keep us all safe from terrible storms, as Mai is safe inside of me.
>
> Help me find a way to tell Daddy. Maybe I should tell Joe first, and when Joe asks me to marry him, I will tell him then. I will ask Joe to be a Buddhist. He asked me many questions about how we pray. He knows you because he has seen you outside at the temple. You are beautiful, Bodhisattva.

But Bodhisattva, I am afraid, too, for Daddy's anger. Sometimes he does not understand my heart. You brought my Joe to me and now, I know, you bring my Mai to me. You are wise. Show me the way.

Cam

She smoothed the note out on her lap, but a great gust of the looming storm snatched it from her, flipped it once, twice, three times in the air, and it flew like a startled white bird onto the agitated surface of the water and disappeared behind the boat.

A moment later her father appeared from around back of the boat—she had not seen him come up out of the engine hold—with a crab net in his hand.

"I fish this for you," he said.

He reached into the basket of the net and took out the sopping letter.

"Daddy!"

He opened it and his eyes ran across the text. Her heart drummed. He said nothing.

He waved her to him.

She stepped on the boat, the wind singing around them, and as she neared him, he put his right arm around her and brought her close.

On the piece of paper she saw the ink she had set there all run into a large, illegible stain, the only words that were clearly readable, "Dear Bodhisattva," and "Keep us all safe from terrible storms."

"You are my daughter," he said. "I will keep you safe."

And she put her head against his chest and heard the wind call her sister's name.

TWELVE

Blow the House Down

The hunting lodge—Cam knew it now like a room in her own house, the mounted buck heads with their glassy-eyed stares, the stacks of *Maxim* and *Guns & Ammo*, the refrigerator stocked with venison and beer, and the bed near the fireplace, Joe's bed, rumpled with its Indian print bedspread.

"C'mon, babe," he said, and took her hand, leading her there. "I worship you," he said, running his hand down the length of her, and she was ready, whenever he felt the moment was right, to lie naked and take him in. He lifted her shirt and patted her belly. "You're amazing," he said.

"Because of Mai."

"My what?"

"My Mai."

"My my," he said softly and leaned over and kissed her on the belly button.

"Mai, my baby."

"Your what?"

"Our baby."

He pulled back. "I must have cotton in my ears. What did you say?"

She smiled at him: first-time dads, she knew, always had a moment of shock. She had seen that on an afternoon talk show on new fathers. The widening eyes, the spreading smile. She waited.

"Baby," she repeated and kissed his forehead.

He sat up. "Have you gone nutso on me?"

"I'm pregnant," she said. "Nobody knows but . . ."

"But who?"

"Angela, Nana."

"They'll blab."

"They're my friends, like my family."

"God help us," he said. "Your family. Your father?"

"I haven't told him."

"God damn, of course not."

"I'm waiting."

"Waiting for what?"

"For . . . a ring."

"What!" He hopped up and glared down at her. On the talk show there had been no discussion of this phase of the male response.

"You look, you look funny," she said. "Joe?"

His brow was knitted and he looked nearly cross-eyed and he spit out: "What kind of trick are you trying to pull on me?"

"Trick? What?" She gathered her blouse up and bundled it in front of her, hiding her breasts. She felt the faintest throb in them, like a pain traveling from her heart.

"You think you can blackmail me into marrying you?"

"We're not too young. My mother and daddy—"

"Are Vietnamese," he cut in. "I'm white. I'm Catholic."

"We love each other!"

"This has just been fun! Christ, what do you think goes on here other nights of the week? You think this place is just for shooting deer?"

"Daddy will give his blessing, do not worry. If you cannot become a Buddhist, I will accept Christ as my savior. I am ready to be christened, many Vietnamese are Catholic. I will be a church girl."

"I've got somebody," he said in a lather, "already picked."

"Picked out?"

"She's rich, her dad owns a lot of timber. She's perfect. It's perfect, don't you see? I can't spend my life as a poor cop!"

Suddenly he fell quiet and got down on his knees next to the bed. He continued softly, despite the wild look in his eyes. "Your daddy knows you need a Vietnamese boy. He's a smart man. You'll have a beautiful life. Your culture, your people. Another baby one day, lots of babies."

"I won't give up this one."

"I'll pay for it all," he said. "Take you, of course. We'll do it somewhere else—I know a clinic in Mobile—nobody will know. If you love me, do this. If you love your daddy."

"Do you love me?"

"Yes, yes, if you do this, I promise."

She stood up and towered over him where he knelt on the floor.

"Can we be husband and wife? Afterward?"

He was shaking as if she were a criminal holding a gun to his head.

"Say we can do that, Joe."

"What we can do," he said, his voice now betraying no emotion at all, "is go on with our lives like we never met."

When the morning came that Clem, Betty's husband, would be arriving at the Gulfport Airport on a commercial airliner, the Cotton Gin floor manager gave the Gin Circle time off. Angela was able to leave from home—her shift had not started yet—and the free time from work would enable her to linger at the airport longer with her friends.

It was on her way there that her phone rang:

"Hey, babe!"

"Frank, oh, I miss you. How are you? I love you so much!"

"Me too, me too, what you up to?"

"Just out for a drive."

"Where to?"

"See some girlfriends." The last thing she wanted to do was bring him down with the tale of the wounded Marine.

"Aren't you supposed to be at work soon?"

"Change of schedule today."

"Where are you heading to that's so damn mysterious?"

"Frank, c'mon now!"

"Tell me, Angela."

"Don't be so jealous, Frank, what do you take me for?"

"I just went online and checked our bank balance," he said.

"What does that have to do with how you're acting?"

"What in God's name are you spending our money on? Buying party dresses? Who for?"

"Stop it, stop it, you know I'm completely devoted to you!"

"My combat pay's going down the drain!"

"I'm working, too, you know."

"What if *I* wanted to buy something? Like an oud. They're not cheap."

"A what?"

"It's Iraqi, like a guitar, real Middle Eastern twangy. It'll be so cool to learn to play. There's a guy in the village famous for making them. He's a master craftsman."

"Then go buy it!"

"That's it? It doesn't matter how much cash I draw out at the PX? Our account's a bottomless well, is that what you think?"

"What's so damn important about an oud, Frank? What about the TV here? It needed fixing, and you said get a new one. A big screen one, you said, with a DVD player, hundred bucks off after Christmas. So I did. And I've got Cam coming more hours for Nana."

"Nana's got her own money," he said.

"Don't try and control every little thing from way over there," she ripped into him. "I'm doing what I can to keep it going here, to stay sane. I love you, Frank, and do you know where I'm headed now? Do you really want to know?"

The phone clicked off.

As she neared the Gulfport Airport, her blood racing, she thought of Rosey's letters, and surely the ones Nana sent in return. Maybe it had been better that way, the solitary meditations and protestations of love with three-week delays from composition to delivery. She tried to keep the picture in her mind of Frank on the Keesler air strip, or poring over weather monitors at his base, but what she saw now was him peering at their bank statement on the computer screen and double-checking every expenditure she made at Winn-Dixie or Dillard's Department Store or on an early-bird-special dinner on a rare night out with Nana and Cam and Mrs. Torres at Bombay Bicycle Club.

The local road from I-10 to the airport was jammed with cars, and as she slowly pulled into the parking lot, she saw a throng of TV and print journalists, a Marine honor guard, and the mascot of the local high school dressed in his tiger suit.

"Damn you, Frank, why did you act that way!"

She glanced at her cell phone. Maybe he was out of range. Had he hung up? No, he'd never done that. Was he okay? Her heart began to palpitate. Why had they lost their connection?

She found a parking spot and went inside and found her Cotton Gin friends. Angela gave Betty a big hug as other friends crowded in to do the same. Outside the casino the Gin Circle looked uncertain, out of place in the bright glare of the airport lights.

"It's landing!" someone shouted.

"Oh, Lord, thank you," said another.

A military band struck up "Semper Fidelis," and people began to clap. A large woman clasped Betty's hand—Betty's mother most likely, Angela realized—and a portly man bent forward next to them, certainly another relative.

Next to her she heard a Mississippi congressman giving comments to a newspaper reporter, using the expressions "fight them there," and "hero," and "grace of God." He said that thanks to the sacrifices of the coalition forces, the Iraqis had triumphantly held a free election—58 percent of the population had gone to the polls. He held up the front page of the day's *Sun-Herald* with an AP photo of a Shia woman with her purple finger in the air, a sign she had voted.

"Here they come!"

Down the long corridor, his wheelchair pushed by an attendant, the U.S. Marine came slowly, waving, smiling. He was only a boy, she realized, no seamed soldier with a world-weary visage, but a young man barely old enough to order a drink in a bar or pull a voting lever. She glanced at her cell phone again, making sure she had not missed a callback from Frank amid the music and commotion.

When she looked up again, she imagined it was Frank in that chair and she became the spouse who'd suffered that close call, surrounded by a town of supporters. He would, at least, be home. Their real lives could begin.

She shuddered, biting her lip, as though others around her had glimpsed that horrible thought. What kind of wife could wish her own husband any manner of harm?

Clem arrived and was swept up in the embraces of Betty and her mother and the man next to them, then encircled by his church group, and Betty's casino workers, then they all fell back and he rolled himself forward to meet the honor guard from his Marine reserve unit.

One of the Marines bent down to embrace him, and Clem put his head on his shoulder and began to weep. When he looked up, wiping his eyes, he spoke to a TV camera pointed right him, saying, "I wish I was still with my buddies over there. They're doing a great job, a magnificent job, and I love 'em, and . . ." He put his head back down.

The other Marines surrounded him, blocking the cameras.

Back at the Cotton Gin, Angela tried Frank repeatedly but was unable to get a response. During her break she ran home and sent an e-mail. Nothing. If she could just leave him a message—"I love you, the stress is what happens with a lot of time and distance, it's natural the other wives tell me, you'll be home soon"—but there was no signal at all.

She did her shift, served her drinks, pocketed the bills, swore to herself to cut back on expenses—she did not need the newspaper subscription, or the weekly outings to Ruby Tuesday with Nana, or a new blouse even if it was for Frank's homecoming. She would do anything to give him peace of mind.

She headed back to her apartment by way of the Biloxi Lighthouse and the historic homes, by the plaque to the cassette girls, those eighteenth-century brides-to-be imported for the Frenchmen thanks to Ursuline nuns, by the pirate ship casino with its lights rising through the jangly portholes, near the sweep of Jefferson Davis's Beauvoir, by Coastal Arms, where Angela thanked God for delivering Nana to her, and toward home.

As the last sun laid down a soft light on the branching oaks and columned houses, over the gentle stitching of sand and beach and road, she thought, "I want to live here forever." Frank teaching at Keesler, their children going to the Biloxi school, their little cosmos of family and friends—what more could she want?

The parking lot of her apartment complex fanned out to view and she saw a familiar figure hobbling with his cane toward the door.

"Big Frank?" she called out her window as she parked and got out to hurry toward him.

"My boy!" he wailed.

"What!"

"My boy, they got my boy! Let me go. I'll tear up every last one of them. Oh, my boy!"

She felt herself moving not walking, floating not running, across the parking lot toward Big Frank, her voice not even her own as she asked, "What do you mean?"—while knowing full well what he meant as he repeated, "Got my boy."

Then she heard herself crying out: "It can't be."

"His leg and his head," said Big Frank, doing his best to stand stalwart. "They couldn't reach you so they had my number and called me and told me it was a bomb, a roadside bomb, blew up under the side of his car where he was riding. My *boy*!"

"But he's alive!"

"His leg and his head. Yes, he's alive."

The door opened, and Mrs. Torres stood there and put her hand to her mouth, repeating, "*Dios mío,*" and helped Big Frank inside. Angela went to Nana, who was staring straight ahead, putting an arm around her grandmother's shoulders, then turned to Big Frank, imploring, "Tell me what they said. Everything. Exactly."

"His head. His leg."

"Who called you?" she pressed on. "Did they leave a number? They didn't call here, Mrs. Torres?"

"Oh, yes, somebody call. I hear the click, but I am speaking with my sister who calls to me from Guadalajara. God forgive me. I am sorry, Angela."

"They're taking him to Ramstein," Big Frank said.

"In Germany," said Mrs. Torres. "The big Air Force base, their hospital."

"They'll fix him up," said Big Frank.

"My boy." It was Nana, mouthing the words softly.

"How can I contact him? Who do I call? Where do I go? Big Frank, Nana, Mrs. Torres, help me."

"They will call back," said Mrs. Torres.

The phone rang.

"Mrs. Semmes?"

"Yes."

An officer's calm, measured voice gave her the news, explaining that Frank had been in a Humvee with two other men heading out to repair some field equipment for the weather station. They seemed to have been making a detour to a local village. The words starting banging inside of her head: "Your husband has been wounded."

"Let me talk to him," she demanded.

"He's receiving emergency medical treatment, Mrs. Semmes."

"I want to talk to him!"

"Mrs. Semmes?"

"I'm calling the general, I'm calling my congressman, I'm calling our senator."

"Yes ma'am, I understand. Someone from the base will be right over to speak with you. Staff Sergeant Semmes is a hero."

"I don't want him to be a hero. I want him to be okay!"

"Yes ma'am."

"I want him safe."

"Yes ma'am."

"I want him home!"

"Yes ma'am. He's very brave."

THIRTEEN

Nightwatch

How long the night was she waited. She went on the Internet and looked up Balad Air Base Hospital. Frank was being stabilized there. She had the picture of a tent hospital set up among concrete barricades. The Air Force website said that insurgents, next to civilians, next to servicemen, received treatment there.

Ten P.M., eleven, midnight in Mississippi: dawn, giving way to early morning, in Iraq.

She had another image in her mind that would not let go: Frank, with his head bandaged, his eyes closed, on a stretcher, but there was no blood. His face was smooth, his color was good, then he opened his eyes and looked at her and she fell into those brown eyes as she had looked into them at the casino, as she had when he turned to her in the glider and said, "I love you."

And she kept falling, feeling the fall, as though she had been pitched out of that glider and was plummeting, spread eagle, the hot wind scouring her face, the gulls she had watched from the Ship Island ferry now watching her, the ground rising faster and the wind streaming around her, "Frank, oh, Frank," but he could not respond, locked away in the base hospital as she was here, falling. Awake, asleep, 2 A.M., 2:30, what to do, she did not know, and when she heard Nana padding about her room—"Where am I?"—she answered, "Oh, Nana, go back to bed."

"What's wrong? Is something wrong? It's about Rosey!"

"No, Nana."

"They said he'd been hurt, wounded."

"No, Nana."

"Rosey . . ."

"No! Nana! Not Rosey! You know it's not about Rosey."

"He's okay, then?"

"Everything's not about Rosey. My husband is dying, Nana, and I'm here, in Biloxi, Mississippi, stuck here in this apartment with you."

Nana sat hard on the edge of the bed and her face crumpled up like a little girl's. "I'm so much trouble to you."

"No, Nana," Angela said, sitting next to her. "You're not trouble, you're my Nana, and I'll do whatever I can, but . . ."

Nana's body began to shake with sobs.

Falling, the two of them, Nana in the small room in Georgetown, where the word had come that Rosey was missing and all she had was the card from the Imperial Japanese Army saying, "I am well, I send my love to my family," Angela in the small room in Biloxi, where word had come that Frank had taken a hit to the leg and the head, and she clutched one of his last e-mails, from what now felt like a very long-ago Christmas morning, "I knelt and prayed, I thanked God," and felt the floor giving way.

Throughout it all, Nana held his head, Rosey's full lips, the dark almond eyes, the wavy black hair, as she saw him gone from the prison camp to parts unknown, a prison ship some said, but what did it look like? A prison on a ship, or a floating jail? Or maybe he had not been moved there at all but had escaped and, uncounted for, was hiding out in the Philippine forests crouched down, repeating in silence his Hebrew prayers asking for deliverance like his family had read aloud in the Passover seder that first and only spring together. It was not Jerusalem but America he prayed for, and at the end of the trek he dreamed it was her own face, as she waited for him and waited still, knowing he could somehow make his way between the gulf of night and the coast of dawn.

And as Frank lay against Angela, his head pressed against her shoulder, she comforted him, stroking his brow, running her palm over the contours of his face, cradling his head—"His leg and his head!" Big Frank's voice kept repeating—leaning down and kissing his forehead, cheek, neck, lips. "Oh, Frank."

She came to, drifted off, opened her eyes to see first light edging through the blinds. Where she'd fallen asleep, Nana lay curled against her, nose against her shoulder.

She felt Nana's warm steady breath, felt her twitch in sleep. Was she dreaming old fox-trots to the champagne swirl of a big band? Or the card from the Imperial Japanese Army saying, "Send love to all my family"? And she thought how delicate Nana was, how frail her shoulders and neck and head, while Frank, all muscle and sinew and resilient strength, was half broken. How could that be?

"You goddamn people who run the war," she said only so that she might hear, even though only Nana, snoring softly, was in the room. "We're the ones at home who carry the wounds, too. When they fall, we fall with them."

Nana curled away, whispered, settled back to sleep.

Morning pooled through the blinds and rose in a pale wash against the cabinets, the dresser, the pictures on the mantel. She stood and looked at them, the light catching up each in turn: Nana and Lucky at the beach in Hawaiian print outfits; Angela in Girl Scouts with her mom and Nana, standing by a fence where wisteria fell in lavender clusters; a youthful Nana in an ancient black-and-white snapshot sporting an extravagant Easter hat, head back like a starlet posing for a glamour magazine in front of the D.C. reflecting pool with the Capitol behind her. How old was Nana in that picture? Twenty-one? Twenty-two? Who had taken it? She imagined Rosey, standing behind a box camera, saying, "Hold still, one, two, three." The presences, she thought, of those not visible in photographs but so present still in the furniture of rooms, the clothes dormant in closets, their memories that suffused the air.

She turned the blinds a notch and looked out, but the world was opaque. She went to the front door. The Biloxi dawn was lost in fog.

She went back in, checked on Nana, glanced at herself in the mirror, and saw a woman twice her age, hair wild, circles under her eyes, and then caught a glimmer of the woman she would be at twice that age again, making her as old as Nana. "But I will not be without you, Frank," she said to the mirror, seeing her husband standing alongside her. "I will not let you leave me, not like this. You wanted to go. Okay. I want you to come home. Do that for me."

She threw on a shift, slipped into her sandals, and stepped outside. The cars and trucks on Highway 90 were green and red dirigibles whooshing through the sea-level clouds. The traffic light at the intersection seemed as distant as a lighthouse—red, green, yellow, red. She clipped across.

On the beach the fog enveloped her, and she felt comfort in being a woman adrift, unseen and without name, witnessed only by foraging gulls. She felt like those characters she had read about in the women-in-history class at the junior college who had waited for their loved ones gone off to fight in ancient places. One girl had been named Penelope, who had worked a loom to pass the time for her Odysseus, which had stretched to twenty years. Surely there were girlfriends and wives—and boyfriends and husbands in her own time—who had done the same on the side of the enemies, too. Those who had waited while father, brother, husband, son, went off to fight. Big Frank in the Philippines, her father in Vietnam, Frank in Baghdad. The yearners, the hopers, the patient and believing. Nana and Angela.

She could not see the water lapping at the shore, but followed its sad music along the shrouded coastline. Frank was in her life like this, she knew, like she was in his, constant even when unseen.

He would survive. He must survive.

When the fog broke and the light of common day returned the coast to its workaday churnings, and she was returning, exhausted, to her front door, she heard the phone ringing with a clear, belling insistence, and she was running, reaching, lifting the receiver, hearing the strange voice from the other side of the globe that pronounced itself coming from Balad Air Base Hospital:

"Mrs. Semmes, we finished surgery a little while ago. Staff Sergeant Semmes, Frank, your husband, came through."

Dear Bodhisattva,

Joe will love me, I know he will. When he sees how my belly pokes out a little with a small hill named Mai, he will be proud of his baby and not be afraid to give me all his heart. I know how he really feels inside, but he wants to live by his tradition. He is like my Daddy in that way, so I understand him. It makes me love him more.

Bodhisattva, please help Joe know how he really feels about me. Tell him in your own wise way. He doesn't need to play games with me. I am already his. Mai is his already. Forever.

Bodhisattva, I have never asked you two things at once, but this is special. Make Frank better so Angela will not have her heart broken. She is the nicest lady, and she and Nana have been so kind to me. I feel happy at their home, sometimes more than in mine. I want Angela to be happy and her husband not to be in pain. She is like a different person she is so sad.

Bodhisattva, thank you for always listening to me and for guiding me with wisdom to this day when my sister's soul is deep inside of me.

Your daughter,
Cam

She looked up. Nearly 9 A.M. Daddy and cousin Thanh had been away for five nights on his boat. She had missed school two of those days and gone in late the third, the morning sickness catching her up no matter what she did, how she turned in the bed or sat near the open window. She counted ahead the months. By the time graduation came, she would be a big cow. How could she hide her rotund form? They would never let her march across the stage for her diploma if everyone could tell. She knew of one girl, Eliza Adams, who'd finished her schoolwork from home while recuperating from stomach surgery—school said it was cancer, but Eliza had left fat and next appeared skinny, so everybody suspected it was fat surgery. Though she wondered now what had really happened to Liza. Had she crossed the line with a boy, too?

She folded up the letter to Quan Am and clutched the side of the table. She could not miss another day without a doctor's excuse, and the notes she forged from her father could only take her so far (she wrote out his English letters for him anyway). But too many, she knew, made for suspicion.

And was that him at the door? "Daddy?" she called out.

He was not due back until the following day.

"Daddy?"

She looked out the back window at the rice paddy hat of old Mrs. Kwan, and far beyond, over the pine tops, at the penthouse floors of the High Chaparral Casino Hotel.

She heard the door open. No voice answered her. She stood and went into the front room.

"Daddy!"

He stumbled toward the chair, clutching its arm, nearly knocking over a lamp, the fumes of his whiskey mixing with the stench of seafood.

"I saw her," he said.

"Who?"

"Last night, when we were bringing up the nets. Out in the water."

"Oh, Daddy."

"Far away I saw her. Waving." He moved his small, tough hand back and forth. "She was swimming to us, but the waves pushed her back. I waved. 'Mai! I am coming to you.'" He got up from the chair now, looking off through the house. "'I am coming.'

"Thanh told me, 'No, you are a crazy man. You cannot swim out there.'

"'I am not a crazy man. She is my child!'" He stepped forward, like he was going to dive headlong into the room.

"Then what?"

"She was gone. Thanh said to me she was not there. It was the light, a reflection."

He turned and trudged into the kitchen and grabbed up a bottle of whiskey from a back shelf. First he held it up to the light, examining its level—he shot a glance at Cam—then unscrewed the top, poured some into a coffee cup, guzzled it. Did so again.

He stood over Cam now, wobbling, wiping the back of his mouth with his shirtsleeve. He turned away and went to the window, peering out, mumbling, "I am coming," then turned again and slumped down, squatting against the wall.

"You are everything," he said, shaking his head, his voice about to break, "that is good in my life."

She felt her body shift and head spin and she went into the bathroom, putting her hands against the wall and closing her eyes, determined not to throw up. But she did.

"Why are you sick?" he said after she had washed up and come back out.

"I'm not sick. I just ate something that gave my stomach fits, I guess. That's all. It happens."

"I saw your teacher at the gas station. He said he hoped you feel better."

"Maybe I had the flu, maybe . . ."

His look silenced her. He never listened, but he could hear things, see things, she did not want him to.

"Tell me what is the truth, Cam."

"The truth," she said, "is that I am upset. Yes, I am sick. I am sick because Angela's husband got hit by a bomb in Iraq and he could be dying right this very minute."

"Oh"—he leaned back his head with a thunk against the wall—
"God."

BILOXI AIRMAN WOUNDED IN IRAQ. Staff Sgt. Franklin Semmes,
U.S. Air Force, who did weather training at Keesler Air Force Base, was
seriously wounded in Iraq Wednesday morning. According to Air Force
spokesperson Lt. Lisa Manetti, Semmes, 26, attached to the U.S. Army
3rd Infantry, was traveling in a Humvee outside of his base near Iskandariyah when an improvised explosive device detonated under the vehicle's left front wheel. Semmes, who was sitting on the driver's side in
the back seat, sustained heavy injuries to his head, left leg and shoulder.
The other two men in the vehicle, said Manetti, were also injured.

Semmes was taken by helicopter to Balad Theater Air Force Hospital, an emergency unit near Baghdad set up in 2003 as a first treatment
center for injured servicemen and others in the area. Often, after being
stabilized at Balad, the wounded are transported to Ramstein Air Force
Base in Ramstein, Germany, where extensive hospital facilities are in
place.

No further report on Semmes's condition at Balad is yet available.

Semmes was deployed to Iraq in spring, 2004. The area where he
was stationed, south of Baghdad, has been nicknamed "the Triangle of
Death" based on the large number of casualties that have occurred in
the region. Since the Iraqi elections on Jan. 30, boycotted by much of the
Sunni population, there has been a rise in insurgent violence against
the Iraqi government and coalition forces.

Angela Semmes, 24, the wife of Staff Sgt. Semmes, is employed in
hospitality at a Biloxi gaming resort. Through Manetti of the Air Force
she issued this comment: "Frank will be okay. I know he will. He is
very strong and very brave. He has an unshakeable faith in God and
country."

Grasping the Biloxi-Gulfport newspaper and reading it over again,
seeing Frank handsome and stalwart on the front page and reading her
quote, she felt like she was holding the news of someone else's life.

Why had she talked about his "unshakeable faith"? Why hadn't she been able to say what she wanted: "God, I hope what he has given his country is worth it."

The words "the price of freedom" kept running through her head. Hadn't those been the words Lucky had used in arguing with her father about Vietnam, about Grenada? "Is it worth the price?" her father had railed back at Lucky, swearing, "I sure in hell don't want to pay it."

But it was Frank's faith that she had spoken of for all the world to hear, and when she stepped outside her apartment, a thin, tall woman holding a Bible stepped forward and introduced herself as being from Back Bay Pentecostal Church and said, "Your husband, Mrs. Semmes, is on our prayer list. You come worship with us anytime you want."

"Thank you."

Since getting the call about the success of Frank's first surgery—morning stretching to afternoon, to the next morning, and three days more of feeling hungover from a bad dream—she did little more than watch the clock, be gracious to her well-wishers, and keep her focus on Nana because, well, what else was there to do?

She felt as though she were an alien inhabiting the body of a woman named Angela Semmes as she opened the letter that came from the U.S. congressman—surely about somebody else's husband—stating, "Staff Sgt. Franklin Semmes is a symbol of all that is good and noble about the United States." She smiled and said thank you, all the while feeling dopey, as the casino's Gin Circle gathered around her when she tried to go back to work and they told her, "No, you don't need to work yet, here, take this, our tips for an entire week."

When she called Frank and they put the satellite phone to his ear and she told him how much she loved him, and how everybody at home was praying for him, knowing he would get better soon, and that she would travel to see him at Ramstein as soon as Keesler gave her the word, she felt like she was playing a role in a movie about a made-up life. There was silence on the other end of the phone. She kept expecting Frank himself to come sauntering through the door.

In addition to the Gin Circle, contributions for "Frank's recovery" and "to help pay the bills" came from Victory Brotherhood, Mrs. Torres's Bible study group, the Biloxi Police Department, Phi Nguyen, and countless others she had never met, but who now knew her, asking about Frank when they saw her in the supermarket, or at the café where she returned to lingering with her laptop, surfing the Web for a place she and Frank could go on vacation when this cruel joke on their lives was done.

The biggest check of all, which could help cover round-the-clock care for Nana if she were able to venture abroad, came from Buck Raheem in Ocean Springs with a picture of grizzly Saddam in jail awaiting trial, and a note: "This is what Frank helped do for us. This token of my appreciation is the least my family and I can do for him."

She was talking yet again into silence on the phone—was Frank even on the other end?—when she heard, like the primal noise of a creature being born, a single, rough syllable, a wrenching "*uh.*"

That was all. Then silence again.

But that was all she needed, like the sounding of a cracked, far-off but treasured bell, to toll her back to who she really was, and what was in front of her—the trip that must be taken, the embrace that must be given, to save all that was precious to her.

When she hung up, she raced to the Sound and danced along on the beach, whirling her arms, kicking up her feet, crying and letting loose, to the shock of a hundred gulls, a big Rebel yell.

FOURTEEN

An Outside Hand

Cam brought Joe to her doorway every way possible in her mind: after his beat, when his shirt was rumpled and his eyes looked tired and he needed her to massage his shoulders and pour him a beer; on a Saturday afternoon, when he was in the yard tending their garden and took a break, his T-shirt slung around his neck like an athlete's towel; and just inside the shut door, too, his morning coffee in hand, naked beneath his bathrobe and putting his cup down as he walked toward her. Their baby would be soundly asleep, snug in her room with pink walls and sky blue ceiling. On the stove a pot roast would be simmering for Daddy's visit later in the afternoon.

"Oh, Bodhisattva," she lamented, "can't you do anything more at all?"

"Cam?"

That was not the voice of Bodhisattva. It was all too familiar.

"Aunt Therese?"

With her French tip nails, short haircut, and tight mauve blouse, Therese looked like city come to country on ordinary Oak Street with its Mississippi fishermen, Asian market storekeepers, and every age of mom keeping after or toting a child.

"Your poor father," said Therese, striding into the room. "He called me from the boat he's so worried about you."

"Was he drinking?"

"What an attitude! You sound like one of your American teen friends."

"I am an American teen."

"You must still show respect to your father!"

"I've felt a little crummy is all."

"You're surely not keeping yourself looking very"—Therese stepped forward and flicked her finger in Cam's hair—"stylish. Let me see your hands."

Therese grabbed up Cam's right hand and peered critically at her nails. "How old are you now?"

"Going on seventeen."

"Clear polish will still do. Not much longer, though."

"There's no problem with boys liking me the way I am, Aunt Therese. I'm plenty stylish for them."

"As long as it's about style, not sex."

"You catch more bees with honey, Nana says."

"Your honey pot, you mean? Terrible!"

Insufferable Therese was her father's oldest cousin—though everyone called her aunt—and no other woman in the Nguyen family had as much status and power. That she owned a restaurant in East New Orleans added to her reputation. In the summer after her mother's death, Cam had stayed with Therese and her slutty daughter, now a pharmacist in Slidell, though Therese had always held her up to Cam as a paragon of virtue.

"What do you hear," Cam asked by way of distraction, "from the cousins in Ho Chi Minh City?"

"I did not drive here from New Orleans to talk about Saigon. I came here to talk about Cam Nguyen."

"I'm making all A's."

"The funny thing, Cam, is that your color looks great, and it's all natural, I know that. You say you're sick, you keep yourself a mess, but you're a rose in bloom. How do we account for that?"

"Rosey," she said.

"Rosy. Yes, rosy."

"It's a name," Cam said. "When you said that, it made me think of him."

"Is that the boy?"

"What boy?"

"The boy you have been with."

"Are you crazy, Aunt Therese? Rosey lived like a hundred years ago. He married Nana and got killed in the war way over in Japan or somewhere."

"Who's your boyfriend?"

"I hang out with lots of different people."

"Which one got in your pants?"

"Nobody got in my—"

"Swear on the memory of your mother."

She looked hard at Therese. "Leave my mother out of this! She was my mother. You're not even a blood relation to her."

"Phi was right. He said to me, oh, and from the boat, so worried about you. 'Come help me, Therese,' he begged. 'I do not know my own daughter anymore.'"

"He loves me," Cam erupted. "He will marry me. I know he will."

"They're all alike," Therese said sadly now.

"You don't even know him."

"Will he be a good father?"

"He'll be a wonderful father." Had she been tricked into confessing her secret? "I'm proud if it, too, and I want the whole world to know."

"Let's tell your father then."

"No!"

"You can't hide it much longer."

"I want to tell Daddy together. With Joe."

"Tell me about this Joe."

As Cam recounted their history—high school basketball games, the lunch room chitchat about rain, the meeting again after so long at Daddy's dock, even the first hunting camp kiss—she watched Therese soften, as though her modish yet scrappy aunt was reliving something of a long-ago romance of her own.

"I see it in your face," Therese said. "All that you're feeling." She clasped Cam's hands. "Let's go make this right, do what we have to. I'll be with you, right by your side."

"You mean . . ."

"Pay Joe a visit. To tell him I speak for the family."

To see Joe again, to go to the police station and find him there, to talk to him plainly, passionately, as the mother of his child. Yes, having Therese there for support, to give Joe the family blessing, was what she needed.

Therese did not stay at the house that night but at the High Chaparral Casino Hotel, and when she showed up the next morning in the same mauve blouse, she looked tousled, her mascara smeared. She opened her compact, adjusted herself, gave Cam a half hug.

"How do I look?" Cam asked, turning around once in her flowered shift and sandals.

Therese nodded. "Get in."

Cam sank back into her passenger seat, looking out as the beachfront slid by, tapping her foot to the light rock that pulsed from the radio. Could Mai already hear the music?

"Can we listen to something," she asked, "a little softer?"

Therese gave her a sideways glance.

Why were they heading now to the bridge from Biloxi to Ocean Springs? She looked back over her shoulder, seeing Highway 90 slipping away behind them in a mercurial ribbon.

"You're turned around, Aunt Therese," she said. "It used to happen to me when I first started driving here."

"We've got to make another stop first."

Therese was in charge. She had no choice. As the car thrummed over the bridge, Cam looked off to the Sound, at the shrimp boats making their way back in. "Isn't that Daddy's boat?"

"Your father slaves for you, you know."

"He's not due back until tomorrow or Friday," she said.

"'Phi,' I tell him, 'you could go back to Saigon and work with your brother. The dollars you've made here, you could live like a king over there.' 'Cam,' he tells me. 'This is Cam's home.'"

"I know he slaves for me, Auntie."

"Think about what this will do to him."

"We're going to fix it, though!"

"Yes, we are going to fix it."

"Where are you taking me!?"

"I know the pretty pictures in your mind, Cam. You, this Joe, the baby, a nice little house with a white fence. But what about this? You alone, a baby, no father, another mouth to feed, your own poor father breaking his back to—"

"Take me to see Joe. Now!"

"We're almost there," she said.

They turned down a side street and pulled into the parking lot of a small, whitewashed building with an unadorned sign out front: "Parkland Clinic."

"Come on," Therese said.

Behind a small barricade alongside the property was a woman holding a sign that read, "God loves the life inside of you." Cam looked at her with puzzlement.

Reluctantly she followed her aunt inside to whatever chore she had to accomplish.

The walls were filled with gentle beach sunset photographs, pictures of gulls banking in the coast air, dunes, and music of Kenny G., soft, tenor sax undulating.

"I called about my niece," Therese said to the receptionist. "I'm her guardian."

"You're my aunt!" said Cam.

"Her mother's dead," she told the receptionist, "her father is at sea. It was me who filled out the paperwork online."

"We were able to work her in. The doctor can see her for a preliminary visit."

The door opened to the back. "Cam?" called out a nurse's voice.

"I don't know what this is about," she said.

Therese took her hand. "Let me be the mother."

At the same time as she put one foot in front of the other, following Therese, she was seeing herself turning and fleeing out the door. Then she realized: her father had, indeed, read her thoughts on the letter to the Bodhisattva before the Back Bay waters had bled away the ink. He had called Therese to ask her to convince his daughter to give up the baby for adoption. Cam folded her arms around her belly, tighter. She would never let go.

They turned into a room where a kindly man with a droopy mustache waited. "Hello, Miss Nguyen, I'm Dr. Ben Juarez, and I've been at the Parkland Clinic for about five years now. As you're turning this prospect over in your mind about terminating the pregnancy, I'm here to answer any questions you have."

"Terminating!?"

"You're here because you want to be. It's your choice."

"You're not touching me."

"She's too young to be ruining her life," Therese said. "But she won't listen to me."

"Then speak to her sensibly and gently, ma'am. She needs your consent, not your directive."

Therese stood. "Maybe you'll talk to him on your own," she said.

"Would you like that, Cam? You're a free agent here."

"Yes sir," she answered quietly.

"Excuse me." Therese pulled out her cell phone and stepped outside the door.

Alone with the doctor, Cam listened as he told her that the relationship between a man and a woman and the fertilized egg inside her body was a sacred trust, a private matter, which, in his view and that of the clinic, and the law, was a matter for the mother alone—though consent was needed, under age eighteen—to decide in the earliest phase. How far along was Cam?

She told him of the first time she had been with Joe, and no protection. Why was she even speaking to him, though?

If she chose to keep the baby, he said, did she have a clear idea about how she would care for it? Was she going to get a job? Was she looking to family members to help her out? And did she know enough, to her satisfaction, about prenatal care? Nutrition? Exercise? If she did consider having the procedure, she would first have a sonogram, as required by law—it would be printed out and offered to her—before she made her final decision. He said he could direct her to websites and telephone counseling, and apologized for having no on-site counselors. "Funding," he said.

His questions made her wonder if she knew very much at all. But it did not matter.

She thanked him, and when the door opened, Aunt Therese was waiting right there. In stark silence, with Highway 90 zipping beneath them, they were headed back to Biloxi, nosing toward the police station.

The town looked different to her now—the historic Saenger Theatre with its fancy arcade, Mary Mahoney's Old French House with its white tablecloth settings in the windows, the marbled columns of a seventy-five-year-old bank where businesspeople strolled in with money matters to discuss, a shop called Great Expectations with mannequins whose big bellies bulged beneath brightly patterned muumuus.

This small wedge of town was neither the snazzy beachfront with its jangly casinos, nor the blocks of extraterritorial Southeast Asia, where Daddy made his home and where she could easily stay put the rest of her days.

This little world in front of her now, she decided, would make a much brighter place for Joe and her to start out together. She even saw their home—a condominium with plant-filled balconies and a swimming pool in its courtyard.

"Oh, I think that's Joe's car!" It was parked near the maternity shop.

He was standing just the other side of his cruiser, completely still, looking dead ahead at something, somebody. As they got closer, she saw a figure crouched down holding a bright object: Daddy, wielding his fish-gutting knife.

"You have taken the honor of my daughter," Daddy yelled, waving his knife in the air.

Joe's hand moved to his hip; no, not just his hip, his holster.

"You have brought shame to my family," Daddy went on, "and now you will do what is right. My grandchild will not be a bastard. My daughter will not be a tramp."

"I'm leaving here this week," Joe said. "I'll send her money. Don't you worry, I'm not a deadbeat, I'll send her money. I'll be in Corpus. I'm going to be married, Mr. Nguyen, Cam knows that, she knew that, I didn't do a damn thing anybody wouldn't do in that situation, just the wrong thing happened 'cause of it. But I ain't a son of a bitch, I'll give her support, my own daddy taught me that much. And I'll be rich enough, too, real soon. Not a cop, either."

"You are son of a bitch," Daddy shouted, the knife seeming to catch a reflection that hit the window of the shop and became a wavering figure unto itself.

He lurched forward now. Joe pulled his gun.

"Stop, stop stop!" Cam cried and rushed between them.

She waited for the slash of the blade, the crack of the pistol, the shattering of lives, but it was as if an invisible presence reached down and put a soothing hand on each man's brow.

They stopped, they lowered their heads. They backed off.

She turned and walked away, moving in a daze through the streets of a town where she would never be Mrs. anybody, but protecting her daughter as Bodhisattva protected her, vowing to go it on her own.

When the phone rings, she waits for someone else to answer it. From the chair to the table is a long way—it has gotten so hard to stand up on her own—and Cam is not there. Mrs. Torres is not there. Angela is not there.

"Hi," says the recorded greeting, "this is Frank, we're not here to take your call, so talk to us now, or holler back again, for me, Angela, or Nana. Later, amigo."

"I'm here," Nana calls out. "I am here."

"Hello," says a familiar voice through the loudspeaker of the answering machine, filling the room with a slow, deep, friendly Southern voice, "I'm trying to locate Christiane Rosengarten, oh . . . Fields."

Like a shot of elixir, the voice picks her up off the chair and she latches on to the receiver. Pressing it close to her ear, she says, "Hello, hello, this is me." The voice moves like a bright streamer in the air, turns, and flutters through her brain. He says he has been trying to reach her for so long, that they have so many years to catch up on, that he is well and feels deeply happy knowing she is well.

"Rosey," she says, and he says, "Yes, Rosey."

"Rosey," she repeats, "my Jewish poet," until he laughs and says he will be coming to see her very soon.

After he has hung up, Angela comes in the door and says, "It's nice to see you smiling, Nana, I'm glad to see you in a good mood."

Nana explains, "I got a phone call."

"And I got a phone call, too, Nana. From Frank! I heard his voice. Three words, he said three words. 'Angela. Home. Me.' They were like gold, better than all of Shakespeare, better than the whole Bible. His voice!"

"His voice," says Nana.

"I'm going to see him," Angela says excitedly. "Mrs. Torres will be here, and Cam's going to come stay here for a little while, too. You'll be okay."

"I knew he would call," says Nana.

"I did, too," says Angela.

"It was Rosey," Nana says.

"Come here, sweetheart."

Angela's arms around her only make her yearn to feel his arms again all the more.

PART IV

Heavy Weather Blues

FIFTEEN

Heart's Destination

Beneath her the Gulfport Airport dropped away, and Angela looked down at the tiny figures until they were blurs: Nana, Cam, Mrs. Torres, Big Frank, the Gin Circle, Frank's friends from Keesler. She clutched her itinerary: Gulfport–Atlanta–New York/JFK–Frankfurt, Germany. This time tomorrow she would be at Frank's side at Landstuhl Hospital at Ramstein.

The plane looped out over the Sound, Frank's Ship Island a mirage. She had told him that Heaven was perfect moments strung together, and hers were bountiful: New Year's Eve at Captain Reggie's with the fireworks igniting the sky, dancing to country rock and Delta blues at their wedding party, blowing beignet powder like fairy dust all over each other at Café du Monde.

As she looked down at the Lego block casinos, the island slivers, and toy boats, she realized that every moment before the fated call from Baghdad had been Heaven enough. Even the disagreements, the fretting about Nana, their moments of marital fighting—it was glorious, all of it, in that they had each other whole.

She settled into her seat and looked over the movies and music the Gin Circle had given her for the trip. She chose something Frank would like: "I Walk the Line," popped it into her laptop, and fell asleep to Johnny Cash's gravelly voice, vaguely aware of the pilot seemingly a moment later instructing, "We'll be starting our approach to Atlanta, please make sure your seat belts are fastened and tray tables up."

"*Exhaustion.*" That's the word that came to mind, body, and soul.

Since the moment Big Frank had come hobbling over the parking lot like a damaged town crier calling out the grim news, she had hardly been able to sleep, her brain always going, fretting, seeing Frank bandaged, bleeding, then hearing his first lone syllable, his brief responses, a few words, then more as the prognosis for his recovery improved and he had eluded blood clots or permanent nerve damage.

How long would he be at Landstuhl? How long the therapy to bring back his speech, his fine motor? She had seen those specials on CNN and PBS about the wounded, but she had always turned the channel. Her story, she vowed, would end happily.

Changing planes in Atlanta, she moved with zombie fatigue through the airport corridor. With her purse chockablock with cards from well-wishers, she kept expecting out of habit to have someone, somehow, know who she was and offer words of support to her, a prayer for Frank. They were only strangers, though, wrapped in their interior lives. On a TV screen mounted overhead at a terminal were pictures of a bomb attack in Iraq, a funeral procession with Iraqis beating their chests. Beneath the screen, passengers sprawled on chairs reading glamour magazines and slurping yogurt cones.

Near the shuttle to Concourse C, she saw a group of men and women in green Army fatigues standing in a cluster. Their presence buoyed her, and she thought to approach them, telling of her mission, but what if they were bound for a combat zone? *"Dear God,"* she silently invoked, *"keep them safe from harm."* She headed to her New York flight.

She settled next to the window, and a frail, elderly woman came down the aisle assisted by a stewardess and took the seat next to her.

Angela felt the woman looking at her. "Don't be nervous, honey," she heard her say as the plane began to taxi. "It's not my time to go, and if it's not my time, it's sure not yours."

Angela glanced over; the old woman smiled. "I was just making a little joke," she said.

They introduced themselves. Rochelle Goodkin was from Brooklyn and lived in Atlanta. "My friends up North can't believe I can thrive in the heart of a red state," she said, "but I tell them we're our own little blue pocket."

The plane rose up. Atlanta became a little Oz beneath them.

"What about you, dear?"

"I'm from Mississippi. I did live a year in Rochester, New York, when I was little, with my dad. My husband's in the Air Force."

"Oh, that's nice, you're going to meet up with him?"

"Yes. You could say that. He's . . ."

Angela bit her lip and looked out the window. A skein of clouds muted the sprawl of suburbs giving way to the patchwork countryside.

She turned back to Rochelle. "He got wounded, a Humvee, yes, in a Humvee. He does weather. Can you imagine? He's the only guy in Iraq eager for a sandstorm, and then the bomb, it just blew up under the wheel of the car. I'm on my way to Germany to, oh God, to see him." She leaned forward and put her head in her hands.

She felt the woman's hand on her back softly patting, and heard the stewardess ask, "Are you okay, ma'am," and Rochelle answering, "Her husband's a soldier who's been hurt in the war. I'll look out for her."

"I'm okay," she said, sitting up and wiping her eyes. "It's just so—"

"Emotional. Of course," said Rochelle.

"Thank you, ma'am."

Out the window the ground disappeared as they were enveloped in clouds, and she was reminded of Biloxi Beach the morning she waited for first word of Frank. That fog had been like a curtain dividing one part of her life from another. Who knew where she would be when they broke through that curtain? She felt a strange tingling in her chest and had sudden shortness of breath. She reached up and fiddled with the air vent, tilted her head back to catch the cool stream in her hair. She began to suck for air.

"Dear, do you want me to page the stewardess?"

She shook her head.

"It's my heart, I think . . ."

"You're having a panic attack," said Rochelle. "Who wouldn't in your situation."

"How do you . . . know . . . how . . ."

"I've counseled prisoners, and patients in rehab. I know. You're feeling trapped."

"And out of control," Angela said.

"And angry," said Rochelle.

"I'm not angry." Her breathing began to steady again.

"*I'm* angry," said Rochelle.

Angela turned and looked at her. "Did *you* lose somebody?" she asked.

The stewardess pushed the drink cart by and they requested sodas and Angela suddenly felt like she had known this woman a long time. Was it Nana she saw, or her own mother allowed to grow old? The tingling left her chest; she felt her body relax.

"Feel better now?" Rochelle asked.

"Yes ma'am."

"You don't have to 'ma'am' me. I'm not a relic."

Angela nodded and laughed.

Even to her own ear, it sounded odd, unexpected—a laugh. It was the first one that had skittered up through her since she had rolled down the car window to hear Big Frank's agonizing news.

"I'm not an old bitty either," Rochelle said, "though I sure look like one."

"My Nana's feisty, too."

"Why are we 'feisty' and 'spry' once we hit eighty, in my case ninety?"

"You're ninety!?"

"One," Rochelle added.

The clouds broke and Angela looked out, imagining she could see as far as the European shores. Only a little bit farther was the hospital—the bed—where Frank waited.

As she told Rochelle about Frank and his tour of duty, and the IED, and Ramstein, the white-haired lady nodded, closing her eyes.

"I'll let you nap," said Angela.

"No, I was visualizing him. It's a form of prayer."

"What church do you go to?"

"Roman Catholic. I'm a sister, a Loretta nun."

"Oh, forgive me!"

"You didn't insult me."

"Do you live in a monastery?"

"No, dear, but I do live in a residence."

They fell silent. The captain announced they were flying over Richmond.

"Why did you ask if I was angry?" Angela said. "Do I seem angry? I was laughing a moment ago."

"I was a friend of Daniel Berrigan's," Rochelle said.

"Who?"

"Father Berrigan, before your time. He was one of the opponents of the Vietnam War. We visited Thomas Merton together at Gethsemani, the beautiful monastery in Kentucky. How they would have risen up and protested against this war. I was even thrown into jail once during a sit-in on the walk in front of the White House. They said we were disrupting traffic. What we were disrupting, I'll tell you, was the complacency of a government that thought it could operate with the arrogance of divine right. Only God is beyond question."

"My husband hasn't done anything wrong," she said.

"No, no, he's a soldier. He did what he was asked to do. A foot soldier, like us all, no matter the branch of service. But it is we, in blessing these soldiers, in praying for their safety, for their healing, who have the right to be angry. Who must be angry."

"But if I'm angry," said Angela, "that only hurts him."

"Then I'll be angry for you. We shouldn't be in the war. The blood of innocents is being shed and no good is coming of it. Only heartache."

Rochelle reached over and put a hand on Angela's folded in her lap. Soon the pilot reported they were passing above Washington, D.C., then, through the sparkling clear sky, the nation's halls of government, the gleaming monuments, were spread out in serene white geometry.

"When I was a little girl," Angela said, "I took a trip with Nana and Lucky, my grandparents, to Washington."

"There's a happy memory."

"And I went with my dad and his new wife—his first new wife—to Manhattan once. I hated it. I got separated from them for, like, five minutes, but it seemed like an hour. I sure never thought my next trip there, even through there, would be because of something like this."

"It's got many wonderful things about it. Maybe you and your husband will take a nice, long weekend there one day. Catch a Broadway show. Stroll Fifth Avenue."

"I guess I am a little bit angry," Angela said suddenly, "but then also I have to believe he did it, Frank did it, to keep us safe from harm. That's what he always said."

Rochelle squeezed her hands harder. Angela shut her eyes and pictured Frank next to her in the glider. When she opened them again, the Manhattan skyline was below. It was just like in countless movies and TV shows: Rachel and Ross, Jerry and Elaine, Harry and Sally, they were all there.

Rochelle pointed out the Chrysler Building with its spire like a big piece of rock candy, the Empire State Building, which, no wonder, was the place King Kong staked his chest-beating claim. She remembered seeing that as a kid, and having that image in her head.

The city rising below did not seem frightening now but grand and approachable, oddly welcoming. She imagined being with Frank in his glider soaring over the peaceful canyons, ten thousand thermals at their bidding.

"There," a man said from the opposite row and pointed toward Angela's window. "That's where it was!"

"The Twin Towers," explained Rochelle.

Angela looked out to a swatch of sky over the Hudson River where they had loomed. Even against the craggy skyline, the World Trade Center void caught her up with a shock. She thought of how the workplace and daily crossroads for thousands of people, as lively as a casino floor, had become a smoldering graveyard.

"Yes," she said to Rochelle. "I did get angry. About that." She pushed her finger against the oval window. "And Frank was angry, too. That's why he decided to do something. He's a man of God, too. Deeply. Passionately."

"I'm sure he is, dear."

The plane changed direction and veered back toward New Jersey.

"What's wrong?" the man across the aisle asked.

"Are we reversing?" another said.

"Maybe it's a holding pattern. JFK gets jammed up . . ."

The pilot's voice came evenly over the loudspeaker: "Ladies and gentlemen, this is Captain Weaver, we want to thank you for flying with us today. We've just gotten word from the control tower that there's a situation at JFK—all's well, but it needs to be checked out—and we've been instructed to land at Newark instead. I'm sorry for this inconvenience."

"What kind of situation?" someone shouted.

The pilot's voice: "We've been cleared for landing. Thank you."

At the terminal they crowded around a gate agent, who told them JFK was temporarily closed due to a terrorist threat. The alert level had been raised to orange.

"Will I be able to make a Germany flight?" Angela asked desperately.

"I'm sorry, ma'am, all departing flights have been put on hold. You'll have to go out tomorrow. We have lodging and meal vouchers for you."

"Look what's happened," she said to Rochelle, who appeared next to her. "Look how they're trying to mess up our lives even now! Yes, I was angry at Frank, too, for leaving me to go off like that. I was angry at him for getting hurt, and at the men who got us into this war to start with, but all this—I saw the Twin Towers fall, I was in Mississippi but I saw them fall—reminds me how important it is what he's doing. It's a threat today, but it could have been the real thing. He helped keep it from being the real thing."

"Here, dear." Rochelle reached into her purse and pulled out two hundred dollars. "Use this for a hotel room in Manhattan. I'll help you find one."

"I can't accept that. I've got a voucher here for an airport hotel."

"You don't need to stay way out here in Jersey, with all you're going through. At least see New York. You'll feel at home this time, I know you will. Take a picture of it for Frank. It's my contribution in honor of your family's sacrifice."

"Thank you," Angela said, finally taking the money. They rode in a cab together and exchanged numbers and addresses.

"We'll say the Mass tonight for Frank," Rochelle said, leaving her at a midtown hotel and giving her directions to Rockefeller Center and to Broadway.

In her hotel room Angela sank against the edge of the king-sized bed and it felt like a vast ocean around her. "Here I am in New York," she said to herself, determined not to cry, "without you." She took a deep breath, called home to tell of the delay, and left a message at Ramstein with her cell number when unable to reach Frank's room. She stood, brushed her hair, put on some lipstick. "Well, I'll see it for both of us."

People streaming by her everywhere—a leggy model in a short red skirt; a large man cradling a Chihuahua in the crook of his arm; a cluster of Japanese businessmen pointing up at buildings, exclaiming and photographing; young women about her in sleek business suits but wearing running shoes with their dress shoes slung over their shoulders. Never had she seen such movement, such quickness, certainly not on Canal Street in New Orleans, nor the corridors of the Atlanta Airport, nor even the casino floor of the Cotton Gin after a slots player hit a jackpot and throngs streamed over, enthralled by the flashing and ringing machine.

Whatever fatigue she had started out with that morning was left behind as she became energized by the quick-moving and stylish people around her. What would it be like to be one of them? To work in an office with views of towering buildings as water cooler colleagues passed gossip of romance and money like in the movies? To take a lunch hour at an Italian restaurant and make her way on any old workaday evening, the lights beginning to glow, to Rockefeller Center? Arriving there, she looked out at the gigantic statue of Prometheus spread out on his side holding stolen fire. She remembered learning his story in high school, how brave he had been, how noble, to bring mortals the gift of heat and light, and safety. In the plaza below Prometheus were festive café tables where New York couples enjoyed a leisurely evening somehow blithe despite the anguish, she knew they must still nurse, of September 11.

"I could do that," she said, peering over the wall at the diners below. Would Frank like the City? Would it be a place, like that old movie with Barbra Streisand and Robert Redford, where she could love her soldier and they would walk hand in hand through Central Park, except they would not argue about this war? They would not argue about anything.

She scanned the hundreds of faces around the plaza, saw the couples being photographed with Prometheus as a backdrop. This was the bull's-eye: Manhattan. Who here had known someone in the World Trade Center? Been on their way to work there that day—so many stories she had heard on the news about near-misses—or had a brother, aunt, husband, child, sitting on the high floors when the planes came crashing through? What Frank sacrificed, she knew, was surely valued here.

But where were the American flags that hung in front of porches on the Gulf Coast? Who here had someone in today's war? She remembered the corkboard at the gas station convenience store in Leroy, Alabama, when she had traveled to Tuscaloosa with Frank to watch Alabama play Ole Miss. They had stopped for gas and snacks, and she gazed at the board filled with pictures of servicemen and women. "Who're they?" she asked the attendant. The lady behind the register had told her, "Sons and daughters of Leroy and Jackson and Thomasville, Alabama, and over the line in Mississippi, all these parts around here—that's my nephew, that there's my cousin, that one used to work at Ed's Drive-In, the boy with the cute grin is married to Martha's sister, Martha works nights here, those two Army are twins—just about everybody here has blood over there."

Is it light from outside that flashes in front of him, catching him unaware in the hospital bed that has become his home for too many long days without her, holds him mercilessly as memory blends with dream—kneeling in the Biloxi Beach sand, looking up at Brother Tim, holding her beneath the illuminated sky—or is it inside his own head, a shower of radiance? He strug-

gles to recall recent days, the drive out from the base across the hot land, the sky startlingly blue, a sandstorm lurking as low winds circled like wolves, the explosion beneath the Humvee that blacked out the world until he came to in this bed, her voice reaching him on the phone with a sweetness known only to those who had listened to prophets and saints. More vivid is a field in Marks, bright and pale yellow, his family's church at the edge, heading there with his mother and father, and his dad ascending the pulpit beginning to preach, then summoning his young son: the Baptismal pool, the water, the immersion, the lifting up and turning to see the congregation with their welcoming smiles, now his brothers and sisters in Christ, as Daddy clasped him, wet as a dog come out of a storm, saying, "Bless you, my child." Then the field is gone and he is with Big Frank and they are watching the mullet leap and slap the water and Grandaddy is saying this is my church, my sanctuary, the bay and the fish, the sun and the rain, us two sitting here like this. Then that is gone, too, and he is with Angela, in the heavens, the sailplane wings banking against the sky, currents of warmth lifting them up like a gospel choir. Then there is only Angela, enveloping him with her light. It spreads out, a holiness no single person can contain, grace and forgiveness, humility and compassion, Christ among them in an ordinary moment, the miracle of healing in the touch of hands, the Kingdom of Heaven an ocean of love, the key now in his hand. Here, he says, reaching toward her. Here, take it, my love.

The sky over New York was darkening, and after stopping for a slice of pizza and watching the mustachioed cook twirl the dough, Angela walked toward Broadway.

She found herself staring straight up at the sad half-masked face of the *Phantom of the Opera* on a theater marquee.

"How much are tickets?" she asked at the box office.

"Ninety-five dollars, orchestra."

"Oh, well. Thank you." She stepped away. What would Frank, lying in his hospital bed, say to that! They could watch a DVD of the movie when he got back home.

A man in a tan sports jacket approached her and said he had extra tickets from his office, that a group had planned to attend but a few in the group were stuck in a meeting in Jersey.

"How much?" she asked.

"Half of what you'll pay at the window."

"Well." She glanced up at the marquee again. Rochelle's gift had covered her hotel room. "Okay," she said impulsively.

He handed her two.

"Oh, no, my husband, he's not . . ." She stopped. "It's just me." She needed to tell somebody, anybody in this swirling city of strangers: "He went to Iraq. He got hurt. I'm on my way to see him."

"You don't have to make up a story," the man said, taking one of the tickets back. "Keep the other one, on me. Our office paid for them anyway. And if it is true? Those bastards."

She had never imagined a theater could be so plush—murals on the walls, a glittering chandelier overhead. She switched off her cell phone and leaned back in the deep maroon seat. The lights went down; the orchestral music went up. She was alone, unknown to anybody, all to herself in the cozy theater as the phantom's haunting voice filled the rafters. He appeared onstage in the opera house depicted onstage. What was so wrong with him except that he was damaged in his appearance, like a man wounded in the head, but whose heart beat ardently with passion for his beloved, Christine?

She had an image of young Nana and the name "Christiane, Christiane," and the man who could not show his face locked away, writing his beautiful and haunting letters.

No matter how Frank came home, she vowed—perhaps his vision ruined, his face half crushed, wanting to hide out from the world—she would always love him, want him, be forever his.

The phantom's voice soared in song. Angela was borne up on it and she knew she, too, would go with this wounded man, already enchanted by his mysterious sadness.

She tried to conjure Frank, but enshrouded in the theater with the phantom's exquisite aria filling her, she could not envision him at all.

Was somebody touching her shoulder? She glanced back but

glimpsed only a row of rapt theatergoers focused on the stage.

She felt the touch again, gently, on her neck, then on her lips, a brush of sensation, a whisper of touch.

A chandelier went swinging through the theater, crashing onto the stage, and everyone gasped at the theatrical effect, but it was the phantom and Christine singing together that held her, their voices calling, responding, interweaving. Her skin tingled as if she were being caressed.

The curtain went down and the applause went up, and the returning lights were a shock to her system. She had forgotten it was a play.

She checked her program: fifteen-minute intermission.

The melody of "Music of the Night" wove through her head. She tasted salt at the edge of her mouth and touched her damp cheeks.

She shuffled out of the theater with the others, wanting to stand outside a few moments to take in the lights of the City. By the marquee passed a man with a limp, another grizzled and lost, another, a woman tall and stately and lonesome looking. Would anyone here think twice about the phantom or any other freak of nature?

She looked down Broadway to Times Square and saw the electronic clock. It was a little after 9 P.M. By now she would have been snug on the flight headed to Germany, Frank only a few hours away. She remembered Rochelle's exhortation to take pictures. She turned on her cell phone and was about to ask a lady she recognized from the audience to take a photo of her with the City behind her that she could text Frank when her phone powered on. Could she possibly, in such a short time, have six new messages?

She pressed the small receiver to her ear and listened through the waves of traffic to the voices of Big Frank, then Mrs. Torres, then Big Frank again, Captain Reggie from Biloxi, a Dr. Sams from Ramstein, all saying, urging, pleading with her to call, that there was an emergency, news they could not leave as a message. When she punched the numbers to get to Germany, Dr. Sams answered, and with his first words, "I'm sorry, Mrs. Semmes," she could not at first speak.

"A blood clot." That's all she heard.

"Mrs. Semmes, are you there?"

"Yes," she answered weakly.

"It was sudden, a blood clot in his lungs, less than an hour ago. He died in his sleep. There was no suffering."

"Thank you," she mumbled.

"Mrs. Semmes . . ."

She closed up the phone.

She started down Broadway.

The faces were phantasmal to her, watery and elongated, as if the whole world had become insubstantial. The sidewalks were wobbling and the lights shaking on the cosmic billboards with actors promoting shows and celebrities hawking running shoes and enormous lips puckered with lipstick and buff bodies modeling underwear, and the words "MTV," "Benneton," "Hanes," "Coca-Cola" giving way to a giant news ticker beneath the ball that fell every New Year's Eve, but now time was stopped, the whole urban kaleidoscope was stopped.

Less than an hour ago. In his sleep. No suffering. In his sleep. Less than an hour ago.

"Maybe I heard wrong."

She opened and looked down at her phone: two more messages. She jammed it to her ear. The first was from Big Frank, he was sobbing: "We'll do him proud. He'll be buried with full honors, Angela. Our family plot's right here in Biloxi. He makes us proud."

The second was from Mrs. Torres, who said, "Angela, Christ be with you and the spirit of Mr. Frank, and your Nana wants to talk to you."

How she could hear her grandmother's small voice within the cacophony of the City, she did not know, but like a child able to detect her mother's voice in a crowded room, she caught her utterance: "I am so sorry to hear this sad news. I love Frank, and I love you, my Angel. You're a good girl."

Good girl? How old was she, thirteen? Yes, thirteen, and news had come just like that: "Your mother, an accident, the hurricane, the traffic, lights all out, he didn't see, right into the intersection. It was instant. She didn't suffer."

Nana had spoken to her then, too.

She found herself on a little island in the middle of the Avenues, a "V" of concrete between Broadway and Seventh Avenue, where a shirtless man maniacally beat a snare drum. He looked like a windup doll unstopping in his rat-tat-tat, a drummer boy gotten old and gone berserk. Near him four teens did break dancing to rap, one slithering on the ground, another doing a handstand.

Out of nowhere an F-16 fighter jet zoomed at her, and she looked up to see film images rolling out above a small building with the words "U.S. Armed Forces Recruiting Station. Be master of the sky. Work with the latest technology. Enjoy your life. U.S. Air Force."

The pictures changed, images tumbling over her of the airmen, soldiers, sailors, Marines, with the names of the service branches and a movie loop of proud men and women taking their nation's fate into their hands. She walked up close, repeating, "Frank, Frank," the recruitment center closed at night, its projections of Americans in uniform looking like one more entertainment at the global crossroads.

Frank.

She leaned back against the doorway with the F-16 zooming over her again and felt a pain in her belly as if she had just been kicked, and she grabbed her midriff. Convulsions began to wrack her body—tears would not flow—and she slid downward until she was against the base of the door. She straightened her legs out, put her hands on the cement ground, and leaned back, trying to breathe slowly.

"Taxi!" she heard someone call, and a clutch of young people laughing and shouting raced over the small island, waving down a cab, stepping over her as if nobody were there at all.

SIXTEEN

Journey of Return

"It's not fair that it's spring," Angela thinks, gazing out over the tarmac of the Gulfport Airport at the Japanese magnolias blossoming beyond the runway, their creamy pink petals like a mockery of the airplane's hard, silver steel.

"Ten—shun!" a commander says, and the honor guard snaps to attention. The transport hold opens. The casket is lifted up, the gloves of the honor guard like doves against the deep red, white, and blue of the flag.

She has been waiting, heartsick, for hours, for days, for this moment. The flag draped over the hard oak surface softens the blow. Its red is deeper than the winter magnolias, blue richer than the Mississippi sky, stars brighter than Orion, which Frank loved to point out to her when they ambled the night Sound.

The photo of Frank in the *Sun-Herald* that morning —"Biloxi Patriot's Final Trip Home"—is in her hand: blue dress jacket, chevrons visible on his shoulders, cap a neat "V" on his head. But the one she holds, clutched with her handkerchief, he gave her one New Year's Eve. It has been little more than two years since then, she realizes, but the calendar tells a lie. They had been innocents, youngsters reveling in the expectation of life without limits. She imagines them as she does when thinking of Nana as a young woman walking with Rosey by the Washington, D.C., reflecting pool. Angela and Frank had been children, their stories from long ago.

The honor guard step forward, bearing Frank toward the hearse, and she reaches out and lays her hand upon him: his shoulder in the bright Mississippi Sound sun as the ferry thrums out toward Ship Island; his chin on a midnight lawn sweeping down to Back Bay with New Year's fireworks in the air; his chest in a French Quarter hotel with a single day spread out before them seemingly without end.

Underneath the flag is only unfeeling wood.

Behind the hearse on the way to Victory Brotherhood, she rides with Nana and Big Frank, a widow now, looking out at azaleas bursting against fences, opening in endless turns against office walls, mechanic garages, trailer park entrances, and antebellum homes. Some poet, she recalls from school, said April was the cruelest month, a bizarre statement when she first read it. Now she understands; on the Gulf Coast it comes in late February and early March.

At the church they meet up with Mrs. Torres to assist Nana, Frank's cousins from Tulsa, and Cam is there, too. They wait together as the flag-draped coffin is lifted out by the white-gloved hands, carried ceremoniously—step, step, a dignified march—into the church doorway. With Angela leading the procession, Frank's mother and sister close by, they enter behind it.

On the altar Frank's father is waiting in his black suit, Bible in hand, Brother Tim beside him, solemn. Every pew is filled, mourners standing in the back, in the balcony. She recognizes many—the Cotton Gin Circle, Captain Reggie, the weather warriors, students from Biloxi Junior College, and people she has never seen, onlookers, she wonders, if Frank even knew.

Her wedding procession—it comes back vividly, the chapel garlanded with white azaleas, the Deep South spring comes rushing round again.

When she takes her seat in the pew, she hears the words "duty," "honor," "flag," "country." She looks around. She catches a glimpse of Cam's father in the back row.

Where's Frank?

When people start weeping around her—Who are they? What loss is it to them?—she has the sensation of standing in a place apart, as though she were on Ship Island and all the others were on the mainland, and they are listening to a music she cannot hear.

But shouldn't she cry? All their eyes are watching, she can feel them, waiting for her to break, "a widow's tears," a Gold Star widow, no less, but she is a newlywed still and he is beside her, touching her on the shoulder, the sign he had given her in the theater.

She is here to renew her vows. "*We will,*" she pledges, "*never let our love grow old.*"

Even in the procession back out of the church, with the flag-embraced casket carried ceremoniously by the plaque that tells how Hurricane Camille left this chapel standing, even as she climbs into the limousine to follow the hearse to the cemetery, she feels like she is going through the motions. She looks out the limo windows, at the sky now brushed with charcoal clouds. "*Hurricane season,*" she thinks, "*will be here soon.*"

Under the cemetery skies the azaleas, like visitors desperate for notice, tumble around the grave yawning wide, indifferent. She feels not like she is in her own body but alongside, an unfeeling twin watching the casket taken out of the hearse and set up next to the gashed earth.

The salute, the troops, the volley of rifle shots by the honor guards— it all begins to pull her back into herself. Her twin is gone; it is only her.

Why are they removing the flag from Frank's resting place? Folding it neatly, crisply, into a triangle, walking toward her with it?

"*No, he cannot go without this flag.*"

The casket stands bare, stark, next to the soil's gaping wound.

No.

Receiving it from the commanding officer, who is saying, "On behalf of the President of the United States, the Department of the Air Force, and a grateful nation, we offer this flag for the faithful and dedicated service of Staff Sergeant Franklin Semmes," she clutches it and folds it to her bosom. It is warm.

She closes her eyes and feels her chest caving in and a rush of sadness like the explosion of a roadside bomb sends her to her knees.

She knows she is letting go of a sound held deep down in her diaphragm for which there's no room now in her body. She hears the keening as though from far off, but it rises up through her throat, the only sound in the world. The triangle of flag in her hands, her life preserver, is all that holds her up in a sea of tears.

When Cam played Mendelssohn, she floated with the music. Within the arc of the notes, melodious and somber, she drifted with her Mai. In exchange for staying at Angela's and Nana's, she spent more hours keeping watch over Nana. Two, three, four hours a day she played the tunes Nana liked, but also the composers that spoke to her own soul— the melancholy Mendolssohn, the stately Chopin, the brooding Liszt. She had been told that music could be heard in the womb.

She pressed her body close to the keyboard as she played.

She glanced out the window, thinking every police cruiser was Joe's. There had been a police escort that led the mourners from Frank's funeral to the cemetery, and she had craned her neck, saying to herself: *"That's Joe. I know it is."*

Since that day she had walked away from the two men in her life in their standoff—the Bodhisattva laying a hand on their brows, the Biloxi streets shimmering with Quan Am's presence—she had not so much as glimpsed him, though. She had driven by the precinct station at odd hours, but there was no Joe. She had listened to a friend's police band radio, but his quick and pressing voice was nowhere.

She thought again of the world they could have made together, a space apart, like those downtown blocks where couples created different kinds of lives. When little Mai did arrive—she did not care if it was a faraway name to Mississippians—she would bring Joe and Cam together.

When Cam saw her father, they rarely exchanged more than an icy "hello."

At Frank's funeral she had been aware of Daddy in the back of the church, his head bowed, and when she had glanced a second time, he was holding his head in his hands. He looked, suddenly, so *Vietnamese* to her, lost among all the mourners of Northern European or African lineage. She remembered how she had felt in gym class at St. Benedict's, dressing out in the girls' locker room, looking up at the mirror to see the lanky carriages and wide German and Scandinavian faces of the athletic blondes and brunettes. By their reflections she was reminded how her family had come from the opposite side of the globe to settle among these Westerners.

Angela resumed her job at the Cotton Gin, also enrolling in a new course at Biloxi Junior College. She had gotten a big check from the government, a payout from the State Department for Frank's death. But Cam heard Angela tell Mr. Flowers on the phone that she was putting it in the bank to buy a house when she was ready, not yet willing to vacate the apartment she and Frank had shared. In the meantime, Angela wanted to keep working, and among those who'd known Frank. Cam heard her tears still at all hours of night, but in the morning, as Cam got ready for school, Angela was up like a mother fixing her lunch, seeing her on her way.

Cam came home one day after school to see an envelope sitting on the piano with Daddy's familiar handwriting: *"For Cam."*

In it was a roll of damp cash.

She took it out—a wad of tens and twenties smelling of fish. She put it back in the envelope and set it on the piano and started to play. "When did he come by?" she asked Nana with annoyance.

"Your father's a nice man," Nana said.

"He's a jerk," she said.

"Now, child."

She bent to her music again.

A week later, when she heard the knock and spied Daddy through the curtain, she stopped playing and went and hid in Nana's room.

Nana rose from the couch and went to the door and opened it. She came back and told Cam, "Speak to your father."

"No, ma'am, I'd rather not."

"Speak to your father. Dammit!"

"Yes, ma'am."

She didn't have to smell the whiskey on him to know he'd been drinking. She could tell by his appearance through the screen, standing slightly at an angle, his brow furrowed, looking off.

She opened the screen and stepped outside. The liquor stench was stronger than the seafood's.

"Cam," he said in a low, breaking voice.

"Daddy," she answered quietly, then asked sternly: "What do you want?"

"I am your father."

"Why do you drink, Daddy?"

"If I had not come here, this would not have happened."

"Then you shouldn't have come."

"If we, we . . . had not come to America. This English, how it hates me."

"You speak well," she said, thinking sadly of how he looked set apart at the funeral, a face from so far away.

"It is not how I say, but what I say. To you."

She waited for him to go on. He expected her to answer him; she could tell. But she would make him twist like a fish on a line.

"I will kill the policeman," he said, "if I see him again."

"Joe . . ."

"Don't speak."

"Yes sir."

"But you are not the bad things I say." He looked at her, eyes red and damp. "You had no mother to teach you. I am . . ." He hung his head.

"Oh, Daddy."

"I am. Ashamed. Not of you. Of me."

"You've been a good daddy. C'mon now. "

"I lost Mai. I lost Kieu. Now I have lost you. If there had been no war, I would have everything."

"You have me. You will have a grandbaby soon, too."

"I am going to the boat. Take." He handed her another fat envelope. "I will be gone for many weeks. To Texas."

She shook her head. "I don't need money."

"What do I work for? Only for you. Take!"

"Okay," she said, feeling sudden tenderness.

He leaned over and embraced her and was gone.

Three days later, when she was at the Asian grocery, buying noodles and ginger and duck to show Mrs. Torres how to fix Vietnamese food, she looked up to see cousin Thanh. Sometimes he stayed back on the short runs of shrimping, but never the long ones.

"Y'all haven't left yet?" she said, surprised.

"I'm not going anywhere," he said.

"But Daddy told me he was going out for a long time. To Texas."

He pointed to his jaw. "A bad tooth, I've been to the dentist twice. Root canal, *argh!* He knew that."

"Then he didn't go?"

"He never said to me he was going."

She drove to the dock but the *Miss Mai* was not there. She drove to the Cotton Gin, parked, walked down to the beach, and gazed out at the Sound.

The horizon was empty.

SEVENTEEN

Hold Me Tight

They sit by the clock that turns but goes nowhere and the shoe boxes filled with offerings—sympathy cards with pictures of angels and crosses and hands folded in prayer, envelopes with memorial contributions in Frank's name to Victory Brotherhood, Sunrise Baptist of Marks, First Baptist of Biloxi, Little Sisters of the Poor, September 11 Fund, Tsunami Relief Fund, Disabled Veterans Fund, American Cancer Society, American Heart Association, VFW, VA hospital, Sons of Confederate Veterans, and a tree planted in his name in the Holy Land. In a big cardboard box are articles from the *Sun-Herald, Hattiesburg American, Clarion-Ledger, Air Force Times*, and *Keesler News* telling of his injury, recovery, downturn, death, funeral arrangements, along with a printout from Associated Press online showing one photo of Angela standing sorrowfully at the grave and another of the honor guard handing her the folded flag.

The news is filled with a fresh Gulf Coast–Iraq story, an Army engineer from Bay St. Louis wounded by mortar fire, and the locals turn their attention to his ordeal. Frank is the public's yesterday.

But not Angela's.

No matter her daily comings and goings—to the Cotton Gin, to class, returning home, helping out like a daughter to Nana and a mother to Cam, back to work—she is still there, the azaleas rampant over the fence, the rifle volley echoing out over the Mississippi Sound, the earth split open. It had not been windy but the azaleas had been stirring, and she had wished it to be more, a miraculous blow, an uplift in the current, a depression, a tropical storm, a hurricane. That's what Frank had needed in his final hour aboveground—the lashing of rain, the explosion of wind.

All that moves through her world now that changes, it seems, is Cam, her breasts getting fuller, her belly bowing out. As spring moves to summer and June is a big damp sponge dragged over the coast, Angela watches how the teen moves more slowly, taking her time going from room to room.

She closes her eyes and imagines it is her; that it is her body, and she is home to a life that she and Frank have made.

At Cam's high school graduation, when her father is still not back, it is Angela and Nana who go as her family, and under Cam's shiny white graduation robe her baby is evident to everyone. Angela can sense it in how quiet the families of the graduates are when she receives her diploma, how, at the punch reception afterward, the parents of Cam's friends nod and whisper when she passes.

At the same time as Angela wishes to defend her—"You hypocrites," she wants to shout, "she didn't do anything your daughters didn't do"—she feels another emotion stirring. She has felt it before, in the year just after her mother died when she looked at other girls at school functions with their moms, and hated them for it; and, already, in watching a young woman with her airman meandering around Biloxi Beach.

Envy—she knows it is wrong. The preachers had told her, her mother had told her. But it's a feeling sometimes like Frank's jealousy had been—irrepressible.

One morning, when helping Cam fix up a corner of the apartment for a bassinet, she has an urge to say, "Get out of here, I should be the one expecting, not you!"

But then Cam turns to her and she recognizes the look on her face—of waiting. Like she waited, like Nana still waits.

Another week passes, and another. Phi Nguyen has been gone more than four weeks, more than five, no one has heard from him. Cousin Thanh has insisted that Phi will come back; that he is probably making a fortune in Texas.

"Don't cry, Cam, don't cry," Angela says, watching Cam put her head on Nana's shoulder and sob. Nana pats her.

"They will all come back," Nana says.

"Nana!" Angela says angrily. "They will not all come back."

Nana looks at her, shrugs. "If you live long enough, they will."

"I want him to come back now," Cam says. "Not a hundred years from now."

"Shh, my child." Nana strokes her head. "Stay calm for your baby."

"You know, Nana," says Cam, lifting her head and drying her eyes, "there's nothing wrong with you."

"Give me that box," Nana says.

Cam goes to the drawer and brings Nana what she requests.

"Come on, my Angel."

Angela goes and sits next to her on the sofa with Cam on the other side. Nana passes the box over to her granddaughter.

Angela runs her hands over the smooth, polished surface.

She looks at Nana, who nods.

Angela unhooks the hinged lid of the triangle of walnut and opens it.

On the underside of the top are pinned Frank's medals: Purple Heart, Medal of Valor.

No one moves.

Reverently, Angela opens her hands and lays her palms on the flag that covered Frank's casket, crisply folded and set snugly into the box. She closes her eyes, feeling the gentle weave of the blue, the pebbling of the stars, the edges where it is tucked into the wood. Back and forth she slides her hands, sensing Frank. Nana's wrinkled and delicate hands lay themselves over the tops of hers, and their four hands move together in a sad duet.

It appeared like a ghost vessel in the middle of the night, up in the marshes along the coast of Louisiana, word coming from a Laotian crabber by way of a Thai seafood plant operator to the Vietnamese community of East New Orleans that a shrimp boat with the name *Miss Mai* had turned up.

The incoming tide had brought it, and its hold was full of shrimp—big, deep water reds still iced, a stick of incense half burned, an apple core still firm, a tiny Bodhisattva correct and enduring on the shelf above the captain's wheel. If the boat had been storm-tossed, someone said, surely the Quan Am would be flipped on her side.

"Nana said he will come back," said Cam as she heard of Daddy's boat from Thanh, who had appeared sadly at the door of Angela's bearing the news.

"I don't know," he said.

"Daddy is alive. Somewhere on land, he must be. He would not leave his boat for good."

"Unless he jumped in trying to swim somewhere," Thanh said. "To somebody."

Cam remembered Daddy's story of seeing Mai in the waves. She shook her head. "I want to go to the boat," she said.

"The boat? It's just sitting there. I talked to Therese."

"She's a bitch."

"What is there to see?"

"Drive with me."

"No," Thanh said. "There's no reason to."

"Then tell me how to get there." He told her, and she was off.

By the ornate Biloxi and Gulfport hotels, the columned shorefront homes of Pass Christian, along the edges of Bay St. Louis with its magnolia and bungalow streets, Cam kept on. Soon the four lanes of Highway 90 became a two-lane ribbon with humpback bridges arcing over marsh.

A blue heron lifted up in front of her and banked with its vast wings against the summer sun. The CSX train paralleled her on a trestle a hundred yards to her right then vanished into the pines.

She came to the Louisiana state line and took a road curving south, into the bayou, where tin roof shacks leaned toward bulrushes and pirogues tied to docks awaited owners to pole them into the swamp. A mossy log drifting in the water revealed itself to be an alligator, its eyes peeping out for prey.

The names of the town were unlike coastal Mississippi's—Violet, Mereaux—and the bait shops that gave way to clapboard churches that gave way to ramshackle juke joints took her to a place that seemed much farther away than the number of miles.

She arrived at a sign with a few other cars parked nearby—End of the World—where the road stopped and jackrabbits skittered and hoot owls called as she got out of the truck and saw it: Daddy's boat.

A few hundred feet away, stuck in the marsh grasses, it tilted for-lornly, a seagoing vessel too big to get back out to the Gulf. It had drifted in on high tide, surely, then as the tide streamed out, got stuck like a whale. The afternoon sun threw gnarled shadows of cypress trees across its deck.

She heard a screen door slam and looked over to see Therese navi-gating the red clay road in her high heels. Behind her was a neon sign, "End of the World," and the words "Restaurant. Bar."

"Thanh told me you were on your way," Therese said, waving her cell phone at her.

"Where's Daddy?" Cam said.

"Your Daddy's gone, poor child."

"He's not gone."

"Look out there"—she motioned to the boat—"it's so sad. He worked so hard." Therese shook her head, holding out her arms. "Poor baby, come here."

"You're not my mother!"

"Do you know why your father is gone? Lost in the goddamn sea like an old drunk?" She stabbed her finger in Cam's chest.

Cam slapped it away. "Go on, bitch, leave me and my baby alone."

"What do you think these are!" Therese went to one of the cars and opened the trunk and lifted up a rattling box of empty whiskey bottles.

"What else do you have there?"

"Nothing. Nothing. Just junk from the boat." She yanked out an old

T-shirt, a blue cap, and the statuette of Quan Am, throwing it all on the ground.

"That stuff should be mine," Cam yelled.

"You want these dead soldiers, too?" Therese shot back, dumping the bottles onto the ground. "A good name, isn't it?"

"You're dead to me," Cam said.

"I don't hear nobody when nobody talks," Therese said, slamming the trunk and wobbling back to the End of the World.

Resting the statuette on the dashboard, Cam sped back along the bayou road, imagining Daddy leaping into the Gulf to grasp at Mai but grabbing only water like Mai had done lunging for Grandmother in the South China Sea. But then she envisioned him swimming back to the boat, grabbing hold of a line left to dangle in the water, and pulling himself to safety.

How had his boat ended up without him in the Louisiana reeds?

She saw Daddy down in the hold of the *Miss Mai* fixing his engine, then leaping up to the deck and mopping it clean. Why would he ever abandon his precious vessel?

Had her Mai been disturbed by Therese's words, too? She felt a thump inside her belly. "Shh," she said.

She spread her hands over her midriff and felt the slow acrobatics.

Mai kicked harder. "You didn't like Therese either . . . Ow!"

Mai turned inside her again, pressing on a nerve, the sensation arrowing down her leg. She slowed the car to keep control, feeling the shooting subside then come again.

She breathed slowly and her body calmed and soon Biloxi was in view. She drove on to Oak Street.

At Daddy's house she went to the medicine cabinet but there was only a rusting razor and a smashed tube of toothpaste and she decided to go walk up the street to buy Tums. The doctor had said exercise was good for the baby.

When she stepped onto the front porch, she felt the stares of all Oak Street—old Mrs. Kwan doddering in her rice paddy hat; two young mothers in jeans and Hard Rock T-shirts, silent behind their matching strollers; sea-weathered men around a beaten card table who'd once borne arms for their homeland and were now gossipy ancients in Asian Mississippi.

She continued to the store and entered, by the racks of martial arts videos and dried seaweed and sacks of rice—"*Gao*," written on a cardboard sign over them—and to the counter with aspirin and cough medicine and antacid pills.

She selected one—the pain again. She stopped, waited for it to pass, then went to the register.

The man who always helped her, Mr. Bob, was Cambodian. He had been a prisoner to the Khmer Rouge for over a year and had escaped one night into mountains and walked through brutal cold to freedom across the Thai border. He kept a meat cleaver visible behind his register: robbers beware.

Mr. Bob was silent as she paid for her Tums, then as she turned to leave, he said, "What a storm in the South China Sea could not do to your father, you have now done by shame."

"My daddy loves me," she said, and left the store, heading to the house.

"Stop looking at me," she wanted to yell at the Oak Street gawkers and, when another pain came, made herself put one foot in front of the other to the front door.

"Mai, oh, Mai."

A kick again, a skittering down her nerve. "*Oh!*"

She sat hard on the counter and it was all she could do to pick up the phone and call Angela's house.

"I think," she said, "I need to go to the doctor. I'm not feeling very—"

"I'll be right there. There's no one else here with Nana, but she'll nap for a couple more hours at least."

"I can drive myself."

"I'll be right there," Angela insisted. "Nana will be just fine."

Ringing, far away. Ringing, closer. Again, like the time she was sleeping in her Georgetown apartment and the ringing summoned her with news that Rosey was missing: the receiver clutched in her hand, the speaker pressed to her ear, her eye settling on the Kiddush cup polished on the pantry shelf, her heart lifted out of her chest and carried like a tailless kite, hurtling and dipping far out over the Pacific Ocean.

Ringing.

"If I answer it, he will be there," she thought, turning over to see the phone islanded in the empty apartment. She does not have to call out for Angela, Cam, Mrs. Torres. She knows—she can sense like a change of weather—they are gone.

She sits up, sees the clock, looks at the window. *Four o'clock in the afternoon.* That's the time when the call came: Rosey is missing.

She reaches out, grasps the receiver.

"Hello?" *Why is my hand trembling?*

"Hello, Christiane?"

"Rosey!"

"I'm in town and . . ."

Laughter.

"I want to come see you."

"Yes, yes."

"Can I drop by? I've got the address."

"Yes, when? Yes, when?" *Be calm, don't repeat yourself.*

"Why wait any longer?" he says.

"I'm tired of waiting."

"Half hour? That makes four thirty or so? I'm just up the beach."

"Half hour," she peals.

"See you then. Bye."

She reaches for her silver brush engraved "CF"—Why not "CR?"—and pulls it through her hair. She begins to sing: "You're nobody 'til somebody loves you. You're nobody 'til somebody cares."

The rest of the lyrics escape her, but she hums the tune and, when she is finished with her hair, goes into the bathroom, brushes her teeth, dabs on perfume, finds a tube of lipstick and touches it to her lips, puckers, then spins out to the closet. No drab old bathrobe for Rosey!

She looks into the adjacent closet. Pretty new dresses, bright blouses, blue jeans. She lifts up one of the dresses—a simple shift, blue and yellow, takes off her nightgown, and slips it over her head. Just right.

Then she sees the shoes—a man's shoes, black leather, buffed to a sheen, and a row of shirts neatly pressed. Waiting no longer.

The doorbell rings and she goes and looks through the keyhole and there he is: still with his full head of hair, though richly silver, his slender face, full lips.

"Who is it?" she asks coyly.

"I'm a few minutes early."

Early. The word makes her laugh.

She opens the door.

He steps in and wraps his arms around her. "Christiane, oh, Christiane, my darling."

"My Rosey," she whispers.

"It's been," he says, "too long."

"You've gotten *taller*," she says as he lets go and steps into the room.

"Shorter! I used to be six-two!"

She follows him in and sees herself in the dining room mirror: the dress is a loose sack that drapes her knees. "How did I get so scrawny?"

"God has given us a great blessing to see each other after all this time," he says. "That we are both, at our ages, even still here."

"I always knew you were here."

"Let me look at you," he says. She turns; his face is close.

As he regards her, she sees in him the boy he was, still is: the olive complexion, the deep eyes. Did he have a purple splotch on the right cheek like a tumbling angel? She reaches up and touches it. "Did you burn yourself?"

"It's a birthmark."

Did Rosey have the birthmark back then? Did the Japanese captors put a brand to his face?

He steps back and she leans into him and presses her face into his neck, breathes deeply: autumn woods with a touch of cinnamon. No, the smell is more like vanilla, a soapy, creamy smell. Has she been recalling it wrong all these years?

"Remember our song?" she says.

"Christiane," he says tenderly, "I am not the same man."

"You are," she says emphatically.

"No. You just want me to be."

"Rosey, Rosey!"

"Yes, I am Rosey but a different Rosey."

"Kiss me! Now!"

She takes his face in her hands and pulls it to her and knows that mouth, full and tender; her lips moisten his.

She feels his hands larger than ever cupping the back of her head.

They linger close.

He pulls back. "Tell me about yourself, Christiane, tell me about your family."

"You are my family."

"The people you live with."

"Oh yes. Angela, my Angel." She glances around. "She was just here. Angela? Angela, see if Rosey wants a Coke."

"I'm fine. I've been eating and drinking too much at the hotel."

"I love fancy hotels, but you know that."

She goes to the couch and on the way sees a picture of her and Lucky on the dance floor in Miami Beach, cheek to cheek. Before Rosey notices, she turns it away.

On the couch she tells him about Angela, how her beloved granddaughter goes to college and needed a place to stay, so, of course, she invited her to stay here. "I take care of her," she says. "And another girl, a young friend who's having a baby. I had a baby, too, you know."

"Yes, I know."

"You've met her?"

"No, no! Mr. Flowers told me."

"I know Mr. Flowers."

"Yes, certainly, your family lawyer. That's how I found you."

"You heard about our daughter?"

"Dorothy, yes, I'm so sorry."

"She never even had a chance to know you. But she liked you."

"What?"

"She saw a picture of us, you in your uniform, I don't know what happened to it."

"Picture?"

"In your uniform. So tall, so proud, like you still are."

"Christiane, sweetheart. You're confused."

"I am not confused. Hell's bells, stop, everybody, telling me I'm confused!"

"Dorothy was not my daughter," he says. "Angela is not my granddaughter."

She looks at the picture turned to the corner. She has an image of Lucky lying against her in bed.

"She could have been," she answers. "If you had come home."

"Maybe I shouldn't have called. Maybe it's too much."

"I just waited and waited," she says. "I knew you'd come. I could tell. I never loved Lucky. I always loved you."

"You loved Rosey. The real Rosey."

"We're together again now," she says and takes his hand.

"So much time, Christiane. Too much."

The big band hour has come on the radio and "Stardust" comes pouring out in a soft cascade of champagne and romance.

She looks at him. His eyes had not been flecked green, but they are now. But his smile is the same, and once again all hers.

Together they rise and he takes her right hand in his left and puts his other hand large as a mitt around her waist and she feels his old certainty.

"Yes," she says.

"Oh," he says.

And they turn to the music.

"They played that at the wedding," he says.

Before he leaves, he writes down his number at the hotel and sets it by the phone.

She is dancing with him still.

"My warrior, my love," she says, floating.

She whispers to the air where his scent of vanilla—yes, that was it all along, vanilla—lingers.

EIGHTEEN

Double Play

"Nana?" Angela called out, stepping into the apartment, met by the droning of big band music on the radio. "Nana," she went on, sensing something was wrong. "Cam's okay, the doctor said she just needs to take it easy, she's been so upset about her dad and all."

The rooms answered with emptiness.

She had never, until now, left Nana alone for more than five minutes. She had been sure it was okay to drive Cam to the hospital. Nana had rarely, if ever, waked during her long afternoon nap.

But in Nana's room, clothes were in a heap on the floor.

"Dear God," Angela said.

She ran into the parking lot with Cam right behind, looking around the sides of the building, asking up the side street if anyone had seen "a sweet old lady in a nightgown who's a little confused."

People shook their heads, started to tell stories of their own grandparents.

"The beach," Cam said.

"She can't cross Highway 90!"

"You know how Nana loves the beach."

"Oh, I can't believe I let this happen! Please, Cam, the doctor said stay off your feet."

"I love Nana, too!"

With Cam beside her, Angela drove frantically around the adjacent blocks, inquired at the gas station, asked two boys on bicycles.

The civil war cemetery was too far for Nana to have walked, but Angela drove there anyway, and when she saw an elderly woman drifting among the headstones, she clutched her chest in disbelief—but it was not Nana.

The Biloxi Lighthouse, the sno-cone wagons, the youngsters flying kites—the coast road zipped by, upended, a nightmare taking hold. Could Nana have called someone in a moment of crystal clarity? Caught a ride somewhere?

She saw a flashing blue light up ahead and a cop car stopped and a truck and a sports car in the middle of the road with people gathering around.

She clenched the steering wheel. "Please, Jesus . . ."

"Stop!" Cam said. "There!"

At the beach, dancing along and waving her hands in the air, was Nana.

"I can't do this anymore," Angela said to herself.

She pulled into a parking bay and they hurried out and down to the water and she threw her arms around the delicate and helpless woman, barefoot, lipstick smeared on, dress twisted to the side.

"He came to see me, Rosey came to see me!"

"Don't ever do that again, Nana."

"I'm happy, my Angel."

"Promise me."

"Don't tell me what to do."

"The highway, it's so dangerous."

"He came back."

"Let's go home, Nana."

"I don't want to go home!"

"C'mon." Angela reached for her hand.

Nana slapped it away. "Don't come near me."

"Do you want to stand out here all night?"

"Maybe I do, dammit."

"Fine, c'mon, Cam, let's go," telling her under her breath: "She'll come, don't worry."

They trudged back to the car and got in.

Nana seemed oblivious to them, though. She swayed and nodded to music only she could hear.

Angela hopped out of the car and strode forcefully back to the beach. "Are you ready yet?"

"He came back," Nana said.

"My dress," Angela answered, "is a little baggy for you."

"It's *my* dress."

"Mine, but you're welcome to wear it."

"I got it from my things, right next to Rosey's shirts all nicely pressed and shoes polished."

"Those were Frank's," Angela said.

"Rosey's."

"Stop it!"

"Rosey's," Nana repeated.

"Okay, Nana," Angela said, finally coaxing her to the car. "Whatever you say."

That next morning, after walking into her closet—her blouses and slacks in disarray, Frank's shoes askew—Angela worried the time had come. Like her discombobulated closet, the life that Angela and Nana had created together no longer made sense.

She eased into Nana's room, where she was curled in the sheets, silver and slight. Angela's heart became a rock sinking in rising waters. How could she possibly, any longer, care for her grandmother on her own?

Nana had moved in and had wavering clarity of mind for so long now, but had been docile enough, easy to manage. She had been the shoulder for her to lean on, sobbing, these first months without Frank. But Nana had been impossible on the beach, insistent about her fantasy. Had she dropped off the precipice of rationality altogether? Love was not the problem; she loved her boundlessly, felt it like the Sound they walked along, savored. What about her safety, though? Her health, hygiene? How much more could she and Mrs. Torres do?

She went back to her closet and picked up Frank's loafers polished to a brown sheen, the left shoe bowed out at the side, the soles scuffed. He had worn this pair when they had wandered the streets of New Orleans. It was these shoes that had shuffled and pivoted on the French

Quarter dance floor when he spun out drunkenly, angrily, after their street corner fight.

That she had ever argued with him at all seemed like the greatest squandering of joy. She could see him walking toward her in these loafers in their French Quarter hotel room, coming close, kissing her neck.

If only she had known it was their last chance to lie together.

"*When was the last time,*" she wondered, "*we made love?*" She tried to fashion a picture of them naked together, but all she could see around her were the insensate clothes.

It was noon. She had the afternoon shift at the Cotton Gin, and though she did not have to be there until two, she decided to call Mrs. Torres. She needed to visit Frank.

She went to the phone and next to it saw scratched on a scrap of paper: "Rosey. 666-6100. Room 809."

She caught her breath. *What?*

She picked it up, looked toward Nana's room. She studied the paper more closely. What kind of ruse was this?

She dialed the number. An operator answered: "Cotton Gin Casino Hotel. How may I direct your call?"

She hung up.

She picked up the receiver again, set it back down.

This time she lifted it and called Mrs. Torres and asked her to come early.

She folded up the number and put it in her pocket.

The depth of summer brought tropical depressions and hurricanes spinning far out in the Caribbean or Gulf. There had been so many this season that Angela had lost track, but each one made her think of Frank. As she turned down a side road to the cemetery, under skies rich with cumulus clouds that would darken by late afternoon, she reached into her pocket and brought out the slip of paper again: Rosey.

"Is Nana crazy, or am I?"

Red birds swooped from a live oak and became a scarlet flag dipping and turning away over the graveyard as she pulled in. She was alone.

Frank's grave had sprouted seedlings, curlicues of green that reached up hopeful into the damp summer air. She plucked one and brought it to her lips. "*Frank.*"

It had a bright, happy scent: mint.

She pulled it apart, pressed it to her nose. What turbulent wind had blown it here to take root? She rubbed it between her palms, covered her face with her hands. Frank's hands, fragrant with soap, widened over her eyes and cheeks and mouth and chin.

She got down on her knees and kissed the earth.

She was trembling when she reached the Cotton Gin, pulling into the lot, and walked through the corridor of sexy swimwear and jangly jewelry and designer dress shops, past the hotel lobby check-in desk and to the elevator, taking it to the eighth floor.

She got off and went down the gold-carpeted hallway: 801, 803, 805 . . .

What a cruel joke this was. It was the room where her groom had lifted her over the threshold.

What jerk could have pulled this prank?

She heard the lock turn.

Out of the room stepped an old man, tall and correct, his silver hair neatly combed, baseball cap set back on his head.

He walked by her with the straight bearing of a retired military man.

It was him, she knew.

As he headed toward the elevator, she turned to see his back—his maroon jersey had "Maccabees" emblazoned across it—and she had an urge to leap on his shoulders and scratch his face off. After breaking Nana's heart for sixty years, how dare he ever show it again?

As she followed him down on the next elevator, different scenarios played wildly in her mind: Rosey coming home after the war but never telling his shattered bride; Rosey returning and telling Christiane he did not truly love her, but she had never accepted it; Rosey shell-shocked, forgetting who he was and finally remembering.

The elevator opened on the ground floor and she stepped out toward the casino. What if, she thought unnervingly, Nana had made up Rosey as a husband altogether? Maybe Robert Rosengarten had been the West Point cadet she had done "something bad" with while tipsy on champagne at the Waldorf, and he had been nothing more than that fleeting "love at first sight."

But what about the letters?

"No," she thought, "*he has returned.*" But how? Why?

Among the craps tables and slot machines she saw him nowhere. It was time for her shift. She went into the employees locker room; changed into her short skirt, fishnet stockings, white blouse, and clumpy heels; and took up her tray.

Within a few minutes, as she was serving dollar slots players near the sports bar, she heard someone shout, "Rosey!"

The tray of drinks began to shake in her hands.

"Rosey," another voice belted out merrily, "you old son of a bitch!"

In the sports bar a group of men were standing in a cluster, drinking and laughing, all wearing the same maroon jersey.

What were they laughing at? Was Rosey telling them about Nana, a foolish and decrepit woman who'd waited for him all these years?

She set down the tray and strode into their circle, pushing her way through the startled men.

"What have you done!?" she lit into him. "Rosey, right? Rosey?"

He nodded, his face going ashen.

"Whose life do you think you've been playing with? Not just any woman's."

"Rosey," one of the men said, "you old cocksman. You win the prize."

"Shut up!" she cut back.

They quieted.

"Surely, miss," Rosey began in the gentlest voice, "there's some mix-up here."

"Robert Rosengarten?"

Rosey looked at her as though a wraith had passed in front of him; his eyes got damp.

"Dear, dear, who are you?" he asked.

"Angela." She could feel her lip quivering.

"Oh, dear child. I do know who you are." He put his hands to his face, then dropped them. "Robert was my brother."

He was Ronald, he told her, and in Biloxi for a reunion of the Maccabees semipro baseball team, Jewish men from Georgia who'd played a couple of seasons in the 1940s just before the war and on into 1942.

His teammates had nicknamed him Rosey, but he'd told them it was not his name to have.

"Robert had been 'Rosey' since high school," he said as they stepped out a side door overlooking the hotel's marina on her break. "Then the war came—I was 4-F, a pin in my leg from an accident as a kid—but Rosey, over in the Philippines, disappeared. I let my teammates call me Rosey after that. It was my way of keeping him close. Every time somebody said my name, well, there he was.

"Growing up in Atlanta—we were eleven months apart—we shared a bunk bed. Rosey was up top, and as a kid he used to lie there flipping through books about airplanes. Through the window next to our bed, he could look out and see them taking off from the airport.

"Our daddy, may his memory be for blessing, had a clothing store— Rose's Haberdashers—on Peachtree. The last thing Rosey wanted to do was be a merchant. I remember the first time we went to an airfield just outside of town and watched this famous barnstormer, Bunky Wilson, who used to do air shows, stunts and things, loop-the-loops. 'That's me,' Rosey told me when we saw him that first time. 'That's me, brother.' It was about that time he started writing poetry, too. He was a dreamer all right.

"Our mama, of blessed memory, was afraid for him. I can just hear her, sitting at the kitchen table: 'You'll kill yourself up there. If man was meant to fly, God would have made him a bird.' Oh, how she went on. I think he joined the Air Corps just to put the matter to rest. He belonged to Uncle Sam now. Mama and Daddy were patriots, no doubt about it. Jews, yes, Georgians, yes, and proud Americans. When he first showed up in his uniform, she cried. If she'd only known.

"Then he met Christiane. What a beauty your Nana was. Ice blue eyes, that's the way I thought of them, yellow hair like cornsilk. Pert. We'd grown up with a few girls who looked like that, real Southern beauties, but they were off-limits. Mama warned him, 'You'll always be a Jew to her. When things get tough and the honeymoon wears off, the arguments will start, then you'll see. 'Damned Jew,' that's what it always ends up as, the name-calling.' 'She's not like that, Mama,' Rosey said. Daddy worried about the children. He was crazy about Christiane, but I don't think he could have seen his grandchildren baptized. But Rosey said, 'She can convert, I know she will, if it means so much.' She was so sweet, Daddy was a little in love with her, too, we all were."

He hesitated. There was a catch in his voice.

"She studied Judaism some when they were engaged, she even tried reading a Hebrew prayer at our big seder—she should have gotten a prize for putting up with all the family *mishigas*, craziness. But they got married in her Presbyterian church with her pastor, a family friend, conducting the ceremony despite their religious differences. Everybody wanted to make Christiane happy. They walked under an arch of sabers, danced to 'Stardust' at the party.

"And for the months they lived as newlyweds in Washington, it was all milk and honey. I'd go to dinner at their apartment in Georgetown. 'My brother,' I thought, 'what a lucky guy.' He'd always been a versifier—me, I couldn't write a Hallmark card—but after dinner he'd recite something he'd written. I remember the look in her eyes, *smitten*. An aviator-poet. Who could beat that?

"'I am not afraid to die,' he would say. 'If I fall from the air in a ball of fire, it will be in glory. For my country.' A combatant's death. A warrior's death. That would have broken Christiane's heart, split it right in two, but I think it would have healed better. Instead she got an open wound. I realize now it never healed.

"December 1941. What came before, and what came after. The dividing line for us, for them, for so many. They were supposed to meet up soon, he had a leave coming, but it never happened, as you know. By then he was marching up the Bataan peninsula. Oh, God, the misery of it all. Christiane went to stay with her mother in Richmond but couldn't keep away from Washington. She wanted to be sitting right there in the window of their apartment if word came of his whereabouts. It did, bit by bit. He was alive. He was in a camp. How was he being treated, though? We'd heard horrible reports of atrocities. Was he starved? Beaten? The Japanese Imperial Army sent out postcards through the Red Cross, typed up forms with items checked about his status. 'My health is *good*.' Check. 'I am eating *well*.' Check. An abomination.

"When I was in D.C., I'd go by to see her, and she'd be holding one of the cards, reading it over and over like it had some hidden message in it. She'd be looking at it, or at one of the pictures of him she had around the house, but I'd be looking at her, Angela. Month by month I could see the ordeal grind her down. She kept up a good front, but it was too much for anybody to bear. Not knowing. Not hearing. One year went by, another. The whole country was transformed by the war—boys going to England, to Italy, to the Solomons, to Okinawa, all over—hundreds of thousands killed or wounded. We were in anguish, too; I can still hear Mama, weeping, repeating, 'Where is my *boy*?' Christiane had two girlfriends whose husbands died at Normandy. She didn't want to complain. But Christiane's war was dealing with the silence inside her own four walls.

"Was he even alive? I asked that question, but she never did. And if he was alive, was he suffering? The Japanese were cruel. You know, my own grandson married a Japanese girl. I had to get over it at first like my parents had to get over Rosey marrying a *shiksa*, a gentile—I don't mean to offend you, but it's true—but they did, and I did. I love Sono like my own now. I had to stop wondering about her people, what they did back then, if one of them had laid a hand against Rosey. Sono never did."

Rosey paused, took a deep breath. The harbor and marina were bathed in soft light. A cruise started out with partyers up top drinking margaritas and taking videos of the casino and shoreline. Rosey waved at them.

"Rosey had gone in spring of 1941. Now it was 1944. Word started getting back of a tactic on the part of the Japanese for aiding their war effort. Slave labor. Horrible. American prisoners were being taken from the camps in the Philippines and shipped to Japan to work in the factories. A ship can be a grand thing—look out there, what a beautiful evening it is—but it can be a dungeon on the water, too. We heard the name *Oryoku Maru*, nightmare stories about POWs herded onto it in Manila. The Hellships.

"On my visits to D.C., I'd started taking Christiane out to dinner— she couldn't sit at home alone every night—and the last time I'd seen her, we'd gone dancing. We'd talked about Rosey the whole time, and when we danced, I knew it comforted her. I'd brought her flowers this time—as a poet Rosey had written plenty about flowers—but when I showed up at the door, she grabbed them and threw them in the kitchen sink.

"'He can't breathe down there,' she started saying. 'I heard how the men are jammed down in the hold of the ship that's for horses and cattle. It stinks down there, it's suffocating down there. They close the hatch. It's pitch-black. He can't get any air! HE CAN'T GET ANY AIR!'

"'Christiane,' I tried to say. 'We don't know.'

"'I know,' she railed. 'I know he needs to be up in the sky, up in God's clouds, flying. Free!'

"She picked up a lamp next and hurled it at the floor, then grabbed dishes. She was wild, Angela, what could I do? Nothing I could say, nothing I could offer, calmed her. I called her mother, who told me to call the doctor. By the time medics arrived, she had collapsed onto the couch, raving. Her family—we all—decided it best."

"What 'best'?" Angela asked.

"The sanitarium she went to—"

"Oh, my God," Angela said.

"Yes. The sanitarium was on a beautiful hillside in northern Virginia, a place where nothing, it seemed, could be wrong. There was no war, no killing, no torture. Hitler's bunker, Hiroshima and Nagasaki— all faraway nightmares. Just the tranquility of the hospital's white buildings and the patients sitting in lawn chairs looking down over the lake. Sometimes she'd start repeating, 'He can't breathe.'

"'Shhh,' I'd say.

"'He needs to be up in the sky, up in the air, flying.' Her voice would get loud. I'd try to quiet her or the nurse would come around and give her another injection."

"You were so kind to her," Angela said.

"As if I had a choice. Or could possibly want one. She was there all spring—the war was over—but there was no jubilation in the streets for our family. We still didn't know what happened to Rosey. I didn't want to leave her alone."

He was looking off into the distance, barely beside Angela.

"I had the key to their Georgetown apartment and went there one day to fetch their mail and a man showed up and said he was looking for Robert Rosengarten's wife. I told him I was Robert's brother and would take her a message.

"The man told me he was a survivor of the *Enoura Maru*, one of the Hellships. He'd been with Rosey trapped down in the hold, and they'd both been sick—just about everybody had dysentery, and most were delirious—and Rosey was raving on about home and the war and seeing his wife in seventeen days and God knows what all else. They were off the coast of Formosa, and he could hear the droning of fighter planes overhead and suddenly the ship was strafed by U.S. bombers not knowing American POWs were aboard. The top hatch of the hold flew open—I think some of the guards were rushing for cover—and some of the Americans jumped out, Rosey one of them. Two of the men were shot dead immediately by the guards, but Rosey made it across the deck and leapt over.

"The planes circled back around and strafed the ship again, this time their fire ripping into the water and tearing up the beach. Was it American fire that hit him? Opened up terrible wounds that sent his blood streaming out into the water? The accounts vary, the man told me, since others had seen it, too. In one, Rosey never made it to shore; in another, he was swimming, swimming, trying to make it no matter how wounded to the edge of a godforsaken wilderness.

"I took the man's name and said I'd deliver the message. I went to see Christiane the next day, and when I drove up, she was sitting in the sunshine. She was so lovely, Angela, exquisite. Her eyes were clear again—such blueness—and her yellow hair was washed and brushed out and long. I wanted to touch it. She looked like her old self. Could I shatter her again?

"Wasn't it better, I figured, that she always thought of him as 'lost at sea,' than dying in such misery? Was it selfish of me? Or loving? I've wondered. All these years I've wondered.

"When I knew we were coming south for our reunion, I found out she was still here through Mr. Flowers. What was I expecting? What was I looking for? To tell her what I knew about Rosey? To see if I should have acted differently, spoken differently? Or to finish a dance we'd started like we were in our twenties again?

"Here I am an old man and Christiane an old woman, and it's like we're right back where we were, like we haven't moved far beyond the last time I saw her. She got out of the sanitarium a few months later, and soon Lucky started coming around. He helped put her back together, but knew he was never number one. He accepted it.

"Me, I keep seeing Rosey swimming, swimming, trying to make it to shore, and I feel like I'm swimming. This Rosey is that Rosey and I'm him.

"Then be him," she said.

"You know"—he shook his head sorrowfully—"I can't."

NINETEEN

Never Let Me Go

If Cam could just throw off the steam bath heat of Mississippi July, ponderous even at dusk, she would feel better. With her feet at the edge of the Sound, and Mai making her feel like she weighed three hundred pounds, she turns this way and that, hoping to catch the breeze. She eases into the Sound, mild as a bath. Against her swollen ankles, even tepid water is refreshing. She looks right, beyond where the coast curves and the Gulfport docks are visible, and imagines she can see as far as Texas, where Joe, she learned from friends, married his witch bride two weeks ago and settled into a house given to the couple by his father-in-law. She knows she should be concerned about the catastrophe that befell the newlyweds—their house caught fire and they dashed to safety as it was gutted by flames, possibly arson, says the news—but she can only think of Joe's brute hand pushing her and Mai away. No arrests, no suspects. She will not even say aloud, alone here on the shallows, Daddy's name.

She steps farther, the water rising to her knees. "Bodhisattva," she says. "You know what is best."

In first darkness the harbor lights blink, red-green, red-green, and the muted sound of the bell-ringing buoy from the far-off channel reaches her like Daddy's call. In her truck is the letter from the attorney at legal aid, Maurice Goldman, saying that Phi Nguyen had instructed him to deliver all proceeds from life insurance and the sale of the *Miss Mai* to his sole daughter and heir, Cam Nguyen, in the event of his death, with details spelled out in a will. Did Cam wish to put in motion a legal claim to have him declared lost at sea? For days she had held the letter, reading it over and again. Daddy is somewhere out there, she senses, but wants no one else to know.

The wind finally rises like the harbinger of a far-off storm and brings with it the smell of seafood, shrimp boat nets, sweet jasmine, the oak trees along the road, sand still warm from the day's bakehouse sun. So heightened is her nose that she feels like a dog, a bitch full to bursting with puppies. Her mother had told her that her own grand-mother had given birth in the middle of a rice field in China. She feels as though she could split open and give birth in the Mississippi Sound.

She trudges out farther, the sandy bottom gently sloping, until the water is up to her thighs, now lapping at her hips. Her belly touches the surface. A caress. She keeps on until the water outside surrounds her like the water inside surrounds Mai.

When the water reaches her aching breasts, she takes a deep breath, lies back, and is buoyed up on the surface. The stars are winking and soon become pin lights in the velvety summer sky.

Her baby is borne of the sea.

In only a month more will be her due date, but she feels a tightening of her belly, a vise around her midriff that won't let go, then eases off. Peaceably she is floating again.

If she could lie here day in, day out—drifting, dreaming, weightless, cool—she could bring Mai into the world gently, she knows. But the contraction grips her again; lets go.

A ship's wave rolls in and she is lifted higher, as on a sofa borne by a flood, and by the time it passes, she has been pushed back toward shore. She stands, trudges in, gets a towel from the truck, and tries to dry off but there's no distinction between where the Sound stops and her body starts. Water is sluicing down her legs.

"Mai," she says, then calls her doctor on her cell phone and leaves a message. She knows she must drive to the hospital, but wants An-gela to know where she is going. Angela insists they come to the beach to fetch her; when Cam says no, Angela instructs her to come to the apartment and they will drive her from there.

"But Nana," Cam begins.

"Will come with us," Angela counters. "It's probably just a false alarm anyway."

"My water."

"Just come on."

Before she can get in her truck, though, she is nearly knocked over by another contraction and sinks to her knees on the beach, clutching her belly, praying to Quan Am not to let her baby come this moment. The seizing passes, and she starts to stand but has a rush of vertigo and sits, taking deep breaths, feeling the dizziness pass, then resolving aloud: "Cam, get up and into the truck."

If Joe had stayed with her, she thinks, if Daddy had not left her, Mai would not be so restless to come. "Do not be angry," she whispers to Mai.

But Mai is insistent; she is violent. On her back, laid low, Cam feels like Daddy's boat marooned in the weeds. Above her the stars lurch.

"Let me be calm," she prays to Bodhisattva.

"Stay calm," the voice answers, and she closes her eyes and feels the hand on her forehead. Small, delicate, cool, the palm soothes her, lets her relax all down through her body, as though bathing her in healing waters.

She cannot make out her features at first, a darkened silhouette with a corona of silvery hair.

The voice says: "It's me, Nana."

Then Angela's: "Let's get you to the hospital."

Twenty minutes later, with Nana and Angela at her side, she is rushed into delivery and feels her tiny girl come pushing out and into the glaring light of the world. Her hands are curled, doll-like, her feet miniature, her single wisp of black hair like a stroke of defiance.

Her five-pound infant utters one essential little cry then is whisked off to neonatal intensive care. Cam gazes at her wondrous but fragile daughter through the incubator glass.

What other name can help strengthen her?

After long hours, as the nurse lifts Mai out to let Cam hold her for a few moments, Cam says, "Mai Rosey," and feeling her daughter's warm breath feathering her neck, repeats it until it becomes a mantra, "Mai Rose."

Hanna, Isidore, Kyle, Lilli, Bill, Danny, Fabian, Isabel, Bonnie, Charley, Danielle, and Ivan—these storms had pushed clamorously, obstreperously, across Gulf waters over the time Angela and Frank had shared together. The dance of wind, the spinning of molecules, the rush of currents—they had shared knowledge of them while together.

Arlene, Bret, Cindy, Dennis, Emily, Gert, Harvey, Irene, Jose—she had charted these tempests alone, going to the websites Frank had used, the different tracking models looking like kite tails dipping and swooping across the screen.

The Gulf storms had become ferocious, as if looking for Frank and howling when they couldn't find him. Between Hurricane Emily and Tropical Storm Gert had arisen Tropical Storm Franklin, and she had yearned for it to sweep into the Sound so she could run out to the beach, no matter the hazards, to greet it.

Before and after.

Her whole world divided itself like that now: before, when she and Frank had walked on Biloxi Beach looking out at the kites zanily swooping and they moved as one; and after, when she meandered the beach all on her own. Before, when her bed had been filled with the hungry warmth of him next to her, and after, when she curled into herself and felt like Nana. Before, when every weather disturbance was a language Frank could best translate; after, when monster storms like Dennis that had brushed them in July, and now Katrina, churning through the Caribbean as August rolled on, filled her with even greater longing to have him meteorologically enraptured at her side.

With classes out until fall at Biloxi Junior College, Angela filled her time when not working by readying a corner of the apartment for Mai Rose.

Rosey had disappeared again, leaving no phone or address—try as she might, she could get no contact information from the hotel—and she watched as Nana stood by the window, gazing out to the Sound, humming her songs. When Nana sat in her room and tried to put on makeup and fussed over which hat to wear for Rosey's homecoming, Angela distracted her as best she could by suggesting they visit Cam and Mai Rose at the hospital. Cam was always there, keeping vigil until the intervals when she could take Mai Rose into her arms.

And she did whatever she could to keep the war away. When her friends in the Cotton Gin Circle spoke of the latest roadside bombs, the fury incited by Shiite against Sunni, Sunni against Shiite, and the Kurds caught in between, she worried for their husbands and sons and brothers and boyfriends, but could not let herself dwell on it. She turned off TV news when men appeared in fatigues, and at checkout lines averted her eyes from magazine covers with battlefield scenes. She had given all that could be asked of anyone.

She continued to visit Big Frank dutifully, sitting with him on the end of his dock as he ritually began to weep and rail at the politicians who had made this war, saying, "These jackasses don't know what they're doing over there, not one of 'em has an ounce of sense FDR had. Yankee or no Yankee, he'd have never gotten us into this quagmire worse than a Louisiana swamp to begin with."

But she could only hear so much of that, too.

He died in vain.

Those four words, the cruelest in the English language, rose up from the blather of a radio talk show that had come on after Nana's big band hour.

Had Frank?

What did it matter if she believed in his cause? She prayed that, up to the end, he had been steadfast in his conviction. Hadn't he touched her shoulder in the New York theater? Didn't that mean that what had befallen him was okay?

But what if the touch had only been a stream of air, or twitch of a muscle from her having been cooped up in an airplane half the day? What if it she had, indeed, implanted doubt within him after their fight at the D-Day Museum? What if he had lain awake those last hours in

Germany waiting for her, only her, to come to him in a faraway place to hear her say, "I am proud of you"?

Had she even uttered those words to him at all?

She remembered their last conversation on her way out to the Gulfport Airport. They had talked about money—their bank account, her new dress. They had fought over nothing.

If she had known that was the last time they'd really converse, she would have spoken of her pride, of their love. She had vowed never to erase the answering machine message and sometimes punched it just to hear his jaunty, welcoming words: "Hi, this is Frank, we're not here to take your call, so talk to us now, or holler back again, for me, Angela, or Nana. Later, amigo."

She had played their wedding video so many times that she worried the tape would rub thin, but their voices were distinct. Captain Reggie had been the amateur videographer with a low-grade mike, but Frank's "I do" pealed forth over and again.

Frank had penetrated so deeply inside her that he could never leave her body. Sex had just been symbolic of how he had entered her.

Only his body had vanished.

But, oh, if she could just have all of him back for five minutes—his smooth, boyish face, his come-to-me smile, his soothing Mississippi voice always a beat slower than her own, as if he knew the effect his easy tone had on her: calming, bringing her closer, right in.

When the mailbox rattled, she went there expecting to find more condolence notes, but just a few straggled in. What she did find now was a postcard with a picture of Ho Chi Minh City on the front. She stuck the postcard in her shoulder bag, got Nana, and hurried to the hospital.

"I didn't read it," she told Cam excitedly in the waiting room, giving it to her.

Cam took it and turned it over. There was no message. She looked at it again, then began to weep.

"What's wrong?" Angela asked anxiously.

Cam raised the postcard to her lips and kissed the handwritten address. "Thank you," she said, wiping at her eyes.

Cam spoke to the nurse of the neonatal unit, who brought them cotton masks. Angela tied on Nana's.

They went in, by a tiny almond-colored baby on his back with bluebooty feet waving; by another so pale and without movement that Angela wondered if he would make it at all; then to the doll with one fist in her mouth and the other seeming to reach out to them, and that little curl of black hair: Mai Rose.

"She's the prettiest of all!" exclaimed Nana.

The nurse reached in and lifted her up and handed her to Cam, who took her and held her close. So small, but growing feisty, her eyes already looking up like the biggest heartbreaker.

Mai Rose fastened her eyes on Nana and made the faintest cooing.

Cam presented her to Nana to hold. "Bodhisattva," she said.

In the Caribbean, she churned through the Dominican Republic, cutting the island in two. Back in the warm August waters, she joggled toward Cuba, then the Keys, missing it in a large arc.

How would the hurricane turn and spin? How many days would it take to come their way?

Mai Rose got stronger in order to meet it. Over six pounds now, she was out of the incubator for good. It would be less than a week until her release, the doctor said, the same time until landfall, predicted forecasters, for the monster storm.

The Cotton Gin put its employees on alert: in event of a projected hit, the casino would close until the National Weather Service gave further word. "Do not leave any personal items in the dressing rooms. Once the casino is closed, it will be strictly off-limits to all employees except security personnel. Seek shelter and await further word through radio and TV announcements and the Mississippi Gaming Association website."

Angela wadded up the flyer and threw it away. In all her years in Biloxi, not once had she seen the houses of chance lock their doors.

She went into her bedroom and found the link Frank had put there that took her to a weaving of lines, red, blue, green, orange, like the colors she used in her daily planner, each from a different weather group showing different bull's-eyes: Biloxi was one; Mobile another; coastal Louisiana a third; Galveston, Texas, another. Ribbons of possibility. Her life with Frank had been like that: each ribbon subject to changes of air pressure, shifts of wind, alterations of current. "You can't control the weather," he had sworn to her. Landfall would come where it may.

An icon popped up showing she had one new message. She clicked on it, not recognizing the screen name: "Hallelujah25." Another old-timer, no doubt, trolling the Bataan website and responding to her ever-lingering posting. What version of Rosey's story or an altered memory of somebody reminiscent of somebody named something like Rosey would she find?

> Hi Angela,
>
> I was a friend of Frank's, in the same unit in Iraq where I am writing you from now. He was a great guy, smart, funny, no bull, watched your back, and knew the Lord. He brought me to faith on Christmas morning. He talked about you all the time and showed me a picture of the two of you in New Orleans. I'm forwarding you a tape he made. I found the cassette in a closet, he'd borrowed another guy's recorder, and I was going to mail it but decided it'd be safer downloaded here.
>
> With sympathy and prayers,
> Simon Pulaski

She shook her head. "It can't be."
She moved the cursor over the attachment icon and clicked.
"Well, here I am, Angela, ten thousand miles from you."
She clicked stop. The room was turning. Frank's voice resonated through it like he'd been at the window looking in, then come to the door sweeping in, embracing her.

She started it over.

"Well, here I am, Angela, ten thousand miles from you. I hope you're sipping a cold lemonade, looking out to the Sound, Nana in a rocker by your side. I think about the wind in the big oaks along Highway 90, eating crab claws, gumbo, and hush puppies, then heading out to the beach barefoot. We take a swim and then I'm thinking about something else, too, that comes next, but can't say it out loud. It's on my mind plenty, though.

"What's it like here? Hot, hot hot, all the days are hot, but this one's like grit under the skin. But you know how I am, it fascinates me, this heat. Man, if we were up in my sailplane, we could ride these thermals from here to where the Tigris meets the Euphrates before we could even think about coming down. The fertile crescent, that's where Eden was. We've known our own Eden, haven't we? Just us two.

"You make me a better man, Angela, I've told you that, but I'm telling you again. I don't drink anymore, and not just because it's regulations. I don't want to, have lost the taste for it. And I'm going to stop being preachy, at least try to. You know I'm a believer, and I have to witness my faith, but I know in your own way you are, too. We have a long life ahead of us, and we'll travel it together, and when we start a family, I'm sure that God will reveal Himself to us in many new ways. I'm counting on Jesus, always have, though I might not have always known it.

"By the time you get this, I'll be heading out with a couple of others to set up tactical weather equipment at another FOB and help with repairs. But wherever I go, I'm right beside you, like when you walk on Biloxi Beach. Or when I take off through the desert landscape and you're alongside me.

"I've got plenty of other company, too. The sand and light, the heat and wind, the air currents and barometric pressure, these are all living things to me, you know. Revelations of God's grace. My key.

"Now I've got a surprise for you. About a month ago, I heard one of our Iraqi soldiers playing an oud, a kind of guitar shaped like a pear.

All twangy and spiritual in a Middle Eastern kind of way. They say it captures the soul of Iraq. I guess it does, like the blues does Mississippi. Beautiful and sad all mixed together.

"Okay, don't laugh. I asked him if he could give me a few lessons. I've been playing up a storm—well, a sandstorm, at least—and I met a master oud maker in a village outside Iskandariyah. He has to lay low, the post-Saddam crowd sometimes doesn't go for his kind of secular music. Weird, isn't it, but I started thinking about Highway 61, Muddy Waters, Elvis Presley, not far from Marks. Remember how Dylan said that God told Abraham to meet him on Highway 61? I doubt my oud maker has heard it; I'll mail him a CD when I get back.

"His instruments are really something, I think he uses mulberry for the body, mother of pearl inlays on the neck. He can only make about a dozen a year, so they cost a bundle. I've persuaded my buddies to swing by that way on our way out so I can buy one—I've got to head over to the PX first to draw some cash, hope it won't bust us!—it'll be a project for me, to learn to play it. To serenade you! That'll be a happy day!

"I've also been thinking about your Mama a lot, that day of the accident. How we went out down that road and saw the yellow VW. Squalls, tornadoes, floods, tropical depressions, hurricanes—I wanted to find out everything I could about heavy weather to stay one step ahead of it. To figure out a way to anticipate it, to beat it, to work with it. It was like all my life was decided in that moment—what I do, what I believe, who I'd meet. She was our guardian angel.

"Gotta go, love ya, hug Nana, Big Frank, bye, love ya."

Reeling from his voice, Angela walked outside and watched the cars zooming by, Mama in one of them. She needed to move about, go somewhere, do anything. Frank felt so present his absence took over the skies.

She got in her car and drove to the store—maybe she needed more bottled water for the storm, she just had to be in motion—but her attention was caught by a storefront near Biloxi Mall: "National Guard Recruitment." She turned in impulsively, got out, went in, and picked up a brochure—"Be a Citizen-Soldier"—then asked for the paperwork. She put it in her purse and headed back home, leaving it on her bedside table. Just to consider. She took the top off a ballpoint pen and laid it on top. For when the right moment came. He would let her know.

Still drunk on his words, she went outside again, goose bumps running down her arms, a prickling at the nape of her neck. Frank used to come stand out here and look at the Sound and feel the heavy weather blues in his blood and bones.

She felt it now for them all.

TWENTY

From the Sea

She heard them out the window, low and throaty, their notes like the lowest register of Cam's piano. She imagined them in the lingering pools of August rainwater, their plump bodies sensing every shift in barometric pressure. The CNN and Weather Channel newscasters were stationed up and down the coast—from the roiling surf of Pensacola to the gyrating magnolias of New Orleans—but their hurricane updates were not as telling as this muddy bass. "Listen," Frank had told her, "for the frogs."

The gulls told the story with their swooping and hurtling bodies, the pelicans in how they folded into themselves against the suggestion of a tumultuous blow, the frogs with their anxious bleat. Her own species showed off storm worries in a different way, but no less obvious: fathers bending to their children, hurrying them on to get in the car, mothers going over hasty packing lists to make sure all was ready for evacuation. They turned to their houses one last time before revving up their engines and zooming away. What pictures did they fix in their minds before leaving places that might be blown away?

What picture had Mama fixed in hers, alone in her car before crossing the intersection that horrible day? Had she been blithe, singing, looking for the first ray of sun to pop out, or delighted to see a shabby gull alight on a fence post like Noah's dove? What had Frank seen riding in the Humvee before the storm exploded in his head? The dance of sand and wind as if it were a dervish whirling for his delight?

The digital clock moved from 7 A.M. to 8 then 9. The Sound was ruffled; Back Bay was rising. The news said landfall by nightfall. Hurricanes, like bawling babies, seemed to come in darkness.

She waited for Cam's call saying it was time for their baby to come home. The bassinet stood in the corner beneath a tape-covered window.

Cam phoned; it would be closer to noon. Paperwork. They would be home just long enough to join the exodus. The phone rang again: Big Frank. Little Frank was picking him up to carry him on to Marks, he said. Did Angela and Nana need help? No, she told him, they had made arrangements and would be fine.

Angela went to her room and played Frank's tape again, turning up the volume, letting his slow, easy voice wrap around her through the humming of the wind, the first whippings of rain, the revving of car engines and pulsing of frogs. Hearing his story, she felt her emotions turn and twist, pressure rising, pressure falling.

She opened her closet, ran her hands over Frank's blue jeans, his USAF sweatshirt. She slipped on the sweatshirt. Too hot. She took it off and slung it over her shoulders; the sleeves hung down the length of her arms. Frank's arms.

She glanced through the crisscrossed window and remembered Mama next to her, showing her how to lay down the masking tape. "If the wind knocks out the windows," she had told Angela, "or sends a branch through it, it won't shatter."

She went to Nana's room and put her ear to the door; all quiet. It was odd for her to nap at this hour of the morning. Nana had been up earlier, standing at the window, up on her tiptoes as if trying to glimpse somebody, then putting her hand against her chest, reeling a moment, then saying she was going to lie down.

Angela tapped lightly. Silence.

She went into the kitchen and got down a plastic jug and filled it with water. The storm, she knew, could still bank left or right, but if the electricity were knocked out, it could affect the reservoir pumps. She filled two glass jars. The rhythms of storm preparation calmed her.

TV news said the National Weather Service had issued an evacuation order for all residents of low-lying coastal areas by 2 P.M. As of 3 o'clock the main north-south corridor would become one-way—heading north. Angela noted the clock—after 10 A.M. already. They could be in Jackson by dinnertime, Memphis by bedtime.

Photographs, a suitcase of clothes, her laptop with Frank's voice forever animating it—she made a mental list of what to pack into the Corolla.

She took out her laundry from the dryer and folded Nana's nightgown.

She went back to her door, tapped again. "Nana? We're going to take a little trip, you, me, Cam, the baby. It'll be fun." No answer. "Let's pick out something pretty for you to wear."

There was a clatter at the front door, and Angela went and opened it. Only a tree branch sprawled on the threshold. Pinecones went spinning. The sky took on an eerie, purplish glow, swirling with the deep colors of a painting by the long-bearded madman from Ocean Springs, Walter Anderson. The colors darkened and Angela imagined a monstrous, wild-haired woman—Katrina she was named—stealing over the ocean.

She stepped back inside and heard a click at Nana's door and hurried to her room; the door was locked. She rapped sharply. "Nana, what's got into you?"

"I'm not going anywhere," Nana said through the door.

She had forgotten that there was a lock. How had Nana even known about it? She reached to the sill above the doorway to find the key but located nothing.

"Open up," Angela said. "Please?"

"I have to wait."

"Wait for what?"

"For him."

"Oh, Nana. I don't think Rosey can get here again."

No answer.

Poor dear. So frightened. "We can't wait too long," Angela said, sugary as she could be, but forceful.

"You go on without me."

"Leave you here all by yourself? What kind of granddaughter do you think I am!"

"I'll have company."

"He can't get through the storm, Nana. You wouldn't want him to risk that, would you?"

"You don't know anything."

"Never mind, you just wait." Lunch would bring her out. "We've still got a while."

Hurricane updates became insistent. Category 4, the forecasters announced, no, Category 5. She remembered a friend of Frank's from California who'd told them he'd take the risk of earthquakes any day over the threat of hurricanes.

"Hurricanes," Frank had said, "in their slow approach, their last-minute decision as to which way to go, test us. How long can you look a combatant in the eye and not blink?"

The phone rang. Cam: another delay. A flooding creek had prevented some personnel from getting to the hospital and the ward was short-staffed.

"When I pick you up, we'll just go from there," Angela told her. "Tell me what you need."

News reported the forward speed had accelerated. Landfall was moved up an hour. Noon came, wore on.

She went back to Nana's room and called out: "Let's have our lunch then go out and get Cam and Mai Rose."

She jiggled the doorknob. *Don't panic.*

She finished packing, loaded up the backseat, then opened the trunk to put a box of food there. Bolted next to the spare tire was a crowbar; she could use it, if need be, to pry open Nana's door. She closed the trunk and went back in, leaving the door open with the sky dancing just beyond the screen.

Beyond Nana's door she heard noise—shoes thumping, a box falling, a clatter and bang.

"Nana!"

"Just a lamp."

"Don't hurt yourself."

More sounds, a scrabbling in the corner, a drawer opening; humming and singing.

The first rain bands were lashing against the house. The clock raced faster as if calibrated to the pacing of the storm.

"Chicken soup and grilled cheese," she said at the door. "How does that sound? Open up now!"

The frogs were braying like mules. The lights flickered. Car horns blared, a collision, the crumpling of metal. Sirens rose.

"Nana? Please?"

A whipsaw of rain.

The lock was turning—*thank God!*—and Nana stood in front of her. She was wearing a floral Sunday hat, a blue dress falling off her shoulders, and smears of lipstick around her mouth. "Is he here yet?" she asked.

Her bracelet slipped over her wrist and clattered to the floor.

"What's your opinion?"

"Let's have a look-see," said Angela, picking up the bracelet.

Nana turned, nearly losing her balance, then steadied herself and faced the front door. "I'm expecting someone," she said.

"Nana, I'm sorry, I don't think so."

"I do think so!"

"Well, let's be good hostesses then," she relented. "You look very nice. I'll fix us lunch." She headed to the stove.

"He's here!" Nana sang out.

"It's just the wind, just the wind."

"Don't be rude!"

The knock at the door was strong, insistent.

"Good, Lord," whispered Angela. She went to the window, peered at an angle. Yes, there was a man. He was a stocky senior with a little mustache, wind battering his poncho. He became clearer through the rain. "General Wheeler?" she said, opening the door.

"Christiane? *Christiane?*" he called.

Behind Wheeler was a young man, lean with wavy blond hair. He introduced himself as Jeff, the general's grandson. "Granddad just had to stop by," he said. "He was thinking about my grandmother and all."

Nana opened her arms and held on to the general. The two sidled into the kitchen and began to talk.

"I don't understand," Angela said.

"My Neenee was just like this," said Jeff. "Granddad cared for her until the end. He told me that your grandmother reminded him of Neenee, that's what we called her, and he was worried. Neenee used to get so upset in hurricanes. But some things even generals can't control."

"I've got on my Army boots," Wheeler said. He held up his left foot. "Still fit pretty damn well. They get me through anything."

"They're so"—Nana clapped her hands together—"bright and clean!"

Angela was taken aback. Nana could hardly see anymore. But the general stood taller, beaming with the flattery. "Spit shine. Can't beat it."

"We all better get going," Jeff said. "You want to caravan behind us? It's getting awful out there."

Angela told him about having to stop for Cam, but Nana hooked her arm in the general's and would not let go. "I'm ready," she said.

"Nana!"

"She can ride with us," said Jeff.

"That's very sweet, but—"

"I'll ride with them," Nana said.

"Nana!"

"Hell's bells, I have an invitation and I'm going to accept it! Who's in charge!"

"There, there," said Wheeler, patting her shoulder.

Jeff looked at Angela, shrugged. "Like I told you," he said.

The wind lifted another notch. "Okay, okay," Angela said. "I'm crazy but okay."

"We won't lose you," Jeff said, "and we'll exchange numbers. We're heading to the Presbyterian Church in Jackson, they've got a retreat center. They'll have room for all of us, if you need. I'm an RN, I've got lots of experience with this."

"What about the rest of your family?"

"Granddad and I, both bachelors," he said.

She looked at him; he had a little scrub of chin whiskers, a calm voice. His green eyes were trustworthy. They rested on her one beat longer than she would have expected, and she glanced over at him again.

"Good-bye, Biloxi," Angela sings out as she drives along Highway 90, her Corolla loaded to the gills, the Wheelers' car right behind, and turns toward Back Bay Bridge and the hospital just beyond. From the bridge she can look out at the shrimp boats bobbing and tossing and men so small before the gathering deluge throwing ropes and tightening knots while others, hoping to ride out the storm, take their boats into open water and set out anchors.

She goes through a yellow light but the Wheelers get caught by the red. She slows for them to catch up, but two more cars push in between them. She tries to call Jeff's cell but circuits are busy. "Please, God," she says.

She arrives at the hospital and Cam sees her coming down the hallway. Cam hears about Nana and the general, the nice boy named Jeff, and then takes Mai Rose outside to meet the wind-tossed world.

She imagines what her baby, cooing and gurgling, is sensing: the bunched dark-cotton sky, the shaking oaks, the starry smiles of giant people, the buffeting of wind and whirring of tires and droning of voices and now the rhythmic thump of music from the car radio, interrupted by hurricane updates, as she is strapped in her infant seat in the back with Cam next to her.

So many cars everywhere, Mai Rose takes in, their red and blue and green tops like shiny ornaments. Cam knows her daughter has no words to make thoughts, but there is something deeper, she knows, richer—the warmth of mother's finger in her tiny grip, the Vietnamese lullaby she is hearing, the humming of wind against the windshield.

"Look, how pretty!" says Cam as they drive by an American flag big as a wave curling at the Gulf. A man is lowering it in advance of the weather. It comes eye level, and Cam sees Mai Rose watching it—a dazzle of colors.

From the driver's seat Angela reaches back, blindly hunting something. Cam watches her hand search over the grocery bag filled with chips and soft drinks, then alight on the duffel. "What you need?" Cam asks her.

"Do you see Frank's flag back there? The case? I just want to know where it is."

Cam digs through the backseat. "No."

Angela pulls off the road, opens the trunk, and roots through boxes and suitcases, taking them out to see better and stacking them on the gravel.

A police car zooms up alongside and tells Angela she can't stop here, that she's creating a safety hazard. When she answers him that she needs to turn around and go back to the coast to get something she's left behind, he shakes his head. "Whatever it is will have to wait, ma'am," he says. "It's not worth the risk for you"—he looks into the car—"and look at this, a new mom and baby, no less. Pack up and keep on the way you're headed."

Cam rolls down the window. "It's my asthma inhaler," she says. "I've got to have it."

He looks at Angela, back at Cam. "Okay, then, just be careful, and start back out as quick as you can. Take the next exit and use the service road."

Angela follows his suggestion and is soon speeding along the empty side road, with a sign to Biloxi High School and nearby, down another road, serene Quan Am and the Buddhist Temple. She keeps on toward the coast by way of Oak Street.

The Vietnamese are staying put. Cam sees old Mrs. Kwan's rice paddy hat, bending in the vegetable patch alongside her house, and the door of the Vietnamese Catholic Church open with parishioners inside, and when Angela asks, "Why aren't these people leaving?," Cam says, "They're afraid their homes will be looted. They have come too far to leave so easy."

When they pass by the house where she and Daddy lived, she looks out to see children peering out the curtains of rain dropping between them and the world. Three, five, six faces she counts and wonders what stories their parents and grandparents have told them about their voyages from Southeast Asia, the wars and sea passages and storms. This hurricane, if it smashes down, will be an image from childhood that will spin after them for the rest of their lives.

Reaching Highway 90, Angela turns onto the coast road, and the sky over the Sound has gone gray, metallic, but hardly quiet. It's as though the Maker has poured dark paint over a dome and there's a swirl of blacks and charcoals and ashes, every shade of gray in motion. It is not the same sky where she and Frank soared—they would be tossed like water bugs by ribbons of thermals.

The casinos are on barges that can in theory be moved, but the once glamorous, electricity-pumping palaces of fantasy are like blind behemoths now, lights off, windows covered, the last Brink's truck making off with the loot, and Angela realizes night has come, strangely early, as the day has taken leave, too, in haste, packed up and fled in advance of the coming artillery.

On the Sound she sees the last shrimp boats struggling in, the laggards gone so far out to Louisiana or Texas and holding out just another six hours, another half day, to make their expenses, at the least before the shrimp boats might be wrecked by the plowing winds.

Still, all is in order, the water in its place, the sand an endless swatch of granules less disturbed than Frank's desert sands beneath crushing treads, the sailboats tied loose to allow for vaulting tides with their halyards clanking like a cowbell symphony and, as she slows, coming to her apartment complex, the tintinnabulation of the frogs.

Their alarm rises from the woods, the gulleys, the docks and twisting azaleas, their pulse catches up with her heartbeat, but the beat soon goes faster. They park. Cam gets out and rocks Mai Rose in her arms, humming the old show tunes, the Hoagy Carmichael and Rodgers and Hammerstein, Nana's songs, to her Mississippi newborn.

Angela turns the key to her apartment.

The flag case. Where is it? Not in the closet, not on the shelf, not under the bed. Then she sees it in Nana's room, in the corner under a spill of paper. Rosey's letters.

She sets the letters to the side, opens the case, lifts out the flag.

Frank's head against her shoulder, his eyes closed after lovemaking, his smooth cheek against hers, his breath against her skin, the soft texture of his hair like a young boy's, the line of perspiration on his brow in the aftermath of holding her, pressing into her, filling her with his heat their bodies rushing hard against each other not wanting a limit the two like wrestlers grappling close but never close enough wanting to subsume each other become the other and the turn of his head ever so slightly and his eyes opening and finding her there and his mouth widening in a smile, saying, "Hey, babe, you're amazing," and reaching over and kissing her on the breadth of her upper chest then dropping his arm and leaning down to plant his kisses on her breasts his tongue his wet and heat his hand on her leg rising up to find her moist ready for him again and he rolls on top of her.

A wind shakes the building—she feels it in the angles of her shoulders and knees—and she presses the flag close to her face, kisses its majesty as gently as she kisses Mai Rose, as she kisses the vanishing image of him, and sets it back in the box, puts Rosey's letters on top, clicks it shut, and grabs it up, hugging it beneath her arm.

"Let's go!"

When they are back in the car, the rain bands are like whips on the windshield, no rain only the beating wind until another lash comes and then it is constant. In the accelerating darkness the road has turned to a shallow stream and the cars that push through it are boats displacing the water of a narrow creek bed. Still, they can slosh along.

Angela sees the Jefferson Davis home like a refuge off to the right, no different in what it offers than the coastal hotels, the few occupied antebellum houses, the sole gasoline station still open with its attendants helping customers pump final gallons of gas—the orderliness of civilization a reminder that, when the storm finally passes, there will be normalcy again.

She goes another few blocks, looking out at the Sound, which has already crept up within a few yards of the retaining wall, then she turns right on the first street she finds, heading to an intersection that will take her back directly to the main highway and then north.

She looks up to see the traffic light ahead a welcoming green.

It is gone.

The darkness all around is instantly thicker, the electricity that bears them all up in a texture of everyday light is absent like a thin tissue of civilization rent by a rush of wind.

Cam is holding Mai Rose close, whispering into her ear, and the radio is static, and only the beams of headlights from other cars slick through the fall of water, and Angela slows, approaching the intersection carefully. "Do unto others," she thinks, and it is her turn to go, looking both ways first, and she starts out but feels a bump—her car dips to the right side—and she is in some kind of sinkhole, and as she starts to back up to go around it, a ghost white SUV roars through the intersection across the path she would have taken. It would have slammed into the passenger side, and she looks at Mai Rose and Cam in the backseat and they are blurring, and she wipes at her eyes and is shaking, and just says, "Yes," when Cam says, "Let's go home."

Back in the apartment, taking what they need out of the car and what they cherish—the laptop with Frank's voice, the pictures—they light candles, put more tape on the windows, fill more jars with water, cook up anything they can find in the refrigerator on the gas burners of the stove, and listen to the chanting of the winds.

The street is turned into an instrument. The pitch rises—a banging joins in a wrenching sound, a metal sign torn off its post like a limb fracturing—and Angela thinks, "*This is crazy*," and tries to dial 911.

The cell phone shows no connection—the towers are down—and the phone, portable and electric, is dead. She has discarded Nana's old plug-in.

She opens the front door only a crack, checking to see if the road is still navigable. "We can try again," but a rough hand of wind rips in and grabs at her and she slams against the door with her whole body to close it, pushing a chair in front of it now, going back to the sofa, where Cam and Mai Rose are snuggled together and curls up next to them, closing her eyes.

Far off in the car with the Wheelers, Nana closes her eyes, too. She has been traveling in this car so long, it seems, on a trip to an unknown place. She is nearly afraid—she feels that old anxiety, a vibration set loose in her central nervous system—and opens her eyes, looking out at the shape-shifting trees, at the endless faces of strangers in cars running alongside them, at the strange young man in the front seat behind the steering wheel. "Where am I?" she starts to say, but then senses the man to her right, his silver head cocked back, snoozing. She cuddles up closer to him, pillowing her head on his stalwart shoulder, all that's certain.

With Frank's flag in her arms, Angela wakes on the couch—her forehead is wet, as though she has been sleeping outside in the rain. But it is the outside coming in, water leaking from the ceiling, first a drip, then a trickle, then a faucet turned low. She hunts for a pan and sets it under the water that becomes a coursing thread; it's joined by another drip, trickle, stream, and there is the noise of the gutter being torn away and part of the building's siding so it sounds like they are in a big airplane hangar being ripped apart.

She opens a kitchen drawer and finds the most primitive of technological inventions—a transistor radio—and flicks it on to catch nothing but static, but as she turns the dial, she picks up a faraway murmuring from a station in Saint Louis.

Through the scratchy distance she hears a voice saying, "I want to send out a song to my husband, Chuck, who's serving in Iraq."

"God bless him," says the radio host. Angela knows that soothing voice, a deejay named Delilah. "Tell me about Chuck. Is he good looking? I bet he's a hottie!"

"Oh, he's a hottie, all right."

"And brave, isn't he?"

"I've got his picture right here in front of me."

"God bless your Chuck, and all the men and women serving overseas, and let me play something to express the feelings in your heart."

Angela clutches the kitchen counter as the roar of the wind becomes a howl and she is kept company in the fray of wind and rain by Willie Nelson crooning a warbly version of "Stardust."

Willie is suddenly gone but the song is in her head, and she begins to hum it loudly to beat back at the jet exhaust wind.

She goes back to the couch and waits next to Mai Rose and Cam.

The wrapping night, the enclosing wind, the encircling rain, the pulsing candles, the rhythm of their breaths interplaying, joining, until they are one breath, steadying, quieting, gentling down, the storm's vortex swirling them in, cradling, lulling, stilling.

Silence.

She is in a village, remote, far-flung on the edge of the planet, and the tanks are grinding forward, aircraft is overhead, explosions, getting closer, are shaking the ground, she is reaching out to protect the people she loves.

She has no protection, she is the protector. She must do it alone.

They are at her door in camouflage suits, their assault over the land in concert with the attack from above. She clutches her family. She will not let go.

The door is kicked in and the assailants are knocking down the walls and the surge of water lifts the couch and they are spinning on top of an unmoored skiff and in the swirling darkness she sees the form of a table, the rocking chair upended, the closets emptied, a ghostly rush of shirts and shoes and a mirror reflecting lightning bolts as though crackling with fire.

She stays calm, holding on, the children close until they are lifted higher still on a tide of manic Gulf and shattered boards and blankets, insulation, CDs, cereal boxes, radio, shower curtain, Scrabble boards, photo albums, laundry basket, watermelon, potato chip bags, stationery, Coke cans, Styrofoam bucket, crab net, dog figurines, rock 'n' roll posters, Sunday hats, restaurant menus, bicycle spokes, pieces of carpet, cookbooks, Holy Bibles, whiskey bottles, a bassinet and a howling cat and a parakeet cage and a stuffed koala and a map of Mississippi and doghouse flip-flops barbecue grill toddler's shoe tennis racket chalk eraser cast net flower vase fishing cork slot machine crucifix switchblade DVD hair curlers eyeglasses magnolia branches tackle box sun visor pool umbrella car keys roulette wheel all shaken and tumbled out by the tidal surge, but her family beside her she still holds tight.

Then she is not holding them.

In the hammering currents she cannot tell the moment they are gone but she churns her legs and flails her arms and is calling out their names.

She is swept away, higher, reaching for tree trunks, for roof eaves, for Heaven, whatever she can grab, and smacks against the highest reaches of a tree with branches clawing her face. A minute passes, an hour, eternity, but she holds on. Frank held on like this, she knows, against the explosion in his head even as the first blood vessels let loose, determined if he could to hold on for her. It is her turn to hold on for them. "Cam! Mai Rose!"

The maw of the water turns and tilts beneath her, won't go back, hangs on and rages; then, like a sated beast, slips back out to sea.

She lets go, falls down, down, into the muck—a mattress, soaked like a sponge, catching her. "Cam! CAAAM! CAAAAMM!!"

When first daylight glimmers, she sees where the Cotton Gin has been lifted up like a child's plaything and set down with a rending of bones on a row of antebellum homes, matchsticks beneath a ship made of paper. Gas stations are stripped bare of awnings and pumps; pawn shops vanished; ruined hotel lobbies are awash with Civil War bric-a-brac; light poles and Greek columns and sailboat masts bob in the shuddering Sound.

She runs and runs, looking, hunting, calling, like the last human on the planet—how can she possibly know where to go?—until she feels a hand pushing her, guiding her in the shallows, and she hears a kitten mewling, no not a kitten, something otherworldly in the sea, tossed up suddenly, just once, and she reaches out to take it and it's coughing, sputtering, as if born of the sea, and she clasps the tiny girl to her and rising right behind is Cam and she leads them to the beach as the morning sun strikes full, and she keeps them close, enveloping them, sheltering them, blessing them as so many, she understands, have laid their blessings on her.

Acknowledgments

The disappearance of my uncle, Major Roy Robinton, U.S. Marine Corps, as a prisoner of war in the Philippines during World War II forever impacted my mother, Evelyn, who was his younger sister, and my dad, Charles, who tried to find out details of his final days on a Japanese "Hellship." That I was named for him, as was my sister Robbie—Roy Robinton's nickname was "Robbie"—is a measure of how deep the loss registered among those who loved him, and surely for his young widow, whom I never really knew.

But it is a long way from family lore to a novel. Although I published a factual story about Roy and fellow servicemen lost on the Hellships, "They Never Came Home," in the *Mobile Press-Register*, on January 13, 2002, one of the ongoing questions—what is the effect of war on the home front as generations unfold?—is one I wanted imaginatively to explore. I used bits and pieces of a handed-down story to invent characters and story lines in service of a fictional truth.

My late mom and dad, and my late sister, Sherrell, my eldest sibling, were closest to the events as they evolved. To them, and as with my other sisters, Becky and Robbie, and all our families, I owe thanks for all their love and supportiveness of this project and all others, and for keeping family stories vivid.

To my wife, Nancy, and our daughter, Meredith, who entered my life well after the era of my late uncle, I owe profound gratitude for being part of my world in every way. Novels are not only grand ambitions, they are also day-in, day-out toil, and Nancy and Meredith, herself a young writer, have given me the love and connection essential to inspiration and joy.

I appreciate the wise counsel and enthusiasm of my literary agent, Joelle Delbourgo; the insights and can-do spirit of my editor at the University of Alabama Press, Dan Waterman, who has published my nonfiction as well as fiction; and the backing of UA Press director Curtis Clark.

Many colleagues in the Spalding MFA in Writing Program in Louisville, and friends from New York City to Mobile Bay, have helped me enter into this work, and the creative process, in ways both literary and personal, among them: Sena Jeter Naslund, Karen Mann, Kathleen Driskell, Katy Yocom, Gayle Hanratty, Luke Wallin, Elaine Neil Orr, Charles Gaines, Mary Yukari Waters, Kenny Cook, Phil Deaver, Jeanie Thompson, Molly Peacock, Richard Goodman, Dianne Aprile, Julie Brickman, Charles Salzberg, Karl Hein, Eli Evans, Andy Antippas, David Weiner, Michael Morris, Karen Zacharias, Ralph Eubanks, Walter Edgar, Jake Reiss, John Sledge, Don Noble, Karen and Kiefer Wilson, Dewey English, George Talbot, Frye Gaillard, Linda Busby Parker, Matt Mosteller, David Alsobrook, William Oppenheimer, John Hafner, Billie and Russell Goodloe, Bill Pangburn and Renee Magnanti, Howell and Krystyna Raines, Walter Kirkland and Judy Culbreth, Rex and Marty Leatherbury, Cori and Lynn Yonge.

During my years as a newspaper reporter on the Gulf Coast, I wrote, among other topics, about hurricanes, immigrants, the changing South, and those who'd lost loved ones in Iraq and Afghanistan, young veterans who came home savagely wounded, and old veterans still wrestling with the ghosts of Korea or World War II. To these men and women, for their sacrifices, and to those who stood by their side, waiting, loving, enduring what may come, we all owe our profound appreciation.

showing the Dundon Hill giant squatting in his boat[10] illustrates better than words how the converging masts of his ship suggest compasses. A line from the point where the masts would converge cuts throught the 'Tongue to the Heart'; it represents the 'chain' or Ray of Light on which the 'key of St. John's Lodge' depends, for June is St. John's month.

This statement in the old Masonic Document that the chain is from the tongue suggests the creative 'Word by Mouth' of the Logos: the Druids believed 'in the Rays of Light the vocalization — for one were the hearing and the seeing'. The Rev. J.W. Ab Ithel in *Druidism* quotes the Roll of Tradition and Chronology as follows, 'It was from the vocalization of God's name that every song and music, vocal or instrumental, were obtained, and every ecstasy, and every joy, and every life and every felicity, and every origin and derivation of existence and animation. God pronounced His name, that is, ⁄|\ ; and with the word all the worlds and all animation leaped from their origination into being and life, with a shout of joy. Where and while the Name of God is kept in memory, in respect of mystery, number and kind, there cannot but be existence, life, knowledge and felicity, for ever and ever.'

Herein lies the secret that has been lost so long; it is time it were recovered, for we read in *The High History* (Branch VI Title 20) that the Master of the twelve ancient knights summoneth Messire Gawain 'by word of mouth, and telleth him that if he delayeth longer, never more will he recover it'.

That brings us to this Orion being the architect god, not only because he holds his arm in the form of a square, and because the 'working tools of a Master Mason' fit him as demonstrated, but because he is 'the giant who beheld the three pillars of Light' or the Word, proving him to represent 'in the earthly Temple of the Stars' a geo-metrician. 'Thus the working tools of a Master Mason teach us to bear in mind, and act in accordance with the laws of our Divine Creator, so that when we shall be summoned from this sublunary abode we may ascend to the Grand Lodge above, where the world's Great Architect lives and reigns for ever.'

Orion in the Somerset Circle of the Zodiac, and 'Jesus'
crozier' the mystic Ray. The legend proves that up to the
seventh century A.D. when the saint's life was written, the
details of its posture, as well as its gold for the sun and
silver for the moon, was still fresh in memory.

As it was one of the sidereal Time gods, perhaps random
extracts from the Book of Dyzan may suggest its con-
ception, and throw light on the whole question of the Holy
Grail from this entirely new angle of 'Time'.

Time was not, for it lay asleep in the infinite bosom of
duration.

Where were the Builders, the Luminous Sons?

The hour had not yet struck: the Ray had not yet flashed
into the Germ.

Her heart had not yet opened for the one Ray to enter,
thence to fall, as three into four, into the lap of Maya.

Darkness radiates Light and Light drops one solitary
Ray into the Mother-deep.

From the effulgence of Light — the Ray of the ever-
darkness — sprung in space the re-awakened energies.

From the Divine Man emanated the forms, the sparks,
the sacred animals, and the messengers of the sacred
Fathers within the Holy Four.

This was the army of the Voice. These 'sparks' are
called spheres, triangles, cubes, lines and modellers.

The one Ray multiplies the small rays. Life precedes
form, and life survives the last atom of form. Through
the countless

rays proceeds the life Ray, the One, like a thread
through many jewels.

(See Seven Stanzas.)

Dr. Angus in his work on *The Mystery Religions and
Christianity* expresses this larger cosmic sense thus:
'Never was there an age which heard so distinctly and
responded so willingly to the call of the Cosmos to its
inhabitants. The unity of all Life, the mysterious harmony
of the least and nearest with the greatest and most remote,
the conviction that the Life of the Universe pulsated in all
its parts, were as familiar to that ancient Cosmic Con-
sciousness as to modern biology and psychology.'

But to return to the 'gold and silver idol'. This map